AND KINGS SHALL BE THY NURSING FATHERS

Marc Estrin

SPUYTEN DUYVIL
New York City

Library of Congress Cataloging-in-Publication Data

Estrin, Marc.
  And kings shall be thy nursing fathers / Marc Estrin.
    pages cm
  ISBN 978-1-941550-13-7
  I. Title.
  PS3605.S77A53 2014
  813'.6—dc23
                                    2014023400

And kings shall be thy nursing fathers, and their queens thy nursing mothers: they shall bow down to thee with their face toward the earth, and lick up the dust of thy feet; and thou shalt know that I am the LORD: for they shall not be ashamed that wait for me. (Isaiah 49:23)

I

Strange.

Very strange.

They look painted on the ceiling — like in the old bedroom. Modya wouldn't do that now, here, in this posh place. They must be real – but outside. Real stars above the ceiling. Like they always were, the Milky Way, the Great Bear, Polaris... I can't see too well with the moonlight, but still... there they are... millions, out there, trembling lights, glittering, polished, rubbed over with snow for the holidays.

And Orion...dear Orion so out there — very well-hung, um-hmm. Yes, yes, that would be something, wouldn't it?

Petya, be good. You can't get that chummy with the stars... Not allowed. Not at your age — though you're not old old. Old enough, but not that old.

When did I last have serious time for the stars? And above the stars? Überm Sternenzelt?

Muss was? Was?? What's up there? Who? I need to know!

Ein lieber Vater, ja, ok, good. Better than an ogre mother. But why so silent, dear Father? Why do I not hear you? Why don't you speak? Is it only the devil who speaks? Maybe it's only the devil I can hear with these weakening ears...

Petya, Petya, Beethoven was deaf, and look what *he* heard — the lieber Vater. The lieber Vater, roaring in music monstrous, solemn...

But ... I fear Beethoven ... and I fear his God. I don't love them, Beethoven *or* his God, his angry

God, God's fits of temper, not for me, not morose enough to be divine. The late quartets maybe, the Grosse Fuge, but Beethoven leaves me cold.

Hmm. I do feel cold. A little cold. Cold. It's cold here.

And what a name — Beethoven. Beet-hoven! Such a harmonious, brass choir sound, fated to impress. But not very exalted: The great Beetfield. "*Van* Beetfield" yet. His little Dutch grandfather must have had a laugh. "I will seize Fate by the throat."

But lieber Vater! that choral movement — that monstrous mangling of Schiller's Ode, that vulgar, tasteless, trivial propaganda. I can't fathom how a genius like Beethoven could... Maybe even *I* did better in that thing I wrote for graduation, I don't remember, it was so long ago...once upon a time. We all tore it up and had a death party for Pyotr Ilyich's *Ode to Joy*.

Herr Beetfield. Despair wearing a mask of optimism. A genius who has lost faith in happiness, who has quit life for a world of impossible daydreams, a realm of unattainable ideals...transparent, pathetic. Ludwig, Ludwig...

You'll see — my Pathétique will take back your Ninth, supplant it. It effaces the Ninth. Finally. Definitively. It ends — like life, in truth, sinking into the lowest tones of beet fields and beyond.

No ideology. No fortissimo prestissimo ridiculo. No, no, no! Reality: reality — Adagio lamentoso.

How deluded can a genius be? Even at his most sublime, he surely understood repression, the force of repression, the crushing, authoritarian, force of "That's how it is." And he offers imaginary freedom — within unfreedom! Florestan's happy release? Release into what? The embrace of the fearsome lieber Vater? The Pathétique doesn't want to spread the voice of the Godhead — for whatever good that does. I don't hear it. I don't get it, the Word of God.

What's the point of speaking five languages if I can't understand the Word of God?

What would it sound like, what instrumentation could catch even the faintest corner of its voice? I don't mean God's Word written into human speech, but "In the beginning there was the Word." *That* word. Voice of the burning bush. What would that sound like? Tomorrow, I'll try to write it down. I just have to get good and drunk.

Maybe once, God's Word was the whole of creation. But the devil must have gotten hold of it, and his Verdi baritone drowns out the Russian bass of God. In Eternity, if there *is* Eternity, if I ever get there, will I be able to hear the lieber Vater's voice alone, solo, without interference? Unlikely. It will be more bass/baritone duet, God and the devil tracking each other in augmented fourths.

My God, we think everything bad on earth comes from the devil — because if we *didn't* attribute everything to the devil, we could never forgive God for playing with us — like a cat tormenting mice. But unlike old Tyuchev, He never lets anyone out of his claws. And then He wants us to be grateful? Grateful for what? For what?

Momma and Papa loved Tyutchev, but I didn't much like him after he brought that tiny bird into the house and left it in the corner near the fireplace. It sat there for days with its weird little wings out. And it never moved, never touched any food. I tried to feed it. Tyutchev didn't bother with it anymore. One day, it was gone, disappeared, and no one admitted throwing it out. I was going to build it a coffin.

Überm Sternenzelt muss ein lieber Vater wohnen...

I remember a story about a hermit who sat with a candle, alone in his cave, sat for years without taking his eyes off the holy book. He slept in a coffin instead of a bed. What a peculiarly tempting idea. I wonder if he cast a shadow. I wonder if *I* still cast a shadow. Damn! Why am I lying here on this couch? The better to get up and work again when the time comes. But I'm so tired. Know thyself, Pyotr Ilyich.

And why all this tropical décor? Modya doesn't live in a place like this, this room with all these hot-house plants, with curtains drawn, with the mirrors turned around, the pictures draped with crepe. It's so damned quiet here. And cold.

Mirrors turned. They do that when someone dies. Why? I'm told people who shoot themselves are often found in a pool of blood right in front of their mirrors. Imagine. Looking at their own images staring out in terror at their faces distorted in fear, faces of the soon-to-be-dead, faces which have lost their "I"s.

For the mourners, dread, strange dread, dread different from the suicide dread piled up inside the victims. The experience of horror in front of the mirror is not for suicides alone.

The icons in this room all look so gloomy staring out of their frames, with their little runs of gold, like piccolos, candles flickering in my shoes. Funny to think of them outlasting my feet, my shoes. But the bones will still be there.

Modya says electric light will come to Malaya Morskaya in January. Two months. Gas is finished. Done. Sentimental archaism. Like Modya.

What will he think of the workmen who come with all their tools and wires? Naughty little brother will have to control himself.

I remember when I first saw electric light, shimmering and perky with its strutting kind of magic. Something otherworldly of course, but also something of the charlatan and clown.

It's so bizarre in here. Something is going on I don't understand, some real weariness. Disilluso. Ansioso. Not the usual fatigue followed by happiness. Something more hopeless, more final. Ha! Like many finales, it feels anticlimactic. I still want to write like before, but when was that? The devil knows what's the matter with me. Some days I feel like my song has been sung, that perhaps life isn't worth living any more. Is that a crackbrained thing to think?

Why is the keyboard locked? Modest, what are you doing? Open the piano.

He doesn't hear me. Modest! Modya! What a devil of a life! There's not one pleasant minute — just melancholy, revulsion... Maybe the end is....

Yes, I *have* been shown kindness of all sorts. Look at them: Bob, Modya, Nicolai, Lev...

But not everyone kind. Some mean, hateful. Back when the stars were painted on the ceiling, I remember the day on the river bank, six boys blocking my every attempt to run away. "Stand still," Mischa yells. Yells. Right at me. In my face. I froze, Yes, sir, yes. Totally submissive.

Then they all took off their shirts, and one of them, who? Some boy, calm, menacing, pulled up my undershirt, and I was cold and naked — under the bright sky, with my cheeks radish red — and another of them pulled a dress out of a paper bag, a blue dress with white dots, frilly hem, with a pink ribbon woven through the lace collar. "Oooooh, woo-woo," someone said. Ivan said it looked like a nightgown. "You're going to make me wear a dress?" "We told you not to talk. Put your arms through the sleeves." "It's only a game, right?" "The more you talk, the worse it's going to be for you, squirt. It's a game, and you're it, but we're the blindfolded ones." "I'll look like a girl." "You bet. So even if you can get away from us, you can't run back to school in a dress, or naked." "What happens if you catch me?"

No answer. They all put their blindfolds on, and there I was, miserable and confused, in a dress. A sweet little blue dress. With a lace collar.

"If you talk we'll know where you are, and we'll get you." They groped around with stiff arms and open hands, and fingers clutching at the air. "It's me," one of them yelled, "Feel for a dress!" "Spread out and hold hands in a circle, and close in. If he's inside..." It was like some grotesque ballet, with me as a maiden to be sacrificed. Ducking under, running as fast as I could — like in a dream, but not my fault. I didn't dare look back. I just kept running, got my second wind, third, lucky to make it. I don't know what they would have done if they'd caught me. It was a nice dress. I hid it under my mattress.

What was that all except meanness? They were supposed to be my friends, but they were hurtful. My throat was sore, I'd cut two of my toes, my knees hurt, my shins hurt. But I wouldn't cry, I just wouldn't cry. I felt the whole stupid world had gone crazy. And it hasn't gotten better. They're still after me. Ghosts threaten. Dies illa.

My tears at the Requiem last winter. Mozart must be the most complete human being the lieber Vater ever fashioned, the most frivolous and at the same time the most profound. Gaiety and desolation. What have *I* done that's truly gay? Fairies and flowers? Nutcracker levity? Mice?

I read a critic in Novoye Vremya who praised Nutcracker as a brilliant attack on the Jews, with

Nutcracker-Tsar winning a war against Jewish rats, healing Russia's economy by rooting out the parasitical vermin so the father of his people can share the fruits of his realm with his children.

Rats? Jewish Rats? He must never have seen a rat. Or read Hoffman. What would Mouse King say? What would my Jewish doctors say? Rats? *I* am Jewish-black-gypsie-gambler-prostitute-artist-rat teetering on the edge of society with my monstrous vices. Carmen, yo — and Petya, ya, olé! What would he say about me, a fairy?

I've always been terrified of mice. I don't know why. But I don't hold that against them. They're animals, for God's sake!

And what makes them animals? Because they're not vegetables? Are they animals because we're allowed to kill them without becoming criminals? We kill vegetables and stay innocent. Are they animals because they have shorter lives, because we can see them being born and dying of old age? Because we can eat them? *I* could be eaten. I could be eaten as easily as a boar. Moreso. Yes, people don't eat human flesh — that would terrify them. But I could be cut up, eaten, chewed, swallowed, transformed into shit. Fear of being eaten is only the shadow of a general terror at the bottom of life, fear of being a body at all, of existing within a puny, helpless envelope. C'est ça. My skin is where I'm over. After that, the not me, the millions of threatening not-mes.

Calm down, Petya, calm down. You're not conducting, you're not in public, your head is not falling off, let's have none of your panic attacks. It's ridiculous to think the lieber Vater created a world around you, or around anyone. If you asked an ant for whom God created the world, it would say "For me, for the ants." And even Modya has ants up here on the sixth floor in his fancy neighborhood. I have ants in Klin. Shall I kill them just because I can, because I need Lebensraum? Should I poison the little crumbs they are so presumptuous to gather?

When Tyutchev wanted food he would meow. I could talk to him, cat talk, and he would make the sound again. It wasn't like two people who can't understand one another. It was more like two things — a cat and a child — who are locked in different forms but can spill over into one another.

That certain personage I married was in love with me like a cat, a sneaky cat. Or Odette. There's nothing silly about being bewitched, changed into a swan. The poor girl likely spent her whole childhood communing with them, with swans. She just slipped a bit too far into the water. Maybe she wanted to suicide herself. Braver than I.

I remember Eugen's beautiful dog, Auntie. She started to act less lively, and one day threw herself in the water and tried to sink by holding completely still. Eugen saw her do it, he swore. He rescued her and tied her up, but as soon as she got loose she went down to the water again and tried to sink herself until finally, forcing her head to stay under, she succeeded in...he saw it. And then she was floating, dead. He watched her commit suicide. Why didn't he save her? Because she wanted so much to die, he said. There was no abuse, she was too old to be in love, he was still there for her...Animals and humans think alike. When Jesus cast the evil spirits into them, the swine just lost their will to live.

It's getting lighter. I'll be happy to see the sunrise. New light is beautiful. Northern light, the night's winter dream. Now Modest can turn off the gas, they can turn off the electricity on Nevsky. Whenever they wake up. When the clock summons. Hey, everyone! The world has rolled ahead. The sun has risen. St. Petersburg, get up take it all in. Take in the sun.

Look at it peeking through the curtains. The earth is an ant to the sun, 300,000 times as big...

What a crowd of zeros that is, and what they tell us, what they say is that *we* are essentially zero, nothing at all. But we're happy to see the sun's light — red, then pink, then white and strong, illuminating the streets and waking up the colors even here, behind closed curtains. Soon humans may come, and I'll see their colors and lines and faces and hands. They'll show how they act, how they live. Show their human warmth in November.

It must be a mistake, all those terrible zeros. It's all right, sun. You don't frighten me. You're not too big for anyone. If not for you, by now we'd find ourselves helpless to do anything ever again. All of us in bodies, all of nature.

Flies and insects have been warned. Beethoven told Schuppanzigh to "play it so beautifully that the flies drop dead in mid-air." Autumn music. The flies drop dead. Up in the trees at Klin and in the fields, struggling life is rustling, restless, working hard not to perish. Existence is busy for a little while yet — until all the legs, all the feelers collapse, and everyone rolls over suddenly, belly up. The giant mushrooms stand there like lungs, semi-alive, naked, lungs without bodies in the crisp air...

Last week's storm, thunder rolling over the house, the Vater playing Beethoven, and then the storm was over, and I walked outside, under the dripping pines. Miserable as I was after giving them my so-called "difficult" Sixth, my God, the joyous sparkle, the scent of rasberries and those mushrooms! And the evening coming on, the blaze of fire covering the sky, the unusual transparency of the air, the trees' long shadows...

II

Someone coming, bumping around. Ah, Rimsky and Kashkin. What are they doing with that box? Handkerchiefs tied round their faces. They look like bandits. The plague is over, my friends, the epidemic is almost done. Stop worrying.

Down near my couch...

Cover off box...

Hey, easy there. Nikolai Dimitryevich, under the arms, under. Where is Bob? Not here yet? And Nikolai Andreyevich, grab under my legs, not by the ankles. You'll break my knees. Let Bob do it.

Where is Bob? Hey, my zucchetto. My zucchetto fell off my head, my gift from Giovannini…OK, good. I am dressed again. Thank you. I need to be well-dressed.

I suppose a plain coffin is better. Looks like a boat, more appropriate than those Russian undertaker wedding cake confections.

"Bob, come help."

There he is, my sweet Bob. I knew he'd come. Good morning, my dear. I hope I didn't get you up too early.

"OK, up we go…and over…and down."

Don't scratch the table. Modest, are you there? Modya? Tell them not to scratch the table.

"We can take the masks off now, but don't get too close."

Bob, my dear darling nephew, incomparable, wonderful Bob. It's so good to see you. I missed you the last few hours. Look, that look of his. Like the kiss of Aurora's prince. Bob will simply drive me out of my mind with his unutterable fascination. So what if he's Lev and Sasha's son — he's family. All the more reason to know and love him deeply. We could be even more fully commingled in one another's blood, in our bodies and souls.

I'm old enough to be his father, yes. Good. He thrives on my wisdom, my guidance, my financial support, and I thrive on his youth, his enthusiasm, his many talents. What's wrong with that? Is that immoral? If Mariya can belong to Mazeppa, Bob and I belong together, too. We don't always have to deny our passions. I love and am beloved, so what? — a happy doom. Let others live in a world where two plus two equals four.

And flowers, friends, yes. Thank you. I do like flowers. Little Russian flowers. Lay on the flowers,

do lay on the flowers, and I'll take them with me when I go.

The closer I come to old age, the more pleasure I get from flowers. At my age, when I'm among flowers, I can enter youth again, even if it means depravity. If my ugliness can still be used and absorbed by beauty, transformed, well...what a temptation, beyond all obstacles. Beauty insurmountable. Flowers.

No smell though. Is something wrong with my nose? Could I have caught something?

Of course beauty itself is a kind of disease. I learned that from him, from the Beetfield. Beauty has to be cured, destroyed. The slow movements of the Ninth, the Seventh, the A minor quartet —

those invasive infections which brought forth his sneezes, his immune attacks, his ghoulish projects of decomposition. Doktor Beethoven had to smash them when they rose in their sickness from the depths of perfection. My music has never come close, I know. Because it's only myself that must be destroyed —for my ugliness, not for my beauty.

I think of this all the time when I pick mushrooms at Klin, all of them growing furiously in the fall, the time of destruction, inflicting the final decay, ridding the world of rot. I read somewhere that the world would be an impassible heap of old rubbish were it not for mushrooms. But beautiful they are nonetheless, so resplendent, delicate, rare tints contrasting with the decaying leaves. And others, pure white, wholesome red, even indigo-blue. When they teach colors to schoolchildren, they should use mushrooms for illustration. I envy the wood frogs that live among such gems. From every gap in the dead leaves some contrivance of color, some unspent richness of the year emptying out.

Beethoven's fear of beauty in the Ninth, adagio molto e cantabile, poisonous, requiring a hectoring chorus to teach us children never to eat the Amanitas, or anything with red or orange tubes. We must be protected after listening from thinking about suicide.

I'm told Amanita poisoning resembles cholera. The death angel, merciful death angel, with its gift of "renal failure", as the doctors so gravely pronounce. Nature is even more clever than Art. I'd love to hear what the flowers have to say about all this.

Arsenic will do too, rat poison for two-legged rats. You can feed us arsenic little by little, and we feel death coming. Stomach trouble, intestinal catarrah. Vomiting and cholera-like diarrhea after stronger doses. One becomes livid, gray, headaches, neuralgia. Profound weakness. Heart attack, coma, delirium... Töchter aus Delirium. It's easy to get at the chemist, arsenic, ten, fifteen grams. Put it in applesauce or mashed potatoes.

Existence changes from the moment when suicide seems natural, normal. At twenty that idea seemed romantic and lyrical to me. But then it became more clear and dry, affected by obvious evidence, and I can't imagine why it ever appeared so strange. It's really the unique solution. All the rest is nothing but provisional. An imbecile who commits himself to death is no longer an imbecile. His inner need for seriousness prepared in the silence of his heart. Like a work of art.

Look at these hands, the hands of a man twice my age. So much unhappiness at play in that wrinkled skin. With every new torment I feel another vein protrude, unroll its deadly length along my hands, my temples. It all makes me think of those terrible, ravaged faces —old Rembrandt, old Beethoven, they who the whole world mocked.

The bags under my eyes wouldn't really matter if not for the misery in my heart. I accept physical decay, of course, why not? I've suffered enough for the sake of spiritual knowledge. More than my share, perhaps. I submit to the disintegration of the body. It's worth it. Work becomes more solid as life corrodes from emotion. That's the price we pay.

The clock strikes nine, and another clock strikes nine, and another strikes nine. Three part canon at the half-step. Quarter-step. Nature's clock is more exact. Inexorable. Always in tune. No counterpoint, no meter. Only one colossal rhythm.

23

Oh dear, it's people. I'm not ready for visitors. Ai, ai, ai — fat Poustiakov. What can I say to him? And Gvozdina, and Petoushkov, Bouyanov...the whole wind section. They're not usually such early risers. The audience at the premiere was hostile. Ambivalent at best. I suppose they didn't know what to make of the lamentoso. They'll appreciate it later, come to respect it at least. I didn't conduct well. But the crowd is always more interested in its own exultation, not in the hard work of exploring. People think they've made an important contribution by shouting "Bravo, bravo!" And if they don't...Well, it's nice to hear, but there were no bravos afterward.

It *is* touching, I suppose, to study them with their sterile ambitions — like Leonardo's machines which longed to fly and were unable, but which still embodied, if not the secret, at least the desire for flight. Seid umschlungen, Millionen. I, too, wrote a fugue on that. I, too, still want to fly.

Look at all these people, staring at me, solemnly clutching handkerchiefs to their mouths. Reverently spitting in them. Modest, you don't have to spray that — whatever it is.

Wind players en masse, protecting their lungs. I've always thought it terrible that when I compose something, there is no way to hear it except at a concert. It's like whispering the most precious secrets of my soul to police officials. Bassoons.

It's good to be separated from them by the denseness of their looks and the thickness of their clothes. It must be cold out. But their pressure is oppressive. I wish they would just go away.

Oop — the lower strings are arriving. Here is Alexei Verzhdilovich with his fine moustache –wavering over me. What, drunk so early in the morning, Sasha? Don't you rehearse at ten? Oh, my goodness, he's bending over. Mmmmm. What a kiss. The groin rises. Alexei, you never told me, I didn't know. I could write you a cello concerto.

Oh my, he's clutching at my face, weeping. I'm all wet. Soaked. Alexei, Sasha, it's nothing. Don't worry. All is well. You've just never seen me this close, oh, two fleshes reaching... Kiss me again, Sasha. On the lips again.

Dear boy, they pull you away, they spray you

and wipe your mouth. Modya, Modya, everyone should do what he likes! How dare you pull him away? And police here...?

What all these people call vice — is it now a crime?? It's only a sickness — a sickness that attacks the highest natures. Sasha, I love your playing, my darling first cellist. Poustiakov, get your fat hands off him. What Socrates felt was not a low passion, or Caesar's weakness, or Michaelangelo's, or Shakespeare's. This same desire surges up in the highest humanity.

Suppose we love a food that's poison to some, but not to us — how dare you punish us? Let go of him. Karabchevsky, stop spraying his handkerchief. One day you'll be ashamed of this barbarous posturing. The great tragedy of life is not that we die, but that we cease to love, that...

"I know it is customary, but under these conditions, it is wisest not to kiss Pyotr Ilyich."

"You should put up a sign, or you'll be wrestling people away all day."

Oh yes. Like naked Greek athletes. In overcoats.

While they were preparing the hemlock, Socrates was practicing a new tune on the flute, and Crito asked him, "What will be the use of that?" "To know this tune before dying," he said. A good answer. What tune are *these people* afraid of? The lamentoso? Even the musicians were suspicious. The brass. Ahnest du den Schöpfer, Gvozdina?

Good. They're leaving. Spitting in their handkerchiefs and leaving. Sasha will be back, I know. He reminds me of Vanya. And too many others. Vanya, bright with all the charm of early manhood — his vibrant moustache, his golden hair falling over a smooth, honest brow. Dark green eyes the same, the two of them, and their mouths, both mouths, soft and full.

When I first saw Vanya during an awful performance of Rigoletto, he felt my gaze, answered it. Oh, did he answer it. I had to turn away in confusion, but not before I took in that warm expression, that flash of human interest, beyond curiosity or distrust. "We are men," it said, "Let us know one another!", an assertion all too rare in this world. I fought the temptation to look again. Green flames danced in my eyes, and a whirlwind roared in my ears, louder than jesters, dukes or daughters. Spellbinding. La Maledizione!

Vanya, Vanya, lovely. One of those people I found myself looking at so openly, it was astonishing what intimacy was admitted.

We did spend some time together, a week or two. Oddly, I was bored when I was with him, but still painfully jealous when I was not. It couldn't last. And so I broke it off. Three days later, he was dead. Shot himself. When I heard the news, I was almost hysterical. This wouldn't have happened if I'd stayed with him, I know. My eyes fill even now with guilty tears. He was young, happy, adorable, healthy, popular. Then suddenly he goes and shoots himself … like Edward a dozen years before.

Oh God, I remember Edward with even more pain, his voice, his movements, but more, worse, the wonderful expression so often on his face. My beloved pupil. Fifteen — at the height of his allure. I think I never loved anyone as much. The death of that boy, the fact that he no longer exists, is beyond my comprehension. However much I've consoled myself, my guilt is unbearable. I loved him. His memory is sacred,

enshrined, hopefully forever, but still, but still... How many have I unbalanced or killed? How many love themes for dead boys must I write? I pursue one living soul, then ever return to my dead ones. It would be better to live without love than to kill because of it. Edward was happy too, the poor boy. He never knew how happy he was.

Fourteen, fifteen, the age to be happy — not dead.

In Venice, little Vittorio would sing songs about Jesus saving him. From what? From me? I hope not. His voice was so sweet and musical. He came to sing for me in my hotel room. His stunning, androgynous beauty, like a redeeming angel. Such a delight to kiss and caress.

We would sit for hours with our arms around each other, talking about the bitter life from which our love had saved us, the happy future we might spend together. The sun over San Giorgio Maggiore seeping through the curtains, the voices of street criers and carriages outside. The fading light has fused forever in my memory with a shiver of emotion at that boy's angelic voice — what a matchless, unalterable, poignant alloy!

But most of those Italian street urchins. They can make love to you and not even know your name. Like the fairies near Peter and Paul, or in the garden squares off Nevsky, or near Zoopark. They tie their shoelaces in large loops to identify each another. But you don't need hints to recognize them in a bunch, prowling in heat.

Nights in Florence when I was feeling more randy than usual, I would go down to the docks for one of my "strolls". I'm always an easy prey for lust, but especially when I'm feeling hopeless or despairing or miserable. At that point, I'm fully

disposed to fall in love like Tatiana with Onegin.
And I usually find some pretty lad.

In dusky light those faces and bodies fulfill
my sweet fantasies— des vrais rêves. We stand
in dark alleys and kiss. I remember one — with
his disheveled hair, looking distressingly lovely.
Sweet, sweet anguish in my heart. We rented a
room — and reality dawned.

While sitting on the bed waiting for him to un-
dress, I was overwhelmed by some terrible emptiness at the core of my being, almost a premo-
nition of death. Then I really looked at him. He
was not unattractive, but in full gaslight I found
him — somehow uninteresting, monotonous. I've
always been charmed by a particular type and the
kind of desire they provoke in me. He — I didn't
know his name, nor he mine — was just a little
off. True, he had everything in the right place,
but there in the room, the thought of putting my
arm around him was surprisingly displeasing: He
seemed so ill-suited for contact. Perhaps it was his
self-centeredness. I felt that his hands, his feet, his
nose, his ears, were organs existing for himself
alone and for no one else. He lacked a generosity
that might suggest his hand as an exciting gift.
Was he prudish? I don't think so. It seemed to me
more a kind of physical isolationism. That mouth
of his belonged to himself alone. Perhaps I was

inventing him. Had I been younger, I might have found great meaning in his version of beauty, and shared his fledgling understanding of his own glory.

How different from piccolo Adriano the next night: "Oh yes...oh yes...please, Oh, I should so gladly do whatever you want. "O sì...o sì...la prego...o, io farei volentieri qualsiasi cosa che Lei volesse." Questo giovane grazioso! That mischievous, love-smitten eye, a living statue by Phidias. His narrow hips and catlike eyes, the handsomeness of his fourteen years. What a deeply decent boy, filled with sharing his here and now.

But I was shocked by the degrading condition of his room: a bed, a pitiful little trunk, a small, dirty table with a candle end and the room's only decoration, a stuffed monkey he won at a fair. But in that moment, this miserable room seemed to me the epitome of human happiness. There was all kind of tenderness there — long, lovely, lingering, enormous kisses, incredible pleasure. Adriano really knew nothing; he understood only those truths to which the heart has direct access. I never felt so happy.

I remember that behind his ear was a lovely beauty mark, and there, the forest of his hair began, first two or three little ringlets and then the curls proper. His neck was not quite clean, but very, very white and delicate. His golden smile, his eyes as blue as an October sky, his early pubic hair, his round little behind. My sweet monkey playmate, with a red ribbon on his ankle.

The next morning, even then...I woke full of remorse, with a deep understanding of the fraudulence and exaggeration of last night's happiness, based on nothing really but Adriano's sexual charm. He had much good at the root of his soul, but, my God, how pitiable he was, how thoroughly debauched! His smile had become a brothel smile for me. And instead of helping him to better himself, I had only contributed to his degradation. My luxuries of virtue, common sense, devotion, magnanimity — there was no way I could make use of any of them.

It's almost as if from my bright civilized world a portal leads to another world where everything is seething, passionate, sweaty, naked. And between people with lives in well-lit spaces and the others, the derelicts, the debauched and filthy, there is always some bridge. Not only that, the frontiers between those lives can be crossed at any moment, and things can become bizarre and queer.

Once I walked some mischievous urchin back to his hovel, Ilya, I think. Wide cheeks and full legs, an alley tomcat, none too nice. His face was untroubled, slightly defiant. He was a lad who would chew the ends of pencils, play broomball or horseshoes, yet my heart was beating very fast. He seemed to give off an aura of divinity, marvelously enchanting in the darkness, himself a source of warmth and living light. Why had his insignificance so suddenly become significant?

A narrow little room he had too, like many of the others, with a rusty iron stove, a rickety bed with paint peeling off the wooden frame, dirty blankets showing through holes in the bedspread...

When we sat down together, I asked Ilya how old he was. He didn't know. This took my breath away. I asked him to stand up. He obeyed, stood up and turned to me. "Hit me in the face," I said. He just stood there, disobedient, perplexed. "Hit me in the face, Ilya!" I yelled. "Why should I hit you?" "Hit me because I tell you to!" I don't know what came over me. "What are you waiting for?" I cried, trying to impose myself on him. Infantile. I stood up and moved right in front of his face, wanting to push him, to say something brutally hostile, to be as nasty as possible. I must do it, I said to myself. Invigorating nastiness, cold as ice! Time was pressing. I must be nasty! But how was I to be nasty to him if he would kiss me, and impregnate me with kindness?

That's the problem dealing with the poor. They're physically so foreign and mentally so exotic. So distant, so small. Whereas in the darkness of that room, I had a sense of growing, growing enormous, gigantic — and simultaneously a sense of overall impoverishment, paralyzing tension, of becoming somehow smaller, being hung by a thread, changing into something, some kind of of transformation, sinking into a kind of rising, as if on a narrow plank being hoisted to the eighth floor, with my every sense alerted. My overwhelming feeling was — emptiness. No wonder I struck out at him.

Instead of hitting me, though, he kissed me roughly, and I calmed down. We lay together on the bed. But after he was asleep, it got even worse: His kind words struck me as being just a line. I was tempted to attack him, sleeping, like a bird of prey. Yet all that cruelty and lust in me had no real object. I didn't want to eat him, God forbid. How then could my wild sensual excitement be appeased? I was utterly bewildered. Now all at once I remembered what had gone on, and I didn't know what to do next. I lay there horribly ashamed. I still am. Horribly ashamed. How old was I? Forty-three, forty-four? To Ilya, I must have seemed like some lecherous old man.

I remember a character one evening at Leiner's, sitting at a corner table staring off into space in a way he must have thought brought out the beauty of his eyes flashing some beautiful, lecherous dream. He sat there flirting at the customers, myself included, with the features, the expression, the smile of a woman. He might have been any age up to a thousand. Beneath all the layers of paint and powder, there *were* preserved some fragments of a beautiful woman in this old fairy — as if some error of nature had introduced her into his body. He worked hard, no doubt, to maintain a semi-masculine appearance. But he could hardly succeed given his taste, his habits of feeling, his way of life. And unlike me, *he* might gorge on human flesh.

Gray hair combed across baldness in a last desperate coiffure, a black mustache, red lipstick, scented like a young fop. Ugliness can be a deep reservoir of beauty — but the fleshy romp of his body had spread like oil, one vice at a time, into the secret recesses of his being. That evening he laughed and laughed, probably because he believed laughter made him look gay. Parading around like an ostrich, wandering the dining room in search of adventures, he affected a plumage so strange that I wanted to snatch him up for the bird house at the zoo. At one moment he would wither the patrons with blazing eyes, and the next he would raise a gloved hand to his face so as to evade the greetings of anyone so indelicate as to question his behavior as anything but some sort of high Art.

To think that I could have been that man to Alexei, a thinner version, I hope, but what a fright!

III

That mirror someone was holding to my lips. Who? Lev Bertenson, maybe. Or was it Vasilly? Can't remember. I couldn't see my face, just my lips. They weren't too bad. Some wrinkling. But what do I look like, the rest of me? After forty, Russian men lapse into monstrosity. We may once have had beauty on our side, but now? I hate looking at all my contemporaries, the "adults". They repel me. I repel me. No more mirrors, please.

Moderato assai.(Tempo di marcia funebre)

We all die soon enough, and are dead. We need to come to an end, I suppose. We shut our eyes so as not to see the hourglass, we shut our ears so as not to hear the ticking of the clock, we abandon ourselves to the illusion of our appearance and all the euphemisms, all the misunderstandings that self-delusion permits.

I pretend not to be concerned by death, but in fact I chase around the circle of passion for life, then lofty, detached serenity, then some blind struggle with my end.

Just like the symphonies. When I look at myself from the outside, like some ballet master of funerals, I'm not any the less on the inside. It's this damn body, my master, whispering its doctrines. A great danger to my mind! Every crisis

I experience comes from or with some change in my body, some disequilibrium...

I don't have mirrors at Klin, because I no longer have the courage of the liar. Alexei dresses me, looks me up and down, and approves my tired body. Or says he does. If God wants me in a weak body, who am I to complain? There's no ointment without a fly in it.

Tired. Exhausted, actually. Deeper than fatigue. At best, I have perhaps one more work in my loins, like an old cannon with one more shot. But my mind is wandering far from here, among its ruins, struggling with the crass tenacity of life, pain, the oppression of formless questions, mingling and crumbling limply away like me. Mirror? This old face reflects nothing but the desire for some ill-gotten rest. Thinning white hair, bloodless complexion, the sinking shoulders of a suddenly old man...

They say old people smell like fish. I don't smell like fish, I think, but then again, the flowers, my questionable nose. Even after my famous Moskva expedition, she didn't mention smelling fish. I told her I'd fallen into the water by accident. And even though I hadn't smelled of fish, of course she believed me, since it wouldn't have suited her satanic, wifely purposes to inquire about my suicide plans, still in motion. Anyone but me would have succumbed, it was so cold, windy, and I soaking wet, freezing, shivering. Where is death when you want him?

The greatest stupidity of my life. Why did I ever marry her? It seems to me now as though some demonic Fate was driving me to that girl. "I can't live without you," she wrote, "and so maybe I'll kill myself. Let me see you that I may remember our kiss in the next world. Farewell, Yours eternally…" I explained I had nothing but sympathy and gratitude for her love. But when I left, I was haunted by the foolish of my conduct. Inconsiderate. If I didn't love her, if I didn't wish to encourage her feeling, why had I visited her, and why hadn't I predicted the consequence? Her next letter convinced me that if, having gone so far, I were suddenly to turn away, I would make her truly wretched, and surely drive her to a tragic end. What a choice: to preserve my own freedom at the price of her death — or to marry her! Was I to be another Onegin? I couldn't. I had to give in, to consent. Besides, my getting married was Papa's only dream. All my relatives. And it would provide a good cover. A great artist should be an honorable man.

So one moonlit evening — despite Modya's advice — I go to her, to my future wife. I tell her openly I do not love her, but that whatever befell,

I would be a staunch and faithful friend. Très noble! I describe my character in detail — my irritability, my volatile temperament, my un-sociability— and my...circumstances. I ask if she still wants to be my wife, the wife of someone who does not love her.

Of course she said yes, the vixen, what did I think she would say? I remember how terrible I felt in the days after that. Completely destroyed. Having lived 37 years with an innate aversion to marriage, how wrenching to be drawn into becoming a bridegroom not the least attracted to his bride. I'd have to change my whole way of life, to live for the peace and well-being of this other person whose fate had become joined to mine! And for me, the most self-centered of bachelors! But if it was to be, it was to be.

At the wedding I was a ghostly bystander until Razumovsky called on us to kiss. Then a kind of pain gripped my heart. I was suddenly seized with such emotion I sobbed uncontrollably. Some people thought I was weeping for joy. Idiots!

I tried to gain control of myself, to calm down. But on the train that night I broke down again. I had to occupy her in conversation as far as Klin — just to earn the right to sleep alone in my armchair, by myself. Myself.

I had hoped that – married — she wouldn't

constrain me — because she was a very limited person, and that would be a good thing: I might be afraid of a really intelligent woman. I stood so far above her, at least I would never be frightened of her.

But who was that man? — the man who in May had taken it into his head to marry this person, who in June wrote a whole opera as if nothing had happened, who in July married, who in September fled his wife, and so on — it couldn't have been me. It must have been another Pyotr Ilyich.

Modya insisted I shouldn't give a damn about what other people might think, that I shouldn't tie up my life in order to appear "normal". But that's true only to a point. If my family doesn't despise me for my vices, it's only because they began loving me as a child, long before I exhibited them. Sasha, for instance. I know she's guessed and forgiven everything. Several others, too. But how painful it is to be "understood", pitied, and forgiven when I am *not guilty of anything*! I thought by marrying, or by a generally open liaison with a woman, I could shut the mouths of all those contemptible creatures whose opinions I don't in the least respect, but who could cause distress in people close to me.

"I am dying of longing," the creature wrote, "and I burn with a desire to see you, to sit with you and talk with you. There is no failing of yours that might cause me to fall out of love with you." The gorge rises. Walking on the deserted bank of the Moskva, I thought I could kill myself without making anyone feel guilty by just contracting a chill. Accidentally. And then pneumonia. So I walked down into the water up to my waist, and stood there until I could no longer take the cold. I really did think I'd die of pneumonia.

I could have used something more certain — something like a gun. But I didn't have a gun, and more importantly, I couldn't stand the idea of a gun so close to my ear. That was the main thing — I was afraid of the noise.

That must be why they're all so quiet here, all these people. All these silent people acting as if they know how afraid of noise I am, how I hate noise. Or that I'm dead.

Who is this one now? Why is he staring at me like that? Look at those eyes — inscrutable. Where have I seen those eyes before? Darkest blue I've ever seen, like sapphires. Trying to touch me. I can't move my hand away, can't move my... Easy, Petya. Take his hand if he wants. He's good looking enough, slim, elegant. His clothes fit him well. But he's too pale, frightening, almost death-like, I like them healthier. Can't move my hand. Can't move my hand...

The hypnotist I went to to be cured for marriage! That's him. He turned me down. Turned me down as a subject. With those metallic blue eyes.

I asked him about treating mental diseases, especially ones of a confidential nature. He asked about hysteria, excitability, depression, addiction. I mentioned my smoking, drinking and gambling, but I wasn't ready to reveal my problem. He probably suspected, warned me against overwork, said he was loath to engage addiction, and he turned back to his desk.

"Why are you so restrictive? I've come..."

"Because without a certain and curative effect," he said, "I don't think it healthful to stir up dangerous curiosity, or vulgar interest in the secrets of one's life. What can accomplish no visible and direct good, what goes only triflingly toward that point, never to reach it — that were better laid aside."

Dangerous. Vulgar.

"You'll be stifling research," I warned him.

"No. I'd be stifling the influence of quacks. I would keep out of their hands fire that should not be played with. Science can be a crime when it is inexact, don't you think? But thank you for your interest. There will be no charge."

Still — here he is. That's he. I'm sure it's he

with those unmistakable eyes. Well, too late to be cured. Or for a cure I no longer need. Or want. But perhaps another cure, a more comprehensive cure for...

I read a Poe story once about evading death, using hypnosis in articulo mortis. To what extent, and for how long a period might death be hypnotically arrested? Postponed. I can ask him. Oh, but he's gone, nudged along... I should have asked him while...

I'm sure this thuggish-looking gentleman has no idea about such things. Broken fingernails, dirty hands, huge, vulgar teeth. Probably thinking of sauerkraut. Wait. I think I've seen him before too, oh dear, yes, probably years ago, snoring next to me. I remember recoiling in horror that morning. I was clearly a disgusting sight myself, but he was too much. And here he is, come back to say hello. Ivan, Igor, whoever you are. Sorry, I've... Don't touch me.

The night before, in that foul pub, smoking and drinking, watching them all play pool... I do like being around real men, powerful, beautiful types, men of the lowest class and the worst character, with equipment as long as kielbasa, gold under filth. I think that was my first time in a fairy dive. We got plenty drunk, and I lay in the arms of one after another, covering their faces, necks, their rough hands, their grungy clothing with kisses, while they caressed me and called me pet names. Little Petrushkii was supremely happy.

After closing time, we regrouped in an alley where the drinking and lovemaking continued even more avidly. But after I wouldn't drop my pants, one of them grabbed me by the throat to keep me quiet, while another one pulled off my jacket, took whatever he found in my pockets, pushed me down, and sat on me. I could have suffocated with my face in the dust. I moaned and struggled with all my might, but they thought it was fun. For the next couple of months, every step I took hurt from the fissures and contusions around my anus. This was no group of rutting boys playing blind man catch the little girl.

When they finally let me go — with only half my clothing — I rushed out through the alley, and didn't stop until I got to a safe, brightly lit street. I was breathless, exhausted, and I swore to myself — no more slumming. Ever. God had brought this about to drive me back to the path of virtue.

I was sitting there for a few minutes when Mr. Sauerkraut, he must have followed me, showed up with my jacket. I think it was he. This one. He said he was sorry for what happened, he assured me of the friendly feelings of the gang. "You're only a baby," he said, "I'll protect you." So back we went to the warehouse across from the alley. I was so touched by his gallantry, so flattered to be one of them, I was sure the assault hadn't been simple malevolence.

I was still afraid of violence — but perhaps there'd be only a gentle rape, not a beating, and I was so drawn to them. Sucking all right — either way — but anus morally horrible and physically painful. Little Petrushkii would draw the line at anus.

The gang was kind, they patted and soothed me as if I were some peevish baby — which I certainly must have seemed, fretting and sobbing in happiness as I rested my head against them. To lie in the bosom of these sturdy young manual laborers, this was the highest earthly happiness I'd ever tasted. All my money had been filched, and I would have had to walk home several miles, but, this sauerkraut gentleman took me to his place, his hovel. And I woke, disgusted, beside him.

I remember thinking how strange life is, about how Mephistopheles had taken me through an experience the same as Faust's. My carnal self had been stirred as never before, and at the same time, I'd never felt such conflict between body and spirit. What animals we are, but that's how the lieber Vater seems to want it. Wollust ward dem Wurm gegeben!

You, Heilige Vater, Remote One, Inscrutable One. What will be the ultimate test, Hidden One? What will be the last adventure? I know quite well he's hearing me, überm Sternenzelt, listening alone in his elegant abode. However distant, he certainly overhears my mutterings. He who understands what we don't, who remains serious about what seems to us ludicrous — like lechery among worms, he whose inscrutable countenance behind its sevenfold veil is undisturbed by earthly woes and all the tears which spring from mournful eyes...

But in this world He always keeps silent, or perhaps it's just devil-noise drowning Him out. At least for someone like me.

After final death, when time no longer exists, will I finally be able to hear Him? If I were really a believer, I'd focus on nothing but God. But even people who don't believe in God sometimes have an instinctive fear of hell. It's the human disease. Perhaps disease itself is the essential condition of life.

Why would Modest be worried about my drinking Leiner's water? Anyway who cares? Hell is hell. I might have picked it up licking bottoms. But who needs that? There are lots of ways to get sick around here. *Desire* is a sickness. How does a doctor examine moral sickness?

I never doubted that homosexuality is a disease. In fact, I took it as a measure of how marvelously objective I am that I could even understand that. But in some other part of my mind I couldn't believe there was any contamination, say, in my love for Edward, or Bob. Everything that happens is a test, the good as well as the bad. The good especially. Like Nadezhda Filaretovna, my vanishing Countess. My biggest test.

Three. Seven. Ace. Wink. I've borne her disappearance philosophically, but all the same, quelle surprise. She'd written so many times guaranteeing me a subsidy to my dying day. Now I'll have to live differently, on a different scale. I may have to take some job in Petersburg. At the Conservatory again. Perhaps she could no longer afford it, perhaps her family wanted her to stop, but I'm very, very hurt.

Women! Widows! My pride wounded, all my confidence mocked. I hope Nadezhda Filaretovna becomes completely ruined so she would need *my* help. You didn't say that, Petya. It's a sick, silly joke, shameful and disgusting. But I hope so anyway. See? I failed the test.

What hurts me so deeply is not that she doesn't write, but that she seems to have lost all interest in me. During the autumn I read through her letters. "Keep well, my dear, my peerless friend.

Get a good rest, and do not forget one whose love for you knows no bounds." What could possibly have changed such feelings? Illness? Misfortunes? Material difficulty? No. Not in the face of such promises. Yet they have changed, those feelings. Perhaps it's just because I never personally knew her that I imagined her an ideal being. Fickleness in such a goddess? Never. It seemed to me that the earth would crumble before she would become someone else for me.

But it happened, it happened, and my attitude toward people, everyone, my trust in the best of them has been turned upside down. Nadezhda's abandoning me has poisoned whatever small portion of happiness had been given to me by Fate. Never have I felt myself so humbled, never has my pride been so wounded as now. And what is most painful of all: I can't ethically tell her because it would so disturb her to tell her my torments. I can't express myself — and only telling her would relieve me. But not a word to Nadezhda Filaretovna. Did she stop sending money because she'd learned of my homosexuality? From her children?

It's all so confused, so complicated. Horrible! I must simply be alone with my music. I don't need to keep up social conversation with wealthy old women. They're such time wasters, even for people who loathe themselves.

I know self-loathing can be a good thing, a kind of cautioning, a nod to some amount of agency on my part. It's probably the only thing which can temper my addictions — some petty sense that I am ultimately in charge of my own destiny, that I have to finally accept responsibility for my actions.

Three, seven, ace. How can an intelligent man like me give even ten minutes of his time to a ridiculous amusement like cards? Well, if one is rational, with a heart of stone, cold and superhumanly cautious like Herman, one can easily win as much as one wants to. I see absolutely nothing wrong with the desire to win as much as possible as quickly as possible. The idea of the well-fed moralist who thinks that playing for small stakes is worse than playing for large ones "because the greed is petty" — this has always seemed very stupid to me. As though petty greed and massive greed were not the same thing. It's just a question of proportion. What is a trifling sum to a Rothschild is great wealth to me. And as for profits and winnings, people everywhere are always winning or taking away something from one another. Since I myself am completely mastered by the desire to gamble and win, even with all the greedy corruption, if you like to call it that, it's all natural to me. I am Herman as well as Liza. What's the use of deceiving myself? I don't gamble like a gentleman, I gamble like a degenerate. I have my monthlies.

We flatter ourselves to think that gambling, or absolutely *anything* can be cured. I used to think homosexuality was correctable, some inappropriate appendage of childhood sexual experiences which could surely be redeemed by the right woman.

But degenerates, sick and obsessed people, are there among heterosexuals as well. Moreso, perhaps. It's just ridiculous public opinion which makes homosexuality taboo, a breeding ground for hypocrisy and crime. I don't feel wicked, and I don't feel innocent. One can pardon oneself for a crime, but not for a baseness.

IV

That gentleman in the corner. Looks familiar. Broad chest, swarthy face, side whiskers, bloodshot eyes, frizzy hair. Look how long his nails are. He keeps looking me up and down, disgustedly, scowling like the sky.

No lieber Vater that guy. Someone should cheer him up.

"You bamboozler, Pyotr Ilyich! I demand satisfaction. Pistols at twenty paces, you hoax."

What? What is this? I don't…I'm too old for …My god, so belligerent...

"You won't answer? I'd slap your face, but in this crowd, they might think it was applause."

Aleksandr Sergeyevich! I knew he'd come for me.

"Yes, my dear. I have the honor to be your most humble and obedient servant, Aleksandr Sergeyevich Pushkin, you turd, and I demand satisfaction. This rencontre admits of no delay."

Why? Why? What have I done?

"What have you done? What do you *think* you've done? Rape my children, you wretch! Two of them. Is that not enough for a challenge? You will give me satisfaction, Sir. I insist upon it."

But Count, two? It was just your son. Just Sasha. Alexandr. We met by accident, late at night, at Greshniki. We each thought the other, I mean I thought he was...I am so susceptible...You cannot upset the Tsar with this trivial...The glorious name of Stendok-Fermor...

"Who? Stendok-Fermor? Who is Count Stendok-Fermor? Alexandr Sergeyevich Pushkin cannot allow your impertinence to continue. I am obliged to address you, vampire. Will you not fulfill the duties of a gentleman of honor? As to time and place I am wholly at your command."

Yes...Pushkin, yes, of course. Not Stendok-Fermor. I'm sorry, I knew...Pushkin. Aleksandr Sergeyevich. You. Who else? Pushkin. But what is my crime? I was a bit confused. The challenge...

"What is your crime? What is your crime? You steal and falsify my *Onegin*. You steal and falsify my *Queen of Spades*. The world swoons at your sappy outpourings. What kitsch! What drippy, mawkish, maudlin...And now, Pyotr Ilyich, my name will be forever associated with *your* debasements, with *your* "compassionate" letter scene — when *I* meant to ridicule Tatiana, confused with *your* poor Herman-in-love, when *my* Herman is, must be, an addict, a gambler exploiting mindless Liza to go after the countess's money...Where are my satires clothed in your sissy garbage? Do you even know what satire is? There is not so much as a hint of it in your stupid love stories. Or your music. "True love thwarted?" You allow yourself "artistic license", do you? Take stories and poems the entire Russian people know and love, and debase them with your loathsome, no-one-understands-me, little girl soul? There are people worldwide who will never know my work, who will know only your assassination of it, and you so proud. I probably shouldn't waste honest powder on vermin such as you, but let's see if you stand up to bullets as well as they say you compose."

No, I…

"If you can't take the heat, Monsieur, stay out of my particular Eden. The name you bear and the society you frequent oblige me to demand satisfaction for your impertinent conduct. Where and when?"

God, I could use a cigarette. A cigarette. I haven't had one since, I don't remember…

La fumée! Dans l'air, nous suivons la fumée qui monte en tournant, vers les cieux! Ah, George, I will never write such a masterpiece…Le ciel ouvert, la vie errante; Pour pays, l'universe; et pour loi, sa volonté. Et surtout la chose enivrante: la liberté! Nothing more beautiful than to think that you're free…

"And nothing more superficial! Pyotr Ilyich, get up. I want to slap your face. Your brother's, too. Where is he?"

Alexandr Sergeyevich, dueling is banned in Russia — since Peter the Great. Surely you know that. "Whoever issues a challenge which inflicts wounds shall be executed." Yes, they often turn a blind eye, but it's arbitrary who, and homosexuals are supposed to be sent to Siberia, but...and I'm a coward, and you already died in one duel and Lermontov...Lensky...and I love your work, its exact proportions, its majesty...

"Twenty paces. Each of us five paces behind our lines, ten paces apart. Once a shot is fired, we must both stand where we are. Whoever fires first has to wait for the other to take his turn."

The seconds lay out their coats for barriers. Maybe that's how I got here, into this room. Lying here with these flowers. These people.

Look at them, lined up like pious sheep with their handkerchiefs. All those people, all these people, Pushkin, Lermontov, what do they want from me? I hate the human race. Why is the doorman letting them in? Why do they look at me that way? So many friends disappeared, gone. Why do they kiss me drily on the forehead, and put their hands on my heart? Why not on my lips like the Sashas? On my forehead —they want to pry into my private parts, my private world of thoughts and feelings, into everything I've so carefully forgotten...all those tortures at school. The School of Jurisprudence. Mother's Institution for Discarding Children. Not very prudential, just wet and moody. If people knew what was going on. Fear, humiliation, contentious "harmony", jail in "the prison room", public floggings. Sixty lashes on a naked boy so pretty. Forty years, and I remember the swish of the birches. The strong young faculty running up, straining one after the other to whack his ravaged body. Even now, my legs grow weak. I feel like I'm going to faint. What did he do, poor boy? What was his name? I can't remember. Maybe he was the one who raped young Zhukov in Pavlovsky park.

But was it rape? What if they loved one another? At that age...is there anything more delicate, more noble than the shy, friendship of one boy for another? The one who loves dares not express it by a caress, a look or a word. He feels some consuming tenderness which quails at the slightest fault of his beloved. Admiration, selflessness, pride, humility, supreme happiness. Secret, melancholy happiness, like the moist, black earth in spring, like subterranean water some chance event causes to rise, sweeping away everything in its path...

But school was the first place away from home we could meet up with something warm and breathing and fragrant, something in which our could take on form and bathe in the beauty of flesh

instead of in the squalor of loneliness.

I'm ashamed how confused I was, bewildered to the highest degree. But still I always sensed things could be otherwise, that there were fine, penetrable boundaries between human beings with feverish dreams prowling in our souls, gnawing at the walls, and tearing open pathways between us. Our boys' horseplay dissolved the tension and our sexual melancholy. And the little jar of petroleum jelly was an obvious clue for anyone to find, method applied to sex, an outward manipulation of an inward state of love.

Panin would come in the night, but he wouldn't want to be kissed. "I don't go for that," he'd say — though in the morning, when we stood together in the bathroom washing up, he'd look at me with an expression that could have been tender-ness. Or maybe just weariness. I couldn't tell.

Before dressing, I'd stand naked at the mirror, wondering if my body was worthy. Perhaps my eyes were "alluring", and there was something attractive about my smile. Not exactly a boy I was, more like a girl, a girl-like Joan of Arc, a devout tomboy, tough in battle, but yielding. Except I wasn't tough in battle.

It's true that big boys who'd scarcely acknowledged me when I was twelve, the giants of my childhood, were suddenly thrashing me at four-teen, twisting muscles in my arms, panting right in my face with maniac looks, and my hands sliding over their smooth, sleek skin. One, gleaming pants buttons pressing down on me, knees burning into my biceps, unyielding, and I put off shouting "I give up" for ten more seconds just to keep breathing in the smell of his sweat. I didn't want his anger, just his body on top of me, the pressure of his crotch on my diaphragm, the sensation of sinking, the feelings of shame and joy.

But I was brave – I was even part of the Secret Suicide Society – we had to lay between the tracks and let the train pass over us to get into the club. And I did it, I actually did it. And when they came running up to see how I was, how it was, I told them I was fine and it was nothing, really easy, though I think I fainted because I remember hearing it coming, the train, and the noise, and then I don't remember anything until they asked me how it was.

And then, what? thirty years later, Dostoevsky wrote that same episode for Kolya Krosotkin just as if he was there, and when the old Suicide Club gang saw the story come out in the Russian Messenger, everyone sent it to everyone else as if Dostoevsky had somehow cheated, and the gang alone remembered the real thing.

Fifteen was the best, a love story. Fifteen, learning to love myself, shy and audacious, as even now, so many years later, I love and desire those fifteen year olds, three quarters sentimentally and one part erotic.

No wonder our class bands together. "The honor of our school uniform." No wonder we hold our Courts of Honor to keep one another in line, away from the authorities. That long afternoon at Tsarskoye Selo, when they proposed my suicide, my Court, and Tomsky handed me the bottle of Paris Green.

Clever fellows, Tomsky and Tchechalinsky, our class doctors. The symptoms of arsenic poisoning, they explained, were just like those of cholera — severe diarrhea, vomiting, renal failure. Quite accurate. Yes. Thank you, doctor. I'd avoid exposure and disgrace over "the Stendok-Fermor affair". And our class, too, The School of Jurisprudence, all upright and professional.

As if Sasha would disclose anything, or his father, attached to the most distinguished regiment in the country, commanded by the Tsar himself...

Something tells me I've been making up a story, just inventing a story about something which once happened to someone named Pyotr Ilyich, which would've been the same story if the someone had no name at all, if it had been told about anybody, nobody, over whiskey, at night to a crowd.

Look at all these people. It's like a herd of them under their overcoats, clutching their fur hats and handkerchiefs. Must be cold out. Even I'm cold. Ah! A priest. My God, look at that gargantuan cross. Is he wrapped in chains like Lev Nicolayevich's? *"People are still arriving. Perhaps they would like to pray. Let us sing a requiem."* Modya, Bob, tell him I don't see any singers. Good, thank you. Now make him go away. I don't like him. *"It doesn't matter."* It doesn't matter? No singers, and it doesn't matter for a Requiem? *"I'll start the service. Perhaps somebody will turn up who can sing. There are students here. But if not, I'll sing myself. Such a great artist, he was, Pyotr Ilyich. All Russia knows him. It's a sin not to pray, not to sing. I'll do it myself. Everything will be fine."* Oh, Lord, patience. I can still be patient. I like the words, I do. They're all singing. Out of tune is ok. They're singing and crying. Weeping. Weeping.

"With the Saints give rest." Yes — my first movement development. The requiem melody. "Eternal memory." They know it! They're on their knees. The whole room. I can't see them now. Stand up! Stand up so I can see you! Up! The priest is bowing to me. What an ugly mug. Like Brahms, blotchy, jowly. Probably alcoholic with a nose like that. Like Brahms wanted all the strawberry jam for himself. Makes me furious that that talentless mediocrity is seen as a genius! When he's in good spirits, he sings, "The grave is my joy." The empty chasm. And what a pianist! A pianist with ten thumbs. He probably thinks me shallow and self-indulgent. At least I have a self. Does Herr Dr. Brahms? Do these people?

This is what the world looks like, stuffed in heavy overcoats, needing more air to sing. Citizens of Petersburg, menacing, apprehensive, embittered, ruining all happiness refusing to accept life as it is. What kind of world is that? Two plus two!

Look at them: Zenkovsky, Trepov, Stepanov, Volokhov, all these characters in this room here together in their saving dullness, completely accidental to one another except for me, chance people concerned with my life. When they leave here, they won't recognize one another.

Day of wrath? Day of whimpering. This face bent over mine. I know her from somewhere. Frail, indistinct, existing provisionally so as not to be itself. I can't see very well. Do not sob, madame. My intention was just to affirm life — not bring order out of chaos, or upgrade creation. Nothing to cry about. Just embrace the life you're given, which is so beauteous once you get mind and desire out of its way. No weeping. My music was supposed to *stop* the weeping. Without music we are dead, you are dead. Not dead like the dead, but dead like the living. Don't cry.

Getting dark again. Dear darkness. But why colder? Has anything changed? There's a star through the crack in the curtain. Just bright enough to know night is falling. It's shivering like a true star, shuddering maybe. Over time, our inner stars dim, we're less and less alive, morally alive, and then night will pull down its blind, and we'll feel no more guilt than squirrels feel stealing the birds' seeds, and we'll be finally without humor or indignation or passion or desire or any heat at all.

But oblivion is not yet.

If I were to die, the dying would be over. But I want to compose something worthy of God.

Like my Bob subject, *con anima. Con anima*!

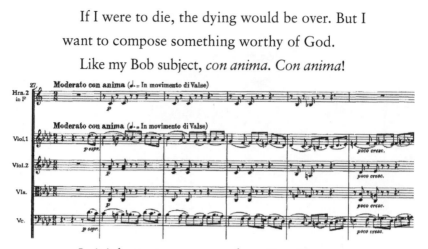

Isn't it better to turn away from Fate, Fate, trumpeting Fate, all the time Fate — and submerge oneself in dreams? Sweet and tender, soulful dreams. A gracious form flits by and lures us on. Bob there! With lovely Bob, how implausible those obsessive trumpets. Put them aside, melt them down — and dreams take possession of the soul. All that was gloomy and joyless and teary — here is happiness! Bob!

And Pyotr. The doubleness of decomposing body and rising soul.

The soul is very very silent, and lying consumes it. Lying or indifference. My soul, seat of my mischief. One thing leads to another and you can never tell how it will end. The cage is too small, too small. Maybe what harms the body leads to salvation.

How valuable music is, how essential for checking our mad impulses. It's God's way of beating in on man, mysterium tremendum unfathomable. Unfathomably obvious. See deeply enough and what you see is music.

What most people love is hardly music, only a kind of sleepy reverie relieved now and then by nervous thrills. It's so hard to make anyone see and feel in music what I do. Music is not just sound – it's feeling. The value of daylight may be great, but daylight truths have no depth, no perspective. No deaths needed in order to reach them.

The hold music has on us is completely mysterious, disrupted by light. Light darkens music. The sign I love a piece of music, that it addresses itself to me, is the need I have when I hear it to get rid of light, turn down the gas, blow out the candles, even if it's night. And if it's day, I want to listen as if in a tomb.

But the mystery music shows us is not of death, it's more of the inexplicability of life, of freedom, of love. The mystery is not "what cannot be spoken of", the untellable, but rather the ineffable. Death is untellable because it's impenetrable, because an unbreachable wall bars us from its mystery. We can't speak of it because there is absolutely nothing to say, we are mute, our reason and language are overwhelmed, transfixed by its Medusa stare.

But the ineffable can't be explained because unlike death there are unending things to be said about it: this is the mystery of music and of God, whose bottom can't be sounded, the inexhaustible mystery of love, eros, caritas, a mysterium par excellence.

From an unsayable negative to an ineffable positive is a distance as vast as that between blind shadow and transparent night, between silence that is mute, throttled, and silence that is tacit. Music takes root in the distant rumor of pianissimo, the border of silence. The opening of the Sixth. The end of the Sixth.

Let there be night then. My time for cruising the docks — and the sky. When I no longer have anything to say, I will stop. All this damn baggage we get attached to and then have to push off, each time a little more fitfully, with a little less energy. My tiny victories are just more and more lifeless accumulation.

Where to move — except where renewal seems possible? I'm tired of dying. I had wanted just a little of death. But nature is taking away my eyes, my ears, my hands, my feet. OK, then. Delay no more. Apply your pitiful "discipline", Petya, since nature made you defenseless against passion. Write another fugue or crab canon or cross motif.

Here I am a man, no longer a boy. What am I doing lying here wasting time and abusing my talent? What use am I making of my gifts? What future do I have if I continue this way? Looking around this hateful room, I feel... Another ballet, maybe, featuring all these big-nosed folks in their overcoats as fairies enchanted.

But in tights, all of them in tights. I do love huge thighs and shapely calves, and bulging crotches. All that sexual power radiating from between the legs. That energy, the rush of blood and adrenalin watching those leaps — genitals tightly bound but flying, twirling in religious aspiration and desire. It doesn't get better than that.

They tell me that I shouldn't idealize ballet so much, that ballet exists only to arouse impotent old men with its lascivious spectacle. But, compared to the docks, say, the ballet is the most innocent, the most moral of the arts. Why else do they always bring children?

Why? Because the fairy tale of our Russian

ballet is truer than life, because life itself is so strange. What better bridges the gap between earthly passion and spiritual transcendence than fairy tale and ballet? I stare at Pavel Andreyevich's legs, his muscles like forked lightning, so free he is, and so adored by all. And then it seems to me that beauty is the highest good, the one thing we all want to have more of or to be — or failing that, to destroy.

Beautiful young love, poignant and doomed — ever my main concern. All the women I am — Odette, even Odile, racial, sexual, crossbreed prisoners, mixtures of animal and man, children of Leda, of animal engendering. That beautiful, painful swan theme comes right from my womb. Tatiana, Joan, Mariya, Francesca, Liza, so do they all, all from my secret womb, all condemned to suffer like me, to be destroyed by the trumpet blasts of fate, Tatiana, Liza, Petya, all of us caught in a net of uncontrollable adversities, unavoidable misery. And death...death.

I remember Sasha's eighth birthday party, when I was nine. She was tall, and I was small, she was a big girl, and I was still Petya, disguised as a child, and girls grow up faster, and she had long beautiful hair and mine was short, and I was tongue-tied in the presence of all her girlfriends in their velvet dresses, their velvet hair, and I wanted so much to be a beautiful girl...

Then will my prince kiss *me* awake, kiss *me* alive? All this now, what's going on in this room, this business is like my Beauty entr'acte, somewhere in the kingdom of magic, everything floating, no rational order, the only thread of coherence the violin high C — there! I can hear it now — the sound which binds everything together, time suspended. But will Sleeping Ugly ever dance? Birth, death, regeneration, salvation? Even for me?

The Russian fairytales, the stories I love. Their purity, so detached from the commonplace world, remaking life in its own likeness, separating good from evil, bringing all fears and terrors to a happy end. Their affinity to painting and music, their sparkling colors and winged phrases. Their riddles, knavishness, deceit, invention and cunning — so effervescent.

Modya's the one I should challenge. To hell with Perrault, he said. "The prince's mother cannot be an ogre who wants to eat her grandchildren." But I wanted that. I want the eating of the children. With my terrifying ogre theme to spice up the end. "Too long," he said.

Why give in? Eating children is basic to all myth, to the birth of art, the source of its metaphors. Maybe I'll do it. Another version. Sleeping Beauty's Wicked Step-Mother, a ballet of its own.

A gamble, but…it's in me. Like my other "it", my "X" — a demon overriding free will, making me do terrible things.

Of course, then I'll deny all responsibility, create Herculean rationalizations, and go home after a disastrous gambling night telling myself I'm the victim of a disease.

An appealing notion — that there's some foreign demon burrowing inside me. Like all addicts I carry my misery stinking within me. And, like all addicts I am a fantastic liar. I lie constantly, atrociously — to hide the results of my habits and assure they can continue. And the person who most readily swallows this shit is me. I can't count the number of times I've had my last spin, played my last rubber, made my last trip to the bank. Three, seven, ace, ha! The Countess bitch gets me every time.

And no, Alexandr Sergeyevich, my Liza doesn't marry "a very pleasant young man somewhere in the civil service with a good income" like yours. My Liza throws herself into a Petersburg canal. Sacrilige? Desecration of your literary classic? Want to challenge me to a duel, maybe? Which is truer, your story or mine? Marriage — or the suicide of a woman betrayed in love? You say "Two fixed ideas cannot exist together in the moral sphere, just as two bodies cannot occupy the same space in the physical world." That's you and me, my friend. *My* Herman kills himself when the trick goes wrong. Yours lives happily in an asylum and spends his life obsessing over the three card secret, "Three, seven, ace, three, seven, ace." Which of us is crueler and more correct?

I think of that blacksmith who placed his head between the blocks of a vise and turned the handle until his skull was broken in pieces. Is there not something awesome, superb about his imagination, his courage? I am not cruel in killing Liza. Who can survive survival? The question must be: Is Death possible? Can I die? Can I say "I can" with respect to death? Can I kill myself? Do I have the power to die?

Well, yes. I could die today if I wished, merely by making a little effort. But it is just as well to let myself die, quietly, without rushing things. What does Kirillov say? Something like "a happy and proud man will not care if he lives or dies." His suicide was only to seek the freedom which makes men lords of the universe. Total freedom. He wanted to open the door, and kill himself — to make a beginning, so that men will understand freedom.

Destruction is an act of absolute power as much as creation. Heaving a brick through a stained-glass window can be just as fertile as designing it in the first place. The suicide has a quasi-divine power over his own existence. Not even God can prevent Liza from doing away with herself. Or me. We are gloriously, pointlessly free. If I desire death, it is to escape not just my sufferings but the monotony of my struggle, to say goodbye to all that eternal lying that allows me to persist. I can finally belong to myself.

Like that suicide on the ship to New York. Can you imagine — I'm the only one among all the passengers who can read German, who can read his suicide note! "Ich bin unschuldig. Der Bursche weiss."

Well, I too am not guilty. The touch of flesh with flesh cuts right through all devious channels of decorum. Flesh to flesh builds the fortress of the I-am, Petya's private own in the midst of all storms...

V

in gravelike darkness,
and whirlwinds of hell
attacking the souls
of those whose reason is eclipsed by passion.
You, Paolo, I, Francesca,
salendo e rigirando la montagna
che drizza voi che 'l mondo fece torti

Out there — a heaven where our appetites are no longer seen as twisted, doing violence to nature, up above the storm and lamentations, the shouts and cries of despair.

Even if I didn't destroy Beethoven's Freude, I surely buried the beetfield pastorale with my storm in *Francesca*. Pitiless toward the audience am I, pitiless toward the musicians, pitiless as Satan toward the damned? Let the critics rage! Master, what do you think? Was I here, at least, more powerful than you? Lieber Vater, is my storm as malign as anything in Job?

Nessun maggior dolore
che ricordarsi del tempo felice
nella miseria...

My Canto V, Petrushka of the dubbiosi disiri?

My own Canto V? There *is* something repulsive about it. It flies like a swan, then it waddles on the ground. The cantabile is lovely, strong. A little heart on the sleeve-ish, but at least not more of Herr Doktor Brahms' inert academicism, so appealing to the taste of the tasteless. Yes, his style is always lofty, yes, he never strives for effect (nor do I, do I!), yes, everything he does is serious, noble — but the most important thing, beauty, is simply not there. Who can say my Andante cantabile isn't beautiful? Glorious?

The Herr Doktor is pleasant enough to me, we share a love for two against three, but we don't really like each other, that I know. Perhaps the very sight of me inspires him with some visceral heterosexual aversion — him with his big cigar — the way strong people hate weak people. That self-inflated scoundrel. Cold, obscure, full of pretensions, and no real depth.

He no doubt doesn't take me seriously either. Ich bin unschuldig. What a talentless wretch!

The fate theme is good. I like the way it crashes

into the cantabile, stringendo, crescendo, fortissimo trumpets. It's more threatening than the steps
of a wife coming up to your door, or a second
lover barging in on a first. "Oh no you don't.
You'll be sorry." The avenging angel bares his
sword. Beware X. Modya, that means you, too.
Our X will surely bring us down.

But yes, then the blaring, frenetic waddle of
the last movement, overwrought, declamatory,
unconvincing. Pyotr Ilyich, you're hopeless. If
Beethoven could do it, why not you? Abominable,
that movement. I loathe it deeply.

The Manfred was better, whatever the critics say. Manfred loved Astarte, Byron loved his
sister, and I...

Thou lovedst me too much, as I loved thee.

We were not made to torture thus each other.

*It was the deadliest sin to love as we have
loved.*

And dancing with Saint-Saens. Rubenstein
couldn't believe our romp. He guffawed and splut-
tered all over the keyboard. I, inspired as Pygmalion, Camille, charming as Galatea, stripped to
the waist, the fat old thing, forty anyway. Nicolai
was bug-eyed with astonishment. I suppose he
didn't realize *I* could actually be a principal dan-
seur. Or that Camille so loved drapery. Too bad it
covered his mighty calves. I relish them as much

as those Saint-Saens thighs, flashing through his dress. Fascinating. I might write a pas de deux for Camille's thighs. Clarinet and English horn over strings and bassoon. A cello solo for what lies between. Good thing it lasted only five minutes. Who knows how it might have transgressed...

But transgression — that was the theme of our story, our dance. Disregard of limits — a sin to which the great and gifted are the most susceptible. Camille and I had only just begun, then he got winded: Pygmalion and Galatea had a child, and the child gave them a grandchild, and the grandchild had a daughter, Myrrha, who called her own father, "dearest, sweetest." Like Manfred with Astarte. Like Byron with his sister. Like myself and that dear fellow over there. Myrrha weaseled her way into her father's bed and then escaped his anger — but with his child in her womb. That wonderful tale — of narcissism, onanism, and incest.

Uncle Petya, do you really want to get into this, with Bob standing ten feet away and Sasha and Lev expected?

Yes, I do. There's magic in the blood of kin, magic we pallidly call love. The same heart muscle thrashing the same blood in the same veins in Bob's dear body and mine. There are some things which just have to be, whether they are or not, have to be even more than some other things that actually are, and who gives a damn whether they are or not?

Incest is not reserved for Uncle Petya. Kings have done it. Dukes. A Pope. There must have been many who've done it, secretly, perhaps suffering for it, dying. Maybe they're in hell for it even as I lie here. But they did it, and now it doesn't matter. Even the ones we know about are just names now, and it doesn't matter.

I love, I'm in love, and I'm beside myself. Even now, in this open box, my insides are burning with love, and I suffer when he leaves the room, when I can't see him. I've gathered myself especially for this time — together with the love virus in the very gland of my consciousness. I can deal with his habits, I can even experience the sweet torture of his longing for women. I don't need him to like men. Just me. Only me. Not even me as a man, but as a discarnate ardor, a pure willingness in his naive, manly, perhaps uninterested arms.

But even when you're not here, Bob, you're close by. Deep in the woods, your image follows me. The light of day, the shadows of the night, everything conjures your charms. Love has spread its poison. J'aime et devant la mort même. I wrote him into my will as if he were my wife.

That word, wife, the "certain personage"

whose name I refuse to utter! How could I ever have cast my lot with so completely unsuitable a partner? I keep asking myself the same question over and over, and whenever she shows up. An act of total madness. I was touched by her love. I thought it genuine. I imagined that in due course I would come to love her. Now I'm completely convinced she never really loved me.

To be fair, she acted sincerely and honorably: she did want to marry me, and she mistook that wish for love. But the harder she tried to win my affection, the more alienated I felt. What to do with my recalcitrant heart? And what if she shows up here, now? My aversion grows daily, hourly, by the minute. I hate her more than I have ever hated anyone, more ferociously than I'd thought myself capable of. If she does come, I'll...

But she did make me realize there's nothing more pointless than wanting to be anything but what I am. Andante cantabile, c'est moi. The self is holy. Sanctus, sanctus, sanctus.

I seem to be getting more religious as I decline. To simply die signifies nothing. It's the path, the path... Bach's Passio secundum Johannem —intense: death, death as a form of joy! This is the refrain I sing to myself. Ich habe genug and *its* Ode to Joy: Ich freue mich auf meinen Tod. Agony crying out in joy! Bach's fusion of exultation and desolation. That's why he's so...normal, so complete.

Certain moments in Bach make me think that everything is only a game that God is playing with Himself. The divinity-in-reality in the Art of Fugue and the Goldberg Variations! When I first heard it, the Goldberg moved me so much I felt I had to go out and walk among the trees — or burst. I closed my eyes and gave myself to the echo of that essential music. Finally, nothing more existed but — what? — plenitude — plenitude alone, without content —the only way to conceive of God, or of what takes place inside Him. After Bach, how can one not believe in God?

And Mozart! The C minor Mass — how can anyone believe that those Kyries, those exalted cries of being, so joyfully ripped apart, are not addressed to Someone, that there is nothing behind them, that they will lose themselves forever in the air? Without Bach and Mozart, theology would have no object, creation would be fictive, and nothingness absolute. If there is anyone who owes everything to Bach and Mozart, to their power of form, it is most certainly God.

Without understanding that, people will never understand stupidity, or evil, or crime. Form governs our pettiest reflexes, sustains the foundations of our whole collective life. Most people think of "art" as works of art, and just so do they narrow the power of form. For them form is only on paper, in the score, and not an emanation from God.

It surprises me that anyone as mentally and morally flawed as I can still exult in Mozart, who lacks the depth and force of Beethoven, the warmth and passion of Schumann, the brilliance of Berlioz, who doesn't overwhelm me or take my breath away. But he enslaves me, makes me feel worthwhile, filled with warmth. When I listen to Mozart, I feel virtuous. Me! Virtuous! The older I grow, the more I love him. Whenever I despise myself, I think about the echo Mozart sets up in me, and I tell myself I'm not so contemptible after all.

Turgenev's Pauline once showed me her autographed score of Don Giovanni. I can't express the emotion that overcame me when I looked through those hallowed pages. It was exactly as if I were grasping Mozart himself by the hand, and talking to him. Certain of his andantes give off an ethereal desolation, a kind of dream funeral from another life. The mystery of his death, the mystery. What a legacy to leave. Writing his own Requiem, if that is what he did. The Christ of music. My pale imitation in the Sixth. Pathetic.

I remember reading a letter Mozart wrote to da Ponte sometime before his death. He says something like "I feel that the hour has sounded; I'm at the point of expiring, I am at term, before having been able to play out all my talent. I'm at the end, here is my funeral chant. I must not leave things behind, unfinished." After that he completed Zauberflöte and was working on the Requiem. "The question is," he asked, "have I anything left to finish?"

Pushkin...dare I mention that name? His little Mozart and Salieri play where Salieri poisons Mozart — to stop the flow of celestial harmony! The murderer's speech burns in my mind, the antithesis of everything I believe: "What if Mozart is allowed to live on and to reach new heights? Will music be maintained at that height? No. It will fall again as soon as Mozart disappears, and he will not leave an heir. Like a cherub, he has brought down a few songs from paradise which will only excite a wingless desire in us, the children of the dust, and then he will fly away. Fly then! And the sooner the better!" Dreadful.

Rimsky has a plan to set the play to music, Mozartean music. I've not looked at it. I couldn't bear to. Much as I love Nikolai, I hope it's never produced.

My worship of Mozart seems contrary to my

romantic nature. But it's precisely because I am a child of my time, spiritually broken, morally ill and out of joint, that I find so much consolation, so much rest in him. In spite of all appearances Mozart is the soul of my soul. He protects me when I go down to the docks to meet my pretty boys.

What is it in him that so touches me? What is the secret chord? The expression of life's joys in a nature uncorroded by reflection? The memory of another world, of something which normal human memory retains no imprint?...We don't know if our memories are true. But we live by memories nonetheless, and not by truth.

So I wonder about the poisoning. That *is* the story. Pushkin believed it — at least enough to write his play.

Karl said his father's whole body became so swollen he couldn't move. That never happened to me. On the other hand, for us both, much vomiting. I hate to vomit. I hate being nauseated. Constanze took him for a drive in the Prater to distract him, and when they were sitting by themselves Mozart, she said, began to speak of death, and told her he was writing the Requiem for himself. Well, we all know that. Who but a dolt doesn't write for himself when he writes a Requiem? And dolts don't write Requiems. But then this eternally gay man began to weep and said he felt he'd been poisoned. Wouldn't that account for the swelling and vomiting? Kyrie eleison! God always finds self-expression in a crucified human body.

Mozart — the most faithful companion of my life.

Getting brighter again. Creamy light. Über Sternen muss er wohnen. Faint light from moist pavement. Is that a streetcar going by?

Sunlight — shining since before Mozart or Moses or Adam and Eve — makes everything seem temporary, perishable, and now it shines through loosely drawn curtains, gaining ground in this little space...Ewigkeit once more.

Quiet here. Damp breathing of the room. The heartbeat endlessly repeating, one breath following another, sleep and waking... It might go on this way for all eternity. The eternal waltz: day, night, sleep, day, night, sleep.

They used to call me "the Russian Waltz King."
What a bad boy I am to write a waltz in five.

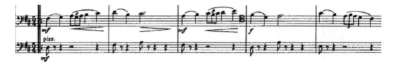

A limping waltz they say, "The Impairment Waltz." But, you know, one can't understand order until one notices the asymmetry of things. Five/four is nothing unnatural to us with our five/four folksongs. All that cosmopolitan, glittering three quarter time gaiety shuts me out. Shuts the real me out. Well let them try to dance to this. In the five/four world, outside of bourgeois time, bourgeois morals can have no meaning. I'm not the old Shakemoffski I used to be, but why should I fear the future? Don't I deserve to have the sun shine on me, too? Prost! All stories end badly.

I'm here. Everything seems mature, fully grown, old, washed out by time. Especially me. Senile. My body seems already slipping away, white hair, wrinkled face — which is part of my body but more than my body. I can't really feel where I end. If I could wriggle my toes...

Hard to imagine some final state where *all* our eyes will be vacant. But the strongest guard is always placed at the gateway to nothingness, to some emptiness too disreputable to be displayed.

Some of my lovers think of themselves as just a passageway for food, a dung-producer, a filler-up of privies. I've slept with them, I know. From these, nothing else comes into the world, there is no real virtue in their work, and nothing of them will remain but full privies. I think Leonardo said that. Something like that. He could also be talking about me. God help us.

The idea that a God exists, and that when called on for help he will respond — that notion is so extraordinary that it alone could take the place of religion. But I do attend mass. Often. The aesthetic solemnity! The liturgy of St. John Chrysostom is one of the most exalted works of art. Anyone following the Orthodox ritual with open eyes and ears, trying to comprehend the meaning of each ceremony, will surely be stirred to the very depths of his being. Especially vespers.

There's nothing like entering an ancient church on a Saturday evening, standing in the semidarkness with the smell of incense wafting through the air, losing oneself in contemplation of wherefore, whence, wither, why? Perennial questions. Sometimes I'm startled by the singing of the choir, and I abandon myself entirely to the fervor of such enthralling music. The holy door opens and "Praise ye the Lord" rings out — one of the greatest pleasures of my life.

Perhaps I'm slated for eternal damnation. Perhaps not. The dead shall be raised incorruptible. If it's true that the lieber Vater has a special love for the sinner, it may be that those like me are especially dear to him.

I'd like to take the ancient Russian chants and harmonize them in new ways, reverently, submissively, the way I did with Ave Verum. To "lose oneself in God" — I know no expression more beautiful. A believer, after all, is someone in love. Not like Romeo. Like a little girl.

It seems to be raining —that same even rhythm Russian rain always has — nothing violent, nothing capricious, just steady, determined... Listening to rain is sufficient activity. I can't imagine why one would want to do anything else. Listen to the rain. Death will come as naturally as the fall of rain. One's whole life is preparation for it.

Hard, though, to resign myself to simply waiting. Why not seek death of my own free will, my right to choose, give death some unique significance instead of passively letting it happen? Kirilov, yes. Why not? One always puts off the decision to choose death., feeling or hoping that one more day, one more hour of life, might offer some kind of unforeseen change, some unexpected opening. We tell ourselves there's plenty of time to die. So the day comes, and we've missed the opportunity to perform the most important act in life. But I still have a crazily persistent wish to kill myself — almost gaily, no real sadness in it, just an absolutely clear sense of ending things. Cleanly.

The suicide lines on my palms. I've never allowed my palm to be read because of them. But the idea of suicide seems like a sotto voce accompaniment to every event of my life, da lontano, serious or frivolous, sometimes urgent. To revoke the self, to do that thing that ends all other deeds. I die, therefore I was. It's much more than the simple thought of getting rid of oneself. It's been a long process of gravitating toward the earth, approaching it, a summing up of many ciphers of humiliation unacceptable to dignity and humanity. It's been a pathway, a way of advancing along a road which has been paved from the beginning.

The truth is — I scarcely belong to this earth, where I'm so deep in exile. It takes the full force of gravity to keep me here and stop me from floating off into another sphere on a another planet. If I stop holding back for a moment, if I even stop working, I'm quickly overwhelmed by depression, boredom, thoughts of the vanity of earthly life, fear of the future, regret over the past, tormenting questions about the meaning of life. I can't stand holidays. On work days I work on schedule, everything goes smoothly, like clockwork. On holidays the pen falls from my hand, I want to be with people I'm close to, or even people I'm not. I feel orphaned and alone, haunted by death. On holidays there's no one on the street. The few passersby are unusually dressed, and I don't know where they're going. On holidays I often weep. I weep when I listen to music and I weep when I compose it, I weep alone in hotel rooms. And always, after a weeping fit, the old crybaby sleeps like the dead and awakens with a new supply of tears. That's my holiday.

Listen to the rain. St. Petersburg November, rainy today, always foggy, often snowy, full of sniffles, coughs, quinsies, sick people eyed by disease and death. Epidemic disease of the spirit, like mine. Depression. Hatred of the human race.

The cholera began in May. It's six, seven months, 500,000 sick, Modya says, more zeros, and half of them now dead.

Using only pure water is the key. Boiled water. Leiner's would never serve unboiled water, even to me, especially to me. Even if I asked for it, demanded it, yelled for it.

Besides, cholera is a disease of the slums, and I'm the most hygienic person I know, scrupulously clean, a true master of cleanliness. But some of the boys — they're not so clean. I wash, though. I spit. I wipe my mouth on clean linen.

"Fecal-oral" the doctors say. Hand to mouth. Or tongue to mouth if one likes to lick around down there. Possible, possible, but not worth thinking about. Better "unboiled water". I'm a sacred, national figure, an internationally respected "ambassador" for Russia and its music. Better "unboiled water." State publication of my Complete Works in leather-bound volumes. State funeral. Grand cortège. Even Papa will be proud. Better than Siberia. Unboiled water, yes.

Koch says it's a vibrio something. How wonderful we should be attacked by vibrations. I must write an opera about vibrios. Do they have sex? Probably not. They no doubt simply split in two — what do they call it? Fission. They fission. Like Dostoevsky's Double, Golyadkin. Golyadkin and

Golyadkin Junior. That was here in Petersburg. At the Ismailovsky bridge where I myself have had many successful strolls.

The Double, by Pyotr Ilyich Tchaikovsky.

Act I: Yakov Vibrioshka falls in love with Clara Pishkova. He feels his heart swelling with emotion, he senses himself growing larger in his love. His and Clara's themes intertwine. He writes her lengthy, longing letters. Orchestral Entracte: the love themes come apart and take up independent existence. Yakov's own theme divides into string and brass versions in which trombones push in to dominate.

Act II: opening in the style of Beethoven's Fourth concerto, strings vs. brass. The crushing of Yakov 1 by Yakov 2. On a cold November night, Yakov 1 throws himself into the Neva. I'll get Modya working on a text. It would be unique. Entrancing. Astounding. Another triumph for German science and Russian art.

Next I'll have Dostoevsky challenging me to a duel.

VI

The devil can make a rock whistle.

When the sun came up this morning I felt

myself completely imprisoned by a legion of devils. Horrible. You don't need much more than devils to explain all of history. For details, then read the historians.

I'm so susceptible, just a battlefield where different evils fight among themselves for primacy. What did Pascal say? "All the evil in the world comes from our inability to sit quietly in a room." Not for me. I've got plenty more sources.

Pantaleyev over there. He looks like an antique marionette going through changes more like those of an insect — from a flaming-haired youth into an entirely different old dotard. Where's the red hair, Anatoly? Yours looks like a tablecloth exposed too long to the sun, ready to be taken out of service. Thrown out.

Time must have some special express train that can bring certain passengers right to a premature old age. Like me. Or Irina Kravchenko there, that old-fashioned coquette now stuffed for the benefit of posterity. Not much difference between her mustache and Trepov's.

But even the youngsters seem soaked in the masks they'll soon take on. Death is already installed inside them, written all over their faces. They all seem as if they are playing roles in some kind of funerary rite.

All these people standing here — holding

themselves perpendicular on legs under skirts, legs within pants, their arms stuck in thick cloth tubes — each of them thinking something, thinking, thinking, observing something, feeling something. Each one something different.

I saw that, Sergei Stepanov, that little touch between you and Gromskii. I know what that means, you sly boys.

I think I saw it. Maybe. Things seem blurrier now — as if they were one text written over another. What am I doing here? If I'm awake, I must be doing something. A person who is awake must be doing something — he has no alternative. I'm swimming in a kind of gluepot, that's what I'm doing, like someone who has got half his body out of a bog, but I can't move my legs, and I may slide back again any time. Give me freedom, whatever crimes I may have committed. I'll scream it. GIVE ME FREEDOM, WHATEVER CRIMES I MAY HAVE COMMITTED!

Nothing. No reaction. Petya is cut off from the land of the living. They all of them fall in step with mortality, with Ewigkeit. Nothing to happen again. Nothing for them to survive. Or become.

That's all right. I'm in no hurry. It would be most disappointing to be dead already, and for everything to continue more or less the same. What's the point of it all if I have nothing more to

look forward to? All I have to live on are memories and hopes, but what is there to hope for?

A fouler mood than ever.

They look more alive than they actually are. Un
poco animato. But under all that cloth, death. Death
approaching. Things, ladies and gentlemen, are not
what they seem. Who knows that better than I? Who
has pulled a trompe l'oreille as outlandish as I?

How long will it take them to hear through
it, my opening to the Lamentoso? A fall nowhere
except in totality. And the waltz which is not a
waltz, only something to trip on.

Is that not the case for us all?

Yes, there was a meeting at which a possible Stendok-Fermor scandal was discussed. Yes, suicide was put forward, almost as a joke, and Tomsky suggested arsenic and could even supply the arsenic. Yes, I was angry, and stormed out angry. And maybe I was upset. So I went for a stroll...

Poor little Petya touring his hovels. Waltzes to trip on. A fall which is no fall — but here we are. Someday perhaps, when there are more and more of us, "inversion" will not be seen by "ethics" as perverted anymore, or judged by a sexuality reduced to "men for women" and "women for men", that somnolent bipole for savages — with its tacky Apparat — feminine charms for women, sordid brutality for males — which makes it impossible for a "normal" person to see half of humanity, sacrifices one half of him to the propagation of the species. Now there's an unbridgeable gap between values and accepted sexual practices. How many saintly victims have fallen in the carnage? Murdered.

Fallen to cholera, too. If certain moderating influences were suspended, the proliferation of Vibrioshkas and other infusoria would rise to its maximum rate, and after a few days, organisms that might have filled a cubic millimeter would become a mass a million times greater than the sun — and along the way would have destroyed all the substances on which we live, so there would exist neither humanity nor animals here on earth. Nor do people understand the catastrophe might be released by the incessant frenzy behind the world's apparent solidity. They busy themselves with their own affairs without thinking about these things, some too small and some too large. Things are not what they seem. But Kant and I know one thing: "Out of the crooked timbers of humanity no straight thing was ever made."

Listen! Listen...in the deepest quiet, someone is singing a slow, slow song. In the silence after the Adagio lamentoso — some inaudible stammering, repeating every sound. I can't make out the words, the language, repeating over and over like a giant saw, slowly cutting through wood. Giant, motionless movement, but I can't tell what's moving. I need to know the words. Words will protect us from what they represent.

Something is coming into being, forming in concealed configurations like iron filings in a magnetic field, in the bottomless pit of things that happen. Things that have happened. Sickness puts you outside your species, Petya, on the verge of zoology. Botany. Is this the approach of death?

The body seems maliciously reliable, recording every heart beat, none identical with the previous one. With every push from the pump the machine wears down, the veins, the kidneys, the eyes use themselves up. The so-called time of everyday life becomes absolute, more and more intensely irreversible. With each forward movement of the second hand, time becomes thicker, heavier. What I dread most is the coming of the cold. It will be hard to live through another winter.

I thought I'd have a Ninth, like all of them. But what can follow the Sixth? I'm done. My symphony is done. Who can take it further? Scholarly Doktor Brahms? Bizet is dead. Berlioz is dead.

Borodin is dead. And I too. I see it coming. I will not write more music. I will be moved into my little cell in the Kingdom of the Earth. Mama, with your beautiful hands, come see — the stars are getting closer. The Sternenzelt is singing. The remnants of constellations. The sawing of the great machine.

I did all I set out to do, Mama, or could do. I could stop here if I wanted and no one would rebuke me with laziness, not even I myself, but of course this is the moment that Fate's trumpets pick out to clobber you.

Will all these people ever leave? I want to be alone to concentrate my mind and prepare myself – reverently – for a solemn Mass, my celebration, my greatest celebration. I want to be alone. You hear that, everyone? I WANT TO BE ALONE TO PURIFY MYSELF AND PREPARE!

To be again without boundaries, outside time, mindless, irrational, escaped from a body which, even after all these years, still clings to the contentment of names, senses, sounds I don't even remember. But it's not only the mind which becomes inured. Holy of holies the body itself, never estranged from the old soft feel of soap and clean linen and something between the foot and the earth to distinguish it from the foot of the beast. I don't really mind my body failing. It could be a pleasure. And I do want to go silent. What a strange and lovely hope, to turn toward silence and peace. No themes, no cries, no obligation to be a credit to the art of dying. My beloved imbecile body doing its best without me. I wonder what its last words will be.

To tell the truth, I'm in no hurry. The task of rebirth seems ominous, full of nonhuman intention. Life will strive to persevere, and in any case, I don't want to die utterly. But it would be good to know if I were going to die definitively or not. I can't really conceive of myself as nonexistent.

This thirst for Ewigkeit is very like love, I think. I want to be myself, yes, but finally I want to be everyone else as well, to encompass the totality of all things, limitless in space and endless in time. This is love among men. To be, to be forever. To be endless. To be like God.

Whenever I contemplate the serenity outside my window in Klin, whenever I look into the eyes of a lover, eyes from which a fellow soul is looking at me, I actually dilate. Dilate. Diastole.

I wrote dilation even into the limping valse triste.
Allegro con grazia — that's what the grazia is.
Humans limping, crippled, full of dilating grace.
I feel my soul's opening bathed in the flood of life.

But if once the voice of mystery whispers to me
"You will cease to be," once the wings of the angel
of Death brush against my body, it's systole that
pushes soul into sound. Contraction. Diminution.

Darkness breaking in. Beware, Pyotr. Love is
the dark side of life, more corrupting than any vice.
Where love blossoms, chaos erupts.

I want to live, somehow, always, forever. I do not
want to be subsumed in the grande salle, in infinite,
eternal matter or energy, or even subsumed in God. I
want to possess God, not be possessed by him, without ceasing to be the I that I am in here. I dread tearing
myself away from flesh, sinful as it may be. I dread
still more tearing myself away from everything per-
ceptible and material, from everything of substance.

They call this pride — "stinking Pride," — and

maybe they look down their noses and ask who are we, we vile worms, to pretend to immortality? By virtue of what? What for? By what right?

Well, by what right do we live? By what right do we exist at all?

It's immortality that's the problem, the only real and vital problem, the problem that strikes closest to the root of our being, the problem of our personal and individual destiny, of the immortality of the soul. Enter trumpets in F minor. Do I really want to persist, immortal — sans teeth, sans taste, forgetting everything, understanding nothing? Not being able to escape myself through all eternity?

I'm having trouble gulping down this obstinately rising sob.

I'm having trouble conjuring up the image of my dear, dead mother.

When I was a child, my mother told me that certain clouds were the souls of the dead going to paradise. I was amazed clouds could have real souls. Now I know it only means a storm is coming. Still, it is amazing.

Souls must detest eternal lying. And feigned indifference — like some premature death, a sin with no real atonement. Maybe this decaying of my body will lead to salvation. The great duet of decomposition and awakening.

Ach, Petrushka, your soul is the seat of all your

problems, pushing you toward your cliff, shoving, guiding your fall. And you can't tell how it will end.

The Universe is too small, that's what. I beat my wings against its bars. Two of my toes are cut, my knees hurt, my shins hurt. And even so, my soul is quiet. Quintuple piano. Almost silent, empty. Adagio lamentoso. The quiet makes me realize it's not mere yearning I've lost, but something positive, some spiritual force, something that flowered in me — in the guise of grief.

How often in your life, Pyotr, when faced with some new and awful event, have you said, "This is it, I can bear no more, this is the end," — and it was not the end. Yet the end can't be far off now. And after that, it will not be like it is now, days following days, out, on, around, in back of, in — like leaves turning in the wind, or pages torn out, crumpled and tossed. It will be a long, unbroken time without before or after, light or dark, without from or towards or at. The old pseudo-knowledge gone. B minor forgotten. Perhaps only dreaming.

I know all this dying business is just a simple trick of physiology. In spite of everything, I'm enjoying myself on this wonderful night, filled with extraordinary lightness, a kind of beatitude before the desiccated life takes hold.

At this stage, my brain is quite in control.

Strange it is.

Strange.

Tell me, please, what means softening of the brain? How can I explain it to you? It's a disease in which the brain becomes softer...dissolves. Is it curable? Yes. Cold douches. Something internal, too. Like a bagpipe, the music ends when you're out of air.

Regret. What do I regret? What can be more heartbreaking than to be left alone, all alone, without anything to regret — nothing, absolutely nothing, because all you've lost was nothing, nothing but a small round zero. Years, months, days, hours, seconds, and the seconds fly off like the wind. Pyotr Ilyich Tchaikovsky, an accumulation of seconds that add up to zero. Nothing.

Thank you, dear Bob, thank you, Nikolai and Lev, for wrapping my legs. I was getting cold. Like Socrates, no? No, not like Socrates. I am besieged by winter. I can't move, though. Strange. Immobility accumulating here. We all seek freedom, you know, whatever crimes we have committed.

Have mercy on me, God. I am sinful in every corner of my being. The gifts thou hast given me were not contemptible. My talent was a small one, and even that I wasted. It's only when our work is mature that we realize we've thrown away our time and squandered our energies.

I know it's absurd for me to cry out I'm alive,

and don't want to be hurled into the dark along with the lost. Libera animas omnium fidelium defunctorum de poenis infernie et de profundo lacu. Ne cadant in obscurum. But, God, it's not me — it's *the life in me* selfishly begging...

More wrapping? That's all right. I'm warmer now, thank you. Nikolai, Lev, leave me alone to finish dying. The dark is already at hand, the dark that will put an end to music, the dark no dawn will follow. Death will cure me of my thirst for immortality.

Earlier, things were drenched in radiant blue, but now the sky is going black. The Sternenzelt dark, heavy matter, implacably black. The stars are

Where?

Where the glitter of background lights?

Endlessly tired. Good. I wait. Waiting is an act of great purity. Dust, resting. Dying on. No more breathing. Just protoplasmic inhale and collapse, inhale and collapse...

Don't wrap my face. Thank you.

One outlives oneself by years, by years, but I'll go there now. I'll wait my turn and go there. I've got to finish it before I, before the, you see what I mean, before what it's about, before it all turns into what it's about.

They sprinkle me, they're putting me in metal.

A metal something. Tin. Lead. They are deserting me, abandoning me to inanimate beings. I can't I can't I can't! It's got to end right here. I've got to go back and make a fresh start when I find out what I was looking for find out what it was all about

They're closing the box.

Howling, no howling. Above all, no howling.

To avoid having to copy and paste the web links embedded in the notes, read them on Spuyten Duyvil's website where you can simply point, click, and listen...

spuytenduyvil.net/kingsfatherlinks.html

NOTES

A Toolbox For Closing A Coffin

(NOTES FOR THOSE WHO ENJOY SUCH THINGS)

Shortly before *And Kings Shall Be* begins, Pyotr Ilyich Tchaikovsky lay on a couch in his brother's Petersburg apartment surrounded by men in frock coats – doctors, relatives, friends, all helping him. While I'm sure he appreciated their attendance, I am also sure he was subsequently happy to be rid of it.

For similar reasons, my feelings grew while writing it that the poem of Tchaikovsky's corpse should be allowed to lie there, unencumbered by any frock-coated, foot-noted scholarly apparatus, as alone as T was at the end.

Still, I think it is a reasonable request from those not pentalingual (as T was), and who don't know the nicknames within the family (i.e. Modya=Modest, his brother and partner in crime) to be further informed about what's going on. So these are a set of notes to provide translations, cultural identifications, and my own commentary, musical and otherwise, as I think may be of interest, entirely separate from the poem.

Why the book, and why this particular book

The death of Tchaikovsky remains a mystery to this day. There is an "official story" as told by Pyotr's brother, Modest, in his "definitive biography" which appeared three years after Pyotr's death in 1893. It is called "the fatal glass of water". In this narrative, the composer died after drinking a glass of unboiled water in Modest's apartment during the cholera epidemic then raging in St. Petersburg. Another variant is told by a friend who attests to being present at Leiner's, an upscale restaurant, when T ordered cold water even if unboiled, was refused, pulled rank, and glugged down a glass, saying something like "Who cares?"

The fatal glass of water immediately raises certain problems. Why would a high-end restaurant serve unboiled water during a cholera epidemic? If Tchaikovsky died of cholera, why was he permitted an open-coffin ceremony in which he was visited, cried over, and even kissed by thousands of his fans, lined up for blocks outside Modest's sixth floor apartment? By medical order, cholera victims were to be doused in disinfectant and sealed in lead inner coffins to prevent the spread of disease.

The plot thickens: In 1979, Alexandra Orlova, a Russian musicologist, published some research which quite unsettled the official story. She had gone back to Moscow and Petersburg and talked with surviving ancients whose parents had been friends of the composer. "What did your parents tell you about Tchaikovsky's death?" she asked them. They all told the same story.

Their understanding from their parents was that Tchaikovsky "had been ordered to commit suicide by a Court of Honor" made up of his old schoolmates — to prevent a national scandal involving a love affair with the son of a friend of the Tsar. Should word get out, both Tchaikovsky's honor, and the honor of the School of Jurisprudence would be compromised. The doctors in the group could arrange an arsenic exit whose symptoms closely mimicked that of cholera, and T would die at the height of his fame, a national culture hero, a martyr to the disease, his music would be preserved, and his name remain at the top of the artistic pantheon. Or he could die whenever, scandalized, his music forgotten. Tchaikovsky was reported to have burst out of that long meeting screaming – and he was dead three days later.

Before Orlova's, there were other suicide theories. The Sixth Symphony, which Tchaikovsky premiered nine days before his death, is seen my many, including myself, and was even referred to by the composer, as his "requiem". In the middle of the development of the first movement there are quotes from the Orthodox Requiem text, and a hint of the Dies Irae. The symphony, especially its radical last movement, the *Adagio lamentoso*, was, is, as despairing and deathy as anything ever written before or after. At the time, his courtly intrigue notwithstanding, he was desperately in love with his nephew, "Bob", his sister's boy. They were living together in a relationship which might become catastrophic for the family. He dedicated the Sixth Symphony to Bob, conducted it, and died. That sequence, too, makes a certain amount of causal sense.

Google "Death of Tchaikovsky" for a quick review of all this, and a good bibliography of the relevant literature, bunking and debunking.

So – cholera, with or without a fatal glass of water? Or suicide, ordered or self-imposed as a way out of emotional/social impossibilities? Because I am interested in false "official stories" – from JFK and 9/11 to Tchaikovsky – I decided to solve the problem. What chutzpah!

111

I — from the sticks of Burlington VT, with only English, French, German and a little Russian — would write a medical mystery, have the detective solve the problem, and voilà, case solved. Next.

An amazing find gave me much encouragement early on: guess who was the doc in charge of the cholera situation outside of Moscow (where Tchaikovsky lived). Anton Chekhov! And the writer was a great fan of the composor. They had been planning to write an opera together. So — Chekhov would be my medical detective solving the mysteries around the death of his friend and hero.

And why? Because Chekhov's patron was Alexei Suvorin, publisher of the powerful newspaper *Novoye Vremya,* New Times, which, two years after Tchaikovsky's death chose to cover, in a daily, sensationalistic way, Oscar Wilde's homosexuality trial in London, thus reminding Chekhov of his dead friend, and the dubious posthumous forensics.

What could be better? Dr. Chekhov solves the famous Tchaikovsky mystery. I get to study up on Chekhov as well as Tchaikovsky, and imitate their thoughts and writing. A God-given assignment for a novelist and lover of Russian literature.

The great edifice quickly came crashing down. All the contradictions contradicted one another. There was no evidential storyline which didn't come up against a wall. For example, Alexander Poznansky (a native Russian speaker and scholar with much greater access to documents than mine) counters the open-coffin problems with an assertion that the epidemic was coming to an end, and that months before Tchaikovsky's death, the burial regulations had relaxed back to open-coffin norms. I can't find the documents, and couldn't read them if I could find them. The various reports of attending doctors contradict one another on details, even on dates. And above all, I was beginning to find the forensics boring – the core of a detective novel.

So I put all the Chekhov stuff into a folder, and proceeded with Tchaikovsky alone – the corpse trying to figure out what has happened to him. Because I didn't know what the real story was, I had to fudge big time, and allow T to consider all the gossip he was aware of after he became sick, and all the suicidal thoughts he had had during his life. Out of all these, the reader will have to construct a satisfactory theory – or just accept not knowing. All possibilities are somewhere in the text.

I do have my own theory: Since the time from infection to death is generally longer than the fatal glass of water of water theory allows, the contagious act must have been earlier in the week or ten days preceding. I'm willing to buy Poznanky's assertion that the epidemic regs had loosened, and that an open coffin affair would not necessarily exclude a cholera victim, especially if his mourning were nationally important. My own thought is that Tchaikovsky likely picked up the fecal-oral disease several days earlier via "rimming" – a tongue-to-anus practice among homosexuals – while "cruising the docks" late at night looking for 15 year old lower-class boys to "fall in love with". He may have suspected this. We don't always know where our diseases come from.

Though this is speculation, I have to say that much of the material in the book was *not* speculation, or fictionally imagined, but was fed directly by voluminous correspondence now published and quoted, especially the stream of letters (keeping his sexuality secret) with his strange patroness, Mme Nadezhda Filaretovna von Meck, and his uncensored communication with his homosexual brother. His biographers have feasted on it, and I on them.

The title

I discovered the title by accident while singing "My Heart is Indicting", a 1727 Handel Coronation anthem written for George II's Queen Caroline. The Isaiah text seemed particularly appropriate, even when twisted into Tchaikovsky's context.

Tchaikovsky was certainly the queen as well as the king of music, feted and nourished by Tsars and kings, nursing mothers to his invert genius. The nobility bowed down to him, as did the people. While T was unsure about the Lord, he had his gods, Bach, Mozart and Beethoven among them, and was tantalized by their visions of a loving Father in heaven. The odd bisexual jolt of kings nursing sets the tone for the piece, even for those unacquainted with Tchaikovsky's sexuality.

Notes on the text

page 5
I

There is a notion in some religions that the newly dead are confused after stepping through the door. The *Egyptian Book of the Dead*, for example, is an instruction manual, a tutorial, a collection of spells for, as the hieroglyphs say, "emerging forth into the light." Some texts may be seen at http://www.africa. upenn.edu/Books/Papyrus_Ani.html.

Tchaikovsky lies here a bewildered newbie. Much needs to be parsed. Confusion haunts him throughout the text, the old life energy swimming in and out of his weakening grasp.

page 5
Strange. Strange.

I had imagined the book beginning and ending with "Queer. Queer." But my old editor, Fred Ramey, convinced me I had to be careful of any anachronistic modernisms in rapidly and regionally changing language around homosexuality. It's not easy to find out what slang words were used for homosexuals in Moscow or Petersburg in the 1890s. Given its current evolution in England and America as a take-back word, "Queer" was probably not among them. Did "stranii" (strange) and its variants overlap with signifiers for homosexual behavior. Finding myself over my linguistic pay-grade, I retreated to the non-word-play of "strange", describing T's seeing stars beyond the ceiling.

page 5
Orion

On a November night, the pre-electric St. Petersburg night is fierce with winter stars, the constellation of Orion chief among them. Hanging from Orion's belt is his four-star sword. It doesn't take much imagination — especially for a gay man like Tchaikovsky – to see the sword as something else. http://goo.gl/U8QsYe

page 5
And above the stars?

The blazing winter sky inevitably draws the imagination outward. So the next question for pre-big bang folks is "What's beyond *that*?" Whatever T first thought in Russian, "Überm Sternenzelt" ("Above the canopy of stars") would be an involuntary simultaneous translation for any classical musician. "Überm Sternenzelt" is a phrase from Schiller's *Ode to Joy*, an evocation often repeated at crucial musical moments in the choral finale of Beethoven's Ninth, B's determined, hyper-setting of that poem.

Tchaikovsky had a special relationship to that extraordinary movement: as a sophisticated but malicious prank, Anton Rubenstein, Tchaikovsky's composition teacher at Conservatory, assigned him to set the *Ode to Joy* poem for a graduation exercise. T was so unhappy with the results that he refused to attend its performance, and happily destroyed his score afterwards. The embarrassment led him to further appreciate Beethoven's no-holds-barred wrestling with the text, though his relationship with the big B was always fraught.

ein lieber Vater

What is there then above the starry sky? Above the canopy of stars, "muss ein lieber Vater wohnen". So says Schiller, so says Beethoven. A loving Father. Must dwell. Must. Tchaikovsky had a loving father, whom he loved so much as to get married (disastrous!) to please him. So — only attenuated Oedipal stuff there. (T was very attached, perhaps pathologically so, to his mom.) But that's "father" with a small f. What about the big-F father, the big-V *Vater*? (alas, all German nouns are capitalized, so the difference is not so striking in German.)

Tchaikovsky's religious stance, like Beethoven's, was something of a muddle. He certainly loved the aesthetics of the Orthodox Church, its rituals, its iconography, and above all, its music. He wrote church music himself, and inserted a quote from the orthodox Requiem sequence into the first movement of his last Symphony. But did he really "believe in God"? I find that unclear. Beethoven, I think, did "believe" in an Enlightenment "Godhead", but Russia wasn't culturally and historically as "enlightened" as the German-speaking lands. Aesthetically at least, T was a believer.

And ethically? Many have commented on Tchaikovsky's generosity and the pleasure of being around him. He did have a few unChristian thoughts when his benefactress, Mme von Meck, abruptly stopped sending checks. But aside from that, and unlike Beethoven or Brahms, you'd certainly want to have him over for dinner.

"Ethically Christian" then, except for one thing, a thing which tainted his entire adult life – his confusion, religious and otherwise, over his homosexuality, a mortal-sin-but-I-can't-help-myself situation. Much pained discussion about this in communications with Modya, his also homosexual brother. Did Tchaikovsky think of himself as an ethical Christian? Some days yes, some days no. On the latter, he had much close embrace from Hell. The storm in his tone poem *Francesca da Rimini* was one he often experienced.

As for the *lieber Vater überm Sternenzelt* – I can imagine a freshman corpse might want to presume His existence. Pascal's Wager. Tchaikovsky's is an amazingly complex psyche and life, and a Google or Amazon search will instantly lead to the most relevant articles and books. But don't forget to listen to the works. YouTube is essential. If you have time to internalize only one, it should probably be the Sixth Symphony.

page 6
better than an ogre mother

One of the funnier disputes between Petya (Pyotr) and Modya was over the contents of his second ballet, *Sleeping Beauty*. Tchaikovsky always identified with beleaguered young girl heroines, and was in continual search for the prince who would kiss him into total wakefulness. But the original Perrault story (*La Belle au bois dormant*) did not culminate with the resurrection of the princess. Some pretty weird stuff goes on.

The wandering prince and his newly awakened princess have two children, L'Aurore (Dawn) and Le Jour (Day), whom they hide from the Prince's mother — who happens to be an ogre (!) Hmm. Once he ascends the throne chez Mama, he is no longer able to keep the secret, and Mama sends the princess and children out to live in a house in the woods. She supplies the little family with a cook from her own staff, whom she instructs to kill and cook the boy for her dinner, using her favorite sauce.

The kind-hearted cook substitutes a lamb (in the same sauce.) Mama loves it, and orders the girl cooked next. This time the cook substitutes a goat, and slathered in sauce, it goes over well. Talk about mother-in-law problems! When her turn came, the princess offers her throat to be slit so that she might join her children whom she thinks dead. The cook pulls a fast one again, substitutes a hind for Mama's meal (in sauce, to be sure), and brings the Princess's family joyfully together at his own little cottage in the woods. But Mama discovers the trick, and for revenge prepares a courtyard tub filled with "toads, vipers, grass-snakes, and serpents" in which to throw the princess and her little family. But the Prince, now king, returns in the nick of time, and Mama the Ogresse, now discovered, throws herself into the tub and "was instantly devoured by the horrible beasts she had ordered placed within it." The Prince is taken aback – she was, after all, his mother – but "he was soon consoled by his beautiful wife and children."

How's that for a show to take the children to?

Tchaikovsky actually wanted that for the end of his

ballet. Modest talked him out of it. The Tsar said the expurgated ballet was "very nice."

page 7
my Pathétique will take back your Ninth.

Taking back Beethoven's Ninth is a major theme in Thomas Mann's *Doktor Faustus*, as his composer, Adrian Leverkühn, descends into demonic creativity. Beethoven's choral movement is such an optimistic conclusion to the symphony, and for all its musical complexity, seems to some, myself included, spiritually jumbled compared to the preceding three movements. (I have an extended essay about this at http://goo.gl/6f0Lbw, if you care to read it. Among my orchestra mates, mine is generally considered a whacko opinion.)

The basic question Beethoven's finale raises is whether its optimism has any except pseudo-reality in our doom-headed time. Leverkühn, his fictive existence recorded just after Nazism and the ravages of the Second World War, could definitely say No! in thunder. For him, as for his author, ours was a civilization only to be mourned. (The end of *Doktor Faustus* contain some of the most beautiful, saddest pages ever written.)

Tchaikovsky, newly dead in November, 1893, had less to mourn than we do. Still, the end of the Sixth, the *Adagio lamentoso*, does take back the Ninth, and whatever drove Mann to end his Faustus as he did must have overlapped with the impulse to T's, devastating and original move.

Which is true, B or T? Which is relevant to our time? Which is most faithful to the human condition? I think even those who live a good, rich life and die a good death, painless, surrounded by love, would judge Beethoven's conclusion to be manic at least, and if inspired, crazed. I put those Mannian words into Tchaikovsky's head because he must have felt his rendering to be more human, more humane, more realistic, more just.

page 8
Florestan's happy release

Beethoven wrote only one opera – *Fidelio*. There again, ten years before the Ninth, he shows his true and constant character as one of a tough guy with a mawkish heart of gold. The gentle giant.

Florestan, unjustly held by the villainous Pizarro, is liberated from prison via some super-operatic plotting via his wife, Leonore, disguised as a prison guard, Fidelio. It's an odd work, written and re-written, not very successful in Beethoven's time, and not very gratifying to Beethoven. But this comment from the conductor Wilhelm Furtwängler in 1948, the same year as Doktor Faustus was published, is worth considering:

"[T]he conjugal love of Leonore appears, to the modern individual armed with realism and psychology, irremediably abstract and theoretical.... Now that political events in Germany have restored to the concepts of human dignity and liberty their original significance, this is the opera which, thanks to the music of Beethoven, gives us comfort and courage.... Certainly, *Fidelio* is not an opera in the sense we are used to, nor is Beethoven a musician for the theater, or a dramaturgist. He is quite a bit more, a whole musician, and beyond that, a saint and a visionary. That which disturbs us is not a material effect, nor the fact of the 'imprisonment'; any film could create the same effect. No, it is the music, it is Beethoven himself. It is this 'nostalgia of liberty' he feels, or better, makes us feel; this is what moves us to tears. His *Fidelio* has more of the Mass than of the Opera to it; the sentiments it expresses come from the sphere of the sacred, and preach a 'religion of humanity' which we never found so beautiful or necessary as we do today, after all we have lived through. Herein lies the singular power of this unique opera.... Independent of any historical consideration ... the flaming message of *Fidelio* touches deeply.

We realize that for us Europeans, as for all men, this music will always represent an appeal to our conscience." (quoted in Wikipedia article on *Fidelio*)

Furtwängler, himself accused of Nazism for having stayed in Germany conducting, honored, and being state-supported throughout Hitler's regime, sees Florestan's happy release as helping to heal the German people through Beethoven's holy spirit evoking a "nostalgia of liberty", a "religion of humanity".

Tell it to the gypsies and Jews, Wilhelm. Tchaikovsky's *Adagio lamentoso* could never be so employed.

page 8
voice of the burning bush

If you want to hear how Schoenberg thought it might

122

sound, check out the Burning Bush singing in his opera *Moses and Aron* (1928-32, unfinished). http://goo.gl/MrHkI9 (BB starts singing to Moses at 1:16, telling Moses to take off his shoes.)

page 10
Malaya Morskaya

No.13 Malaya Morskaya was the address of the then upscale apartment house where Modest lived in a top floor apartment. The neighborhood today has become more pedestrian. http://goo.gl/Z4SbyM. The corner room at the top is the one in which Tchaikovsky's corpse lay. There is a superb BBC documentary called *Who Killed Tchaikovsky?* which you can find in five parts on YouTube. In the second segment (2/5), starting at 2:54, you will see a moving, if comic-awful, exploration of this once snazzy apartment: http://goo.gl/gYvQq8. I'd definitely advise watching all five segments.

page 11
I first saw electric light

One of my more frustrating searches was trying to find out if the room in which Tchaikovsky lay was lit by electricity or gas. I was able to determine that Nevsky Prospekt, St. Petersburg's Fifth Ave, inaugurated electrification in 1893. But when in 1893, and what other neighborhoods were wired and when? There may be records buried away in some Petersburg archives somewhere, but there were no books I could find on the subject. So I decided to go with gas. If I've got a thinking, talking corpse, I've got some fictive leeway. http://goo.gl/bqfMO0

page 11
It's so bizarre in here.

The music this brings up for T is the rather weird opening of the last movement of his First Symphony, (http://goo.gl/P2FlA 33:06), an odd moment in an otherwise energetic symphony — as in the next selection (first movement, 9:05). This alternation between vivacious and grim is at the core of Tchaikovsky's fractured heart.

page 12
Bob, Modya, Nicolai, Lev

These were all people surrounding Tchaikovsky immediately before and after his death. Bob was his beloved nephew, the possible cause of a possible suicide, of whom more later. We've already met Modest, Modya, his brother, in whose apartment T died, and was laid out. Nicolai was either Nicolai Rimsky-Korsakoff, the composer's composer friend, or Nicolay Figner, a singer friend who had helped with the early preparations. Lev was Lev Bertenson, one of the Bertenson brother MDs, who attended T through his last illness. It was problematical, both for Tchaikovsky's fate, and for the subsequent forensics, that neither Lev nor his younger brother, Vasiliy, had ever attended an actual case of cholera. They were doctors to the upper class, and cholera was a poor person's disease.

page 12
the day on the river bank, six boys blocking my every attempt to run away

Hoping that he might become a civil servant,

Tchaikovsky's parents enrolled him at the Imperial School of Jurisprudence (http://goo.gl/E9yHi4) when he was ten. He graduated at 19, a titular counselor, on the bottom rung on the civil service ladder.

Those nine years began traumatically with Pyotr's separation from his mother, an event which never ceased to pain him. Because he was only 10, he had to spend his first two years at the preparatory school, 800 miles from home. He remembered his dragging himself along behind his mother's departing coach, screaming "Mama, don't leave me!" He spoke and wrote about this for the rest of his life.

There are many reports from many sources about pupil experiences at boys' private schools, about the bonding, sexual and otherwise, and the often sadistic treatment a young student might receive from classmates and teachers. I have woven several of these together to create some fictive memories for T's corpse. For instance, at weekly dancing classes, some boys had to take the role of the girl. For a child like Pyotr, this was not a simple experience. Communal showers gave kids a lot of opportunity to study the physical changes going on in their own and their classmates' bodies. There were iconic jars of vasoline. And there were public floggings for malfeasance, with much morbid fixation on young male buttocks.

The School of Jurisprudence years turned out to be traumatic not just for the pre- and adolescent boy, but may have been the cause of his death, forty years later. Because of the serious punishments by the staff, pupils regularly held "Courts of Honor" to resolve issues without bringing in the administration. These courts would strictly uphold the honor of the school and of their particular class, and continued post-graduation, lifelong. It was just such a court of the class of 1859, a group of late-middle aged, accomplished men, that according to Orlova (see initial note, above) ordered T to commit suicide, and provided the chemical means.

page 13
My tears at the Requiem

Presumably, from what fictively follows, T had attended a performance of the Mozart *Requiem*, and broke down in tears. My choice of that particular requiem stems from Tchaikovsky's particular worship of Mozart, and the popular story of Mozart being visited by a stranger dressed in black, who commissioned him to write a requiem, the stranger being interpeted by Mozart as Death, and the requiem being understood as his own. There are those among the Who-Killed-Tchaikovsky? community (myself among them), who think of the Sixth Symphony as a consciously written requiem for self.

page 13
Nutcracker *attack on the Jews*

You can't make stuff like this up. I include this tidbit as an illuminating glimpse of the nationalistic energies Tchaikovsky was surrounded with, and the antisemitism often attached. Tchaikovsky was frequently criticized as being too "European" a composer using classical western forms, and worshipping French and German musical gods. He travelled too much out-of-country. Ironic, then, that he eventually became the icon of 19th century Russian music.

page 14
Carmen

T thought *Carmen* to be the greatest opera ever written, and likely the greatest which ever could be written. Again, he identified with the tragic heroine, this time a lower-class beautiful young girl, rejected by polite society, and eventually murdered by a jealous, dominating male. That she worked in a cigarette factory was a bonus: Tchaikovsky smoked like a fiend.

page 15
Klin

For his last year and a half, Tchaikovsky's country home, 53 miles northwest of Moscow. http://goo.gl/apSbwj It is now a much-visited museum.

page 15
That certain personage

Antonina Ivanovna Miliukova, Tchaikovsky's short-term, but too-long-lasting "wife". He hated her so much, and himself for marrying her, that he avoided referring to her by name. He sometimes called her simply "the reptile" or "the creature". The story of their "marriage" is one of the most horrifying in the annals of psychosexual neurosis. I hint at it here and there throughout T's monologue, but all Tchaikovsky biographies treat it at length. Sad, sad, sad.

page 16
lost their will to live.

Tchaikovsky was a great animal lover. So I include a story I found somewhere of a suicidal dog in order to introduce the question of suicide – which so dominates the Tchaikovsky death debates. The music quote attached is the heart-sinking last measures of the Sixth, his last work. (http://goo.gl/16Q1L5 10:25-end.) He conducted its premiere nine days before his death. I will link to this work several times, later.

page 17
Schuppanzigh

Ignatz Schuppanzigh, Beethoven's friend, teacher, and first violinist of Count Razomovsky's string quartet. Poor Schuppanzigh! Beethoven never ceased making fun of "My Lord Falstaff"'s growing obesity. He once composed a short choral piece dedicated to him called "Praise to the Fat One." He must have been a pretty good player, though, to premiere all those late quartets and lead his gang through the *Grosse Fugue*. He grew so fat that he could no longer play. But by that time (1830), Beethoven was three years dead.

page 18
Kashkin

Nikolay Dmitriyevich Kashkin, professor of piano and theory at the Moscow Conservatory, and a music critic very supportive of Tchaikovsky. I think I made up his helping move T into a coffin. He would certainly have been one of the early visiting colleagues come to pay respects.

page 18
The plague is over

This declaration gives the reader (you) the chance to consider Poznansky's assertion that official restrictions around the funerals of cholera victims had been lifted by the time of Tchaikovsky's death, and that open coffin services would not then contradict the cholera or "fatal glass of water" narratives. I find Poznansky convincing enough to have adopted my rimming theory, but since I don't really know, I do not commit my Tchaikovsky character to spilling the beans and revealing "the truth."

page 19
zucchetto, gift from Giovannini

a little skullcap, worn by Roman Catholic clergy. I gave him a skullcap to wear around the house, so he could refer to little gifts given him by his Italian boy lovers. His anointing it a *zucchetto* accords with the habitual joking around for which he was known.

page 20
Mariya, Mazeppa

Mazeppa, in Pushkin's poem, Poltava, became the title character in a bloody Tchaikovsky opera from 1883. More tragic love and political intrigue. In the end, Mariya, who loves her father's friend, Mazeppa, goes insane, and Mazeppa leaves her. Another very put-upon young woman in Tchaikovsky's collection.

page 20
lay on the flowers

You can't say "flowers" — even if you are Tchaikovsky's corpse — without calling up the overly famous "Waltz of the Flowers". (http://goo.gl/Tr4mk6 beginning at 1:17)

The odd thing about the *Nutcracker* ballet is that is a late work, premiering before the Sixth Symphony, and less than a year before his death. The other odd thing is that while it was not originally very success-ful, it has become – at least in the post-60s US — as *de rigeur* for Christmas time as the national anthem is at sports games, annually performed by many bal-let companies, a major money-maker, a must-see for the children. What is it with merry America that even Messiah is forced into being a Christmas piece? Kvetch, kvetch, kvetch. Tchaikovsky did love flowers, though.

page 20
Beauty has to be cured, destroyed.

This is part of my rant against the choral movement of Beethoven's Ninth, and Tchaikovsky's fictive need to "take back the Ninth" with his Sixth. More in my essay, cited and linked to above.

page 21
pick mushrooms

Another possibility for the reader who wants a sui-cide theory without the help of the Court of Honor.

Tchaikovsky, like many Russians, was an ardent mycologist, and would surely have known the danger – and the uses – of certain mushrooms. Several species produce gastrointestinal symptoms leading to acute renal failure, a syndrome he suffered in the last days, and which could easily pass for cholera, especially with doctors like his, inexpert at the disease. Arsenic is mentioned a little later as another cholera-imitator, and was – if you believe it — the gift given him by his doctor Scholl of Jurisprudence brothers at the posited court hearing, though, as T mentions, it is easily available at the druggist's. BTW, "Gift" in German means "poison".

page 22-23
work of art, Look at these hands

The music is the lonely horn solo opening the Second Symphony, the folk song "Down by Mother Volga." One pictures the slow, worn, crooked hands of a Russian peasant. The movement will take the theme through many vicissitudes which might well describe a Tchaikovskian path to the loneliness to which the piece returns and ends. The next two musical earworms glimpse moments along that path. http://goo.gl/3gl4bT, if you care to hear it.

The use of printed music in the text is only to suggest what themes are bubbling up in Tchaikovsky's ebbing mind throughout. Germans call these "earworms", an excellent word.

page 24-25
Poustiakov, etc

Most of these are just thrown-in names that show up in Tchaikovsky biographies. I have no idea who came to pay respects. From the description of the lines up the stairs and down the street, it would appear to have been hundreds, if not thousands. The only exception to fictive use of names is that of Alexei Verzhdilovich, whom several writers describe kissing and breaking down over Tchaikovsky's corpse. I imagine Tchaikovsky would have loved the osculatory attention from this handsome young man and talented cellist.

page 27
Ahnest du den Schöpfer?

Another line from Beethoven's Ninth: Do you sense the Creator... (Beethoven/Schiller continue : ...world? Look for Him over the canopy of stars. Up there. He must dwell up there..." This earworm continues T's run-in with the *lieber Vater.*

page 27-35
Vanya, Edward, Vittorio, Adriano, Ilya...

This particular incident is described in one of T's letters to Modya. The earworm brought up by Edward's name is T's love theme from *Romeo and Juliet.*
http://goo.gl/1LdSeh (beginning 7:47) Tchaikovsky himself wrote of that connection. Vittorio appears in letters to Modya, though I may have mixed in some details from other encounters. "Strolls" is how Tchaikovsky referred to his scouting for lovers. This section is about such strolls.

page 31
I never felt so happy.

The music is the upbeat conclusion to the Second Symphony, which began in such loneliness (above). Again, http://goo.gl/PViTjn, beginning at 25:42. Of course, being Tchaikovsky, it doesn't stay so simple and innocent.

page 36
No more mirrors, please.

Beginning now to understand that he is dead, the very weird funeral march that begins his Third Symphony comes to mind, develops in uncanny intensity and morphs into doubtful declaration. http://goo.gl/6Jqnkx. Doubtful because why, after all, start with a funeral march as context?

page 38
I told her I'd fallen in the water by accident.

In despair over what he'd gotten himself into by marrying "the creature", Tchaikovsky thought he'd kill himself. But, being nice-guy-Pyotr, he didn't want anyone to feel guilty about his suicide, so he decided to wade one cold night into the Moskva River, and catch fatal pneumonia. No blame. What a nice guy. It didn't work, and he never even caught cold.

page 48-51
Nadezhda Filaretovna, Three. Seven. Ace.

Nadezhda Filaretovna von Meck was a rich widow

133

and patroness of the arts. She supported Tchaikovsky for thirteen years, generously enough that he was able to leave teaching and devote himself full-time to composition. Well, full-time when he wasn't on strolls.

Is this the standard story of a flirting artist milking a rich widow for money? Far from it. It was one of the most extraordinary dimensions of Tchaikovsky's hypercharged life.

While her letters make it obvious that she was in love with him – in love with the person that wrote such music – she stipulated that they must never meet. Over the years, 1,200 letters went between them, a biographer's treasure trove. What a deep and penetrating Platonic embrace. And they never did meet, though it is possible that their carriages once passed one another on the road. Tchaikovsky was deeply grateful for her love and support, but remained uncomfortable about all that she continually bestowed on him. Consider the subtle, but penetrating shame of an intensely felt, longterm "How can I ever thank you?"

And yet, one day in 1890, three years before his death, she sent him a year's subsidy in advance, and wrote that she would no longer be writing. None of T's further queries were answered. In spite of the fact that he was now famous and well-off, he was hurt, and even offended by her abrupt departure. His speculation centered around her having discovered his homosexuality – a subject he had bracketed in his otherwise honest, intimate letters.

At this point in his coffin, he is confused enough to

be conflating Nadezhda Filaretovna with the old, rich Countess in his opera, *Queen of Spades*, libretto by Modest, based on a story by Pushkin. The main character, Herman, a gambling addict like Tchaikovsky, hears tell that the Countess has a "secret formula" for winning at cards. Insert elaborate opera business here. To discover the secret, Herman invades her bedroom, scares her literally to death, and thinks the secret has died with her. But her ghost returns to whisper to him the secret formula, "Three. Seven. Ace." Armed with this information, Herman returns to the gambling house, and runs up the stakes to an insane level. The tension is high as he bets the last card to break the house and all winning records. "Ace," he confidently says. The card is turned over. Ace? No. It is the Queen of Spades. The card winks at him, the Countess's ghost laughs at her revenge, and Herman commits suicide. The Countess in her beautiful youth was once known as "the Queen of Spades".

Tchaikovsky betrays his own good self by thinking of Nadezhda Filaretovna's departure as the old, rich Countess's trick.

page 51
absolutely anything *can be cured*

Petya and Modya spend a lot of time in their letters discussing their homosexuality, how to behave around it, whether it is a disease, and if so, whether it is curable.

page 51
That gentleman in the corner

With a Don Giovanni-Commendatore fanfare (the startling opening of the Fourth Symphony), http://goo.gl/yjYaEL a stranger enters the scene.

I often conceive of a novel with one, usually silly, idea, and this was it. Pushkin will challenge Tchaikovsky to a duel over T's insults to the Pushkin works he has polluted with smarmy sentimentalism.

Pushkin fans, and Russian literature cognoscenti do get upset about this the way certain folks (myself included) get upset about the Disneyfication of... just about anything, folktales and masterpiece stories. ("The Little Mermaid" is the one that most gets my goat. I'll spare you another rant. But if your family has ever embraced that red-haired, little half-nymphette, I urge you to read Andersen's actual tale.)

In the Pushkin-Tchaikovsky case, it is not so much a happy-ending, PG "G" rating (no parental guidance required (= more take at the box office) issue), but rather a determined extirpation of Pushkin's ironic critique of sentiment. Tchaikovsky found deep sentiment in everything, and in his dramatic works, put the spotlight on it. No doubt Pushkin would have been pissed, but he died three years before Tchaikovsky was born. He was killed in a duel he initiated.

A prime example of Tchaikovsky's tranformations of attitude re Pushkin's heroines is his setting of the famous "letter" scene in *Eugen Onegin*. Pushkin shows his cards thusly: (http://goo.gl/D1SrwH)

XXVI   *I see another problem looming:*
to save the honour of our land
I must translate — there's no presuming —
the letter from Tatyana's hand:
her Russian was as thin as vapour,
she never read a Russian paper,
our native speech had never sprung
unhesitating from her tongue,
she wrote in French... what a confession!
what can one do? as said above,
until this day, a lady's love
in Russian never found expression,
till now our language — proud, God knows —
has hardly mastered postal prose.

Pretty snide. Yet here is what Tchaikovsky will do with the "letter scene" – hardly true musically to Pushkin's character or text: http://goo.gl/evMKBv (Letter begins at 3:15.)

Only Pushkin and fanatic Pushkinites could not fall in love with this Tchaikovsky-Tatiana. Worthy of a duel, n'est-ce pas?

page 53
Stendok-Fermor

At this point, Tchaikovsky is confusing Pushkin's accusations of rape with those rumored to be evoked by his recent affair with Alexei Stendok-Fermor, the son of Count Stendok-Fermor, a close friend of the Tsar. It was this potential scandal that putatively brought the fatal Court of Honor into session — if that was the case. Pushkin, of course, has no idea of what T is referring to. A fictive Countess, a very real Count. What a psychic mish-mosh. Tchaikovsky was uncomfortable in aristocratic circles juggling his culture-hero role with his fear of exposure.

page 54
I could use a cigarette.

As mentioned above, Tchaikovsky was an addicted smoker, and given his deep love of *Carmen*, his mind drifts to the cigarette girls, and Carmen's seductive, but duplicitous *Seguidilla* http://goo.gl/9IkFnv with which she convinces a smitten, confused Don José to help her escape from prison. Again, Tchaikovsky identifies himself with a young girl breaking free from society's strictures. An outlaw. A victim.

page 55
The seconds lay out their coats

The image of coats focuses T's sight on all the overcoats crowding the room. The poet Lermontov, whom Tchaikovsky imagines there, was also killed in a duel. Why, he wonders, do people keep wanting to pry into his private life? This sniffing around at him brings his wandering mind back to his experiences at SoJ, its tendernesses as well as its cruelties. The next earworm that comes into his head is the beautiful, yearning them of the second movement of the Fourth, the *Andantino in modo di canzona*, simple, he annotates, but full of grace. http://goo.gl/UgBzUP.

page 59
Kolya Krosotkin, the Suicide Club

Kolya is a character in *The Brothers Karamazov*, a daring, if posturing, leader of a gang of boys which impact the young lives of the brothers, especially Alyosha. His was the trick of lying under an overpassing train. I transposed this into a fictive moment of Tchaikovsky's boy-life, and then had the audacity to make Tchaikovsky blame Dostoevsky for the whole thing. His inner laughter about the memory bubbles up in the Scherzo (ital. "joke") of the Fourth Symphony. I believe it's the first symphonic movement ever written in which the strings play entirely pizzicato. http://goo.gl/zywbNe Very original, and fun to play.

page 64
con anima.

Though dedicated to Mme von Meck, the emotional urgency of the surprising turn from fanfare – which T identified in letters with ominous fate — to writhing waltz (http://goo.gl/yjYaEL at 1:45), turns his thoughts to his current anima, life, soul, his nephew, Bob.

page 64
decomposing body and rising soul

This breathtaking (for who would dare breathe?) moment ending the exposition of the first movement of the Sixth poses an existential halt! to the listener. As the melody falls, the dynamics go from *p* (soft), to *ppp* (very, very soft), and from there to *pppp* (very, very, very, very soft), to *ppppp* (very, very, very, very, very soft), to *pppppp* (very, very, very, very, very, very, very

139

soft) as the one remaining clarinet drops into its lowest register. I don't know that *pppppp* appears in any other score, orchestral or otherwise.

Where is he? Where are you? http://goo.gl/J5HvuQ
9:57-11:00

(I like weirdo, always-unshaven Gergiev as a conductor, but I think he should take more time after the clarinet fermata measure to bathe in nothingness. The visual of his windup for the next fortissimo doesn't help. But this is a good recording/video of the entire work, worth experiencing in its entirety.)

page 66
The opening of the Sixth. The end of the Sixth.

Again, go back to the last link, or many, any, other YouTube performances of the work. You'll not regret internalizing this Symphony. (And I'm not a big fan of Tchaikovsky.)

page 68
Odette, Odile, Tatiana, etc

All heroines of Tchaikovsky's ballets and operas. The Odette/Odile, white swan/black swan, good girl/evil girl pair (usually performed by the same dancer) is particularly interesting in the light of T's psychic projections.

page 69
violin high C

http://goo.gl/gNK8OO, at the end. Nice little concerto slow movement thrown in there.

page 70
my Liza.

The heroine of both Pushkin's and Tchaikovsky's *Queen of Spades*. The difference between them again illustrates the difference between the poet's and the composer's approaches.

page 71
Kirilov

One of the conspirators in Dostoevsky's *The Devils*. Interesting character, of relevance to Tchaikovsky's life/death dilemma. He believes that will is the only reality, and that one can evade the fear of death only when he is able to take his own life. In accepting death, man achieves Godhood.

page 72
V

The chapter opens with an earworm from T's greatest storm, the whirling catastrophe in his tone poem, *Francesca da Rimini*.(http://goo.gl/WKZlHS   1:25 ff) (Man, those Venezuelan kids can really play!)

The story of Paolo and Francesca (Dante, *Inferno*, Canto V) was of such interest to Tchaikovsky that he composed this extraordinary symphonic fantasia the better to understand it, and himself in it.

P&F: a hateful marriage, an illicit affair with a relative, death of the miscreants – what's not to like if you're Tchaikovsky? Eternally swept away by whirlwinds as they were swept away by their passions – this is something T had to probe as deeply as he could, even if the passions here were heterosexual.

page 74
My own Canto V

He begins to hear the passionate sections of his own Fifth, the earworm here the emotional climax of the second movement (http://goo.gl/T13aO6, 10:10-11:23). Pretty persuasive, but the fact is Tchaikovsky didn't really like this piece, or rather he liked it until he finished it and performed it – and *then* he didn't like it.

Here is a program note I wrote for a recent performance, requested, but too racy to be printed:

SOME NOTES ON TCHAIKOVSKY'S FIFTH

"There is something repulsive about it."
This was the composer's comment about his Fifth Symphony after returning from a European tour conducting it.

True, Tchaikovsky was often neurotic about his compositions, announcing his joy with them to his brother, Modest, then doubting them — and himself — after performances. Schizy. He could fly like a swan, but once on the ground, he would waddle.

Waddling is one thing, but what is "repulsive" about the Fifth? Some clues present themselves.

In a notebook page dated 13 April 1888, the year of its composition, Tchaikovsky outlines a scenario for the first movement: "Introduction: Complete resignation before Fate, or, which is the same, before the inscrutable predestination of Providence. Allegro: (1) Murmurs of doubt, complaints, reproaches against XXX. (2) Shall I throw myself in the embrace of faith??? A wonderful program, if only it can be carried out."

A hopeful beginning. In opening the work, Tchaikovsky cuts to the core. The opening theme in the low clarinets recurs in every movement, commenting on other themes, or challenging them.

Thus, the opening theme carries a narrative function beyond its musical one, and it doesn't take much imagination to hear it as embodying the Fate Tchaikovsky invokes in his primordial program. So let's call it the "Fate theme", and see how it functions throughout the piece.

Tchaikovsky always wore his heart on his compositional sleeve: the sublime slow movement is the expressive core of the whole work. The opening string chorale before the famous horn solo warns the audience to take this movement seriously, even religiously. Halfway through this erotic movement, the orchestra begins a stringendo and crescendo culminating in fortississimo (fff) trumpets blaring out the Fate theme. It's worse than hearing the steps of your parents en-

143

tering the room when you are making out with your lover, or a cuckolded spouse returning home early. There's only one possible effect of this interruption: to scare the hell out of the audience, and make it regret its emotional vulnerability. "Oh no you don't. You'll be sorry." The avenging angel bares his sword.

If that's the way the Fate theme can function, what is the meaning of its triumphant takeover of the last movement? Critics have always found this part the least successful. Is it because it's overwrought and only barely convincing? Protesting too much, and as such, repulsive?

I think there is little mystery what the XXX refers to in Tchaikovsky's note to Modest. Throughout their extensive correspondence, both closeted gay men dealt in code with their "sickness". X, it was called, or sometimes Z, in unmistakable contexts. But in this case, there is more to it than that. What was going on for Tchaikovsky at this time?

It had been three years since Tchaikovsky had produced a major orchestral work — his Manfred Symphony. Manfred, a strange, programmatic inclusion in the series of numbered symphonies. Why Manfred?

Manfred is the subject of a dramatic poem by Byron, the story of a Swiss nobleman tortured by mysterious guilt. "Thou lovedst me/Too much," he declares concerning his sister, "as I loved thee: we were not made/To torture thus each other, though it were/The deadliest sin to love as we have loved."

Tchaikovsky was sympathetic to Byron's love for his half-sister, and this for him brought up the dangerous theme of incest. At the time of writing Manfred, Tchaikovsky was already deeply in love with his nephew, Bob, his sister's son, then 15, Tchaikovsky's favorite age for sex with boys. The composer dedicated his Sixth Symphony to him, and awarded him the lion's share of his will. Problematical family dynamics. XXX indeed, and a perfect vehicle for Tchaikovsky's brooding about his sexuality. The noble outsider, rejected by a conventional world. He later disowned the piece, calling it "abominable...I loathe it deeply." Sound familiar? Repulsive?

And what followed the Fifth? His fantasy overture, Hamlet, overlapping the scoring of the Fifth, and beginning again with a "Fate" theme. Over the first page, Tchaikovsky had written. "To be or not to be?" The Fifth — sandwiched between Manfred and Hamlet.

Within five years, Tchaikovsky was dead, probably by his own hand or tongue, possibly of arsenic, possibly of cholera, nine days after premiering his death-haunted Sixth Symphony, his Requiem.

Again, Gergiev has a provocative recording of the whole: http://goo.gl/QQNidd.

page 83
Mozart – the most faithful companion of my life.

The earworm that arises is Tchaikovsky's orchestration (http://goo.gl/cQ4Qx1, click on 3. Prayer) of the short choral setting of *Ave, Verum Corpus*, Hail True Body, which Mozart wrote six months before his death.

The text must have been particularly interesting to Tchaikovsky's corpse in puzzling over its own body in the light of Mozart:

Ave, verum corpus
natum de Maria Virgine,

Vere passum immolatum
in Cruce pro homine,

Cujus latus perforatum
fluxit aqua et sanguine,

Esto nobis praegustatum
in mortis examine.

Hail, true body
born of the Virgin Mary,

Who truly suffered, sacrificed
on the Cross for man,

Whose pierced side overflowed
with water and blood,

Be for us a foretaste
In the test of death.

He included this orchestration as the "Prayer" movement of his fourth orchestral suite, *Mozartiana.*

page 83
The eternal waltz.

The first earworm is the lovely third movement waltz from the Fifth Symphony. http://goo.gl/PviT2U. The bad boy limping waltz, is, I believe, the first waltz in five ever written. http://goo.gl/ddOQ91.

page 85
Praise ye the Lord

http://goo.gl/pa1vP0 I'm sure Tchaikovsky also got off on the young boys choir which likely did the singing.

page 86
same even rhythm

The rain brings the gentle rhythmic pattern early in the second them of the second movement of the Fifth. This will build to the climax he heard (above), but for the moment, it gently pulses in the strings behind the oboe/horn duet. http://goo.gl/60CV9f 2:08-2:35

page 93
a trompe l'oreille as outlandish

The opening of the last movement of the Sixth, the *Adagio lamentoso*, is surely one of the remarkable aural illusions ever penned. Surely, no naïve listener hears anything but a descending line, F#__ E, D, C#, B, C____. http://goo.gl/iKuq9J . A glance at the score in the text demonstrates that that melody appears nowhere. That is, it appears out of everywhere, patched together by the ear from alternating notes in each of the violins, supported by harmonies in the lower strings. Why does Tchaikovsky open this, his most crucial movement in such a snake-like way? What's with his resorting here to trickery? Are these measures his arcane reference to hiding, the great theme of his social and sexual life?

page 96
the silence after the Adagio lamentoso

The end of this, his last symphonic movement, disappears into the earth (http://goo.gl/16Q1L5 10:25-end.)

Next printed earworm just before that: 9:10-10:18

page 99
Contraction. Diminution.

Again, the ending of the Sixth, as above.

Grinding the Face of the Poor:

A Reader in Biblical Justice

Edited by
W. R. Brookman

North Central University Press
Minneapolis

ISBN 0-9762461-3-9

Library of Congress Number 2006900364

1. Biblical justice 2. economic justice 3. I. Brookman, W. R. II. Title

Printed in the U.S.A. by
Morris Publishing
3212 East Highway 30
Kearney, NE 68847
1-800-650-7888

Published by
North Central University Press
910 Elliot Ave.
Minneapolis, MN 55404
1-800-289-6222
www.northcentral.edu

Unless otherwise noted, the Biblical texts are from the New Revised Standard
Version Bible, copyright 1989, by the Division of Christian Education of the
National Council of the Churches of Christ in the USA, and is used by per-
mission.

Cover Photo: Grinding Coffee Beans - Lalibela, Ethiopia - photo by Pat
Brookman

*To my mom & dad
who always supported me
in anything I ever attempted*

*To Pat & Kelly,
the two women in my life
both of whom have taught me
some things about justice*

Contents

Foreword

It has been clearly demonstrated to me on numerous occasions throughout my twenty-six years of teaching that when academic colleagues get together, interesting things can happen. These interesting things are even more likely to occur when those colleagues are actually very good friends. Such was the case when Bob Brenneman, Nan Muhovich and I first began to conspire together.

Over time, our regular departmental meetings at North Central University gained an interesting momentum toward a like-mindedness with regard to a new project we were discussing. The conversation evolved, and it was almost as if we shared together a series of moments reminiscent of something you might have read in *The Three Musketeers*; you know, "One for all and all for one." At times I felt a bit like Athos, with Aramis and Porthos at my side. However, I wouldn't carry the Athos analogy too far. For while we could say that in Athos, Dumas provided us with a fascinating character who was distinguished in almost every way – intellect, appearance, wit, bravery, swordsmanship – yet, unlike me, he was seemingly tortured by some sort of a deep melancholy, the source of which escapes the reader, at least this reader.

Yet, to be sure, our conspiracy was not of a subversive nature, as many conspiracies are wont to be. Rather, our scheme was one of noble endeavor. We simply wanted to contemplate and explore a new direction for the Department of Intercultural Studies and Languages as we were sensing the subtle whisperings of the Spirit. As it is well known, the discerning of the Spirit can be a tricky business. However, after considerable dialog, prayer, and incubation of ideas, we agreed that the three of us all sensed the same thing; this is quite a remarkable feat in many Christian circles.

Somewhat to our own surprise, the notion of biblical justice came up again and again in our discussions. It happened that over a period of months, as we considered how we could best prepare students for a lifetime of ministry in a cross-cultural setting, this topic of biblical justice seemed continually to be a central element within our deliberations. So it was that the three of us began to discuss a plan of action in which we would attempt to bring issues of biblical justice more directly into the curriculum and co-curricular activities of our department. Thereby, it is our hope that the very essence of biblical justice will be instilled into the lives of our students as a part of their education at North Central University.

Many ideas came to the forefront as we brainstormed about possible avenues toward this end. One of the early ideas we agreed upon was the creation of a new course. We wanted to build a class that would provide a good overview of biblical justice and also directly engage various justice issues or topics in a creative and practical way. We agreed that topics such as human trafficking, prostitution, homelessness, poverty, AIDS/HIV, child labor, etc. would be incredibly germane for our students. Occurring on both a local and global level, these are issues which our students, as witnesses to the Gospel, would be encountering throughout their entire lives.

Thus, we wanted this class to provide students a way to explore what the biblical text has to say about justice in general, and at the same time, offer practical experience opportunities for students to engage issues of biblical justice in real-life settings. Naturally, the setting of North Central University within the urban center of Minneapolis would afford a more than ample supply of such opportunities. Beyond that, our hope is that after students participate locally in a service-learning experience through the course, a global vision for ministry which is well rooted in the principles of biblical justice would become a reality in their lives.

This book is a result of our conspiracy and the subsequent planning for such a class. Hopefully, the content herein presents students with a rather handy and accessible portal into the world of justice as the Bible presents it. While there is nothing particularly novel about what I have done (see the Introduction), I would expect this volume to be a rather effective vehicle to get one's feet wet in the world of biblical justice.

W.R. Brookman
Kingsriter Centre, 2005

Introduction

Without a doubt, a thorough study of justice encompasses a rather large and complex domain of concepts and issues. In Western thought, the notion of justice has been rather tightly tied to the political nature of the state. For example, in his two dialogs, *The Republic* and *Gorgias*, Plato made justice a prominent theme. In one instance he put into the mouth of Thrasymachus the following words: "...justice is nothing else than the interest of the stronger." While a rather scary thought, that very notion continued as a dominant view of justice for centuries. For after Plato, a number of other thinkers including Aristotle, Hobbes and Spinoza also addressed the issue of justice from this sort of framework. Thus, oftentimes, justice was considered as the interest of the stronger or as a conforming to the will of the sovereign. Naturally, the implications of this line of thought lead to what has been called a "might is right" approach to justice.

Another central theme to most philosophical considerations of justice is that of conflicting interests. According to Hume, Mill, and others, these conflicts of interest are what present us with the issues we lump into the realm of justice. While the previous names, I am sure, are familiar to you, one should also be aware of a less widely known philosopher, recently deceased[1], who has written the best analysis of justice in the 20th century. John Rawls is a name you may not recognize, yet his work, *A Theory of Justice*, is now generally considered to be a standard work in the field.

Aristotle held that justice is essentially "treating equals equally and treating unequals unequally" (*Nicomachean Ethics* Bk. V, Chap. VI), albeit

---

[1] His obituary in the Harvard University Gazette (11/25/02) included the following remarks: "Philosophy Department Chairman Thomas Scanlon, the Alford Professor of Natural Religion, Moral Philosophy, and Civil Policy, said that 'John Rawls was widely recognized as the greatest political philosopher of the 20th century. His work revived and reshaped the entire field, and its profound influence on the way justice is understood and argued about will last long into the future. He was also a remarkable teacher, who inspired countless students, and an unfailingly generous and devoted colleague. We will miss him greatly and are all deeply grateful to have had the privilege of being around when he was here.'" And also, "Dennis Thompson, the Alfred North Whitehead Professor of Political Philosophy and director of the University Center for Ethics and the Professions, stated that in his view Rawls 'will be in the canon for centuries, along with Hobbes, Locke, Rousseau, Kant, Mill, etc.'"

only if this were done in the correct measure of the pertinent differences. For instance, if two individuals are in equal need, they must be treated equally. If there is unequal need between the two people, for example, one is in critical need of medical help and the other only somewhat in need of medical attention, then there should be unequal treatment. Yet, one needs to assess needs fairly. Rawls saw a problem in how one assesses the situation.

For Rawls, an important aspect of justice is fairness, and he perceived that the classic utilitarianism that had dominated Western ethical thought for so long was an open door leading to unfairness. As a result, he developed an ethical approach he called "justice as fairness" to be an alternative to utilitarianism. He wanted to remove personal biases from the equation. But how does one eliminate human bias? Rawls reasoned that if people made decisions without knowing anything about their own personal condition, e.g. their wealth, social standing, race, political views, etc., they would act fairly. It is a person's personal knowledge about his or her own situation that will naturally influence ethical decision-making. This concept of reasoning without one's personal biases he called, "The Veil of Ignorance."

While Rawls was in the social contract tradition of Hobbes, Kant, and Locke, he separated himself from their particular brand of social contract by saying that a truly just social contract would result only if it were one to which we would agree if we were completely unaware of our own place in the society. This veil of ignorance is referred to as the "original position," and in this original position the individual would have no knowledge of their own standing. In the original position this individual would be totally ignorant of any of the variables that normally influence one's ethical decision-making, e.g., their religious beliefs, their physical health, their nationality. As a result, personal interests and biases are removed.

Rawl's theory is complex, and what you have just read about it here is a mere tidbit which, in no way, suffices in any substantive way. In fact, Rawls rethought and re-articulated some of his positions in the aftermath of the publication of *A Theory of Justice*.[2] Yet, it could be cor-

---

[2]Rawls, John. *A Theory of Justice*. (Cambridge: BelKnap Press, 1999). In addition, see the

rectly said that this is somewhat true of the entire ocean of justice studies, not just of Rawls'; it is a complicated matter. What can be seen as one wades, even just knee-deep into the waters of justice, is the immense variety and complexity of ways to talk about justice.

Fortunately, for your sake as well as mine, it is not the intention of this book to be a comprehensive primer for a headlong dive into the murky pool of justice. To be sure, there is an immense literature on justice. Yet, narrowing the field somewhat, one may engage a more manageable subset of the rather daunting arena of justice in the broad sense and focus upon what is known as biblical justice. As the center of attention for this little volume, biblical justice is introduced to the novice through a collection of texts that may provide a foundational basis for further study. In fact, this work is very simple in its design and goal. The aim is to provide a first step for the one who wishes to discover the world of biblical justice. I would judge that people, even those just vaguely familiar with the Bible, would have a sense that Scripture has much to say about the concept of justice. However, I also suspect that most would be surprised at the depth and breadth of its position within the biblical corpus. It permeates Scripture at a level that is surprising once the entire landscape is surveyed. Yet, it is exactly the surveying of this landscape that can prove to be a formidable task.

In Appendix A you will read some passages which address the concept of justice from Thomas Aquinas' great work, *Summa Theologia*. While you may be familiar with his name, and maybe even the title of his famous work, my suspicion is that you may not have actually read any Aquinas. While reading this will be a challenge, I selected this passage for inclusion in this book for several important reasons. Aquinas presents us with a Christianized theory of justice which draws upon earlier Greek and Roman thought on the universal law of nature; and it is simply my opinion that an educated Christian, even in the 21st century, should have some exposure to him. Aquinas' systematizing is an interesting, and for most of us, a novel way of thinking about things.

Suggested Readings section at the end of this book for a brief and manageable list of works on justice you may find to be very helpful if you decide to pursue the study further. While the literature on justice truly is immense, you will need look elsewhere for a comprehensive bibliography; it is not within the scope of this book to provide such a list.

I have also included, in Appendix B, selected paragraphs from the 1986 pastoral letter composed by the U.S. Catholic Bishops entitled, *Economic Justice For All*. It focuses most specifically upon economic issues, particularly from the American Christian frame of reference. Certainly, there are many good things written about biblical justice which just as well could have been included in a reader like this. However, I consciously wanted students to read a few things that they, in all probability, would not have otherwise read. For example, well-educated, thinking Protestants should read Catholic thought. In fact, when it comes to issues of biblical justice, I would judge that Catholics are quite ahead of Protestants in their thinking and in their actions. Of course, this is only my own anecdotal opinion. Yet, at the very least, it could be argued that we Protestants have much we could learn from our Catholic brothers and sisters in this facet of Christian thought. Thus, the assembling of these texts into a handy, little volume seemed to be a good step to take.

The idea of this type of collection is not new, and it certainly was not my conceptual invention. To be sure, this task had already been undertaken. A quarter of a century ago, Ronald Sider edited a diminutive volume entitled, *Cry Justice*. While I had seen references to that book, I had never actually looked at it until after I had independently assembled the texts I wanted to include in this book. A quick comparison will demonstrate that Sider included some texts which I had decided were slightly peripheral to what I wanted to include. Plus, I included several texts that he had not incorporated into his book. That did not surprise me. What did surprise me was the layout of the texts I had decided upon before seeing Sider's book. If the two volumes were to be put side by side, one would notice the similarity of a concise title (centered) followed by the Scripture reference (flush left). The two layout designs are eerily the same. In fact, on some occasions the titles are the very same for particular passages. I assure the reader and Mr. Sider that this stems from the content of the text and not my conscious or subconscious reliance upon his book, for I had never seen his volume before the creation of my titles for the texts. Some of these I have rewritten, others I have left as is.

This book presents a collection or an anthology, as such, comprised of selected materials that have been gleaned from Scripture, non-canonical texts, and from secondary sources. Taken together, these texts will provide an entryway into the world of biblical justice. Needless to say, this is not an all-encompassing collection of texts germane to biblical justice; it is merely a manageable start.

Responding to biblical justice

I have a serious concern. I have just read the parable popularly known as "the Rich Man and Lazarus" (Luke 16:19-31), and I perceive that my culture, in general, and individuals within that culture are, in large measure, playing the role of the rich man. America is, in my humble opinion, in a nasty predicament. This situation is not, however, one which is generally recognized by Americans. Our reading of the parable is skewed by our presuppositions and by our merely being American in culture. If you haven't read the parable in a while, take a look at it, and consider the rich man.

There was a rich man who was dressed in purple and fine linen and lived in luxury every day. At his gate was laid a beggar named Lazarus, covered with sores and longing to eat what fell from the rich man's table. Even the dogs came and licked his sores.

The time came when the beggar died and the angels carried him to Abraham's side. The rich man also died and was buried. In hell, where he was in torment, he looked up and saw Abraham far away with Lazarus by his side. So he called to him, "Father Abraham, have pity on me and send Lazarus to dip the tip of his finger in water and cool my tongue, because I am in agony in this fire."

But Abraham replied, "Son, remember that in your lifetime you received your good things, while Lazarus received bad things, but now he is comforted here and you are in agony. And besides all this, between us and you a great chasm has been fixed, so that those who want to go from here to you cannot, nor can anyone cross over from there to us."

He answered, "Then I beg you, father, send Lazarus to my

father's house for I have five brothers. Let him warn them, so that they will not also come to this place of torment." Abraham replied, "They have Moses and the Prophets; let them listen to them."

"No, father Abraham," he said, "but if someone from the dead goes to them, they will repent."

He said to him, "If they do not listen to Moses and the Prophets, they will not be convinced even if someone rises from the dead.

Think about the rich man for a moment; his sin was not that he oppressed the poor. The biblical text has much to say about those who oppress the poor. However, that is not necessarily the case in this parable. The American pickle is, in part, that we, like the rich man in the parable, are guilty of *neglecting* the poor. Many might recoil with a shocked expression and exclaim, "But America is the most generous nation on earth. How can you accuse us of playing the role of the rich man?" First, of all, the assertion that America is the most generous of nations is factually wrong.

In 1992 at an Earth Summit in Rio de Janeiro, 22 nations of the world approved a program under the sponsorship of the United Nations Article 21 in which they agreed to set their Official Development Assistance (ODA) at 0.7% of the gross national product (GNP). Technically, they now use the term Gross National Income (GNI) rather than the older, yet similar term GNP. This measure is the most widely accepted way to measure a country's "generosity." Last year (2004) five nations met their targeted obligation. Unfortunately, the U.S. has never met the target. As if that were not enough, the U.S. has typically, each year, been near the bottom of the "generosity" listing. The following are the most recent rankings.

Aid as percentage of GNI:

Norway	0.87	Germany	0.28
Luxembourg	0.85	Canada	0.26
Denmark	0.84	Spain	0.26
Sweden	0.77	Australia	0.25
Netherlands	0.74	Austria	0.24
Portugal	0.63	Greece	0.23
France	0.42	New Zealand	0.23
Belgium	0.41	Japan	0.19
Ireland	0.39	United States	0.16
Switzerland	0.37	Italy	0.15
United Kingdom	0.36		
Finland	0.35		

Source: *Official Development Assistance increases further - but 2006 targets still a challenge, OECD, April 11, 2005–World Bank*

So there we are, number 21. The trouble is, just about any way one would try to massage the data, this is about where the U.S. ranks. Now the air is cleared; we are not the most generous nation. Frankly, we are not even close. Notice that Japan, which definitely could not be characterized in anybody's mind as a Christian nation, ranks higher in this generosity index than the U.S. If we look for the good news in these ranking, we do rate above Italy, although just by the smallest of margins.

All of a sudden, the rich man of the parable is a closer approximation of our nation, our culture, and ourselves. If you don't see even a little bit of the rich man in yourself and in your country, you are probably not very authentic in your introspection. Of course, there is more to biblical justice than just generosity, and we need to consider the full measure of things. Hopefully, the readings in this volume will nudge each of us in that direction.

Reading and contemplating the texts within this book should provide a vivid call to biblical justice. The real challenge is how one responds to this call. From the very subtle neglecting of the poor such as we see in the above parable, to the more dramatic act of actually grinding the face of the poor, each of us must actualize a response to injustice. Where we have been guilty of injustice, we must change. Where we are aware of injustice, we are obliged to work for change. Where we acquiesce to the injustice of others, we must change, and change requires a conscious movement against inertia. While inertia is a powerful force, the force of the Holy Spirit is more powerful.

Grinding the face of the poor

What is meant by "grinding the face of the poor"? I think the words actually speak for themselves, and a fairly graphic image should emerge in your mind as you consider the phrase. As the prophet Isaiah has expressed Yahweh's perspective, I can't help but catch on to it that Yahweh is a champion of the poor and down-trodden, and He is not very happy with the way in which people, in general, tend to interact with the poor. Not only is there subtle inaction, as characterized by the rich man's posture towards Lazarus, there are the more extreme cases of actually grinding the face of the poor. Perhaps most of us would readily admit that, yes, at times, we too have not acted in ways that we could have or should have. Maybe, on rare occasions, we also exhibit the behavior of the rich man in the parable. Yet, most of us would tighten up and pull back at the very idea, the very suggestion, that *we* are guilty of this despicable and extreme behavior. After all, we have never gone to the extent of actually grinding the face of the poor; only really bad people do such horrendous things. However, the argument can be made that the act of grinding the face of the poor could, in fact, be construed to be exactly what the rich man did to Lazarus. That is, what if his mere inaction were actually perceived by Yahweh as taking his sandal and pressing it against the back of the neck and forcing Lazarus' face into the dirt? All of a sudden, even our subtle inactivity, of which most of us are culpable from time to time, becomes almost freakishly important and relevant.

I think it is important for you to understand that your reading of these texts *is not* a call to guilt. Rather, it is a call to action. It is a call to change behavior and attitudes. It is a call to seriously contemplate your role in our culture. The reading of these texts constitutes a clarion call to follow, to doggedly pursue, the ideals of biblical justice. The wonderful thing about biblical justice is that, wherever you find people, you can experiment with it. In this sense, the world is a bit of a laboratory, and you can reach out and initiate research and trials in which you attempt to enact true justice.

So, for instance, when the Bible says, "If you close your ear to the cry of the poor, you will cry out and not be heard." (Prov. 21:3), please don't roll your eyes and think, "This Scripture doesn't apply directly to me because I don't close my ear to the poor." For I suspect, that if we start forthrightly examining ourselves, we just may uncover some of that subtle inactivity of the rich man. Yet, I suppose that someone could, at this point, protest and say, "Wait a minute! The cry of the poor is so overwhelming, there are so many poor people in the world, we simply can't address all of their needs."

Indeed, the plight of the poor does appear to be of such an extent that the problem is unsolvable. The level of poverty in the world is so overwhelming it's almost as if we are dealing with what one might call imaginary numbers. They are imaginary numbers, first of all, because they are so large. But also, they are imaginary numbers because most of us, as Americans, will never directly encounter such overwhelming numbers of poor people. Consider this; every day, every single day of the year something very extraordinary happens in the world. Every day about 30,000 children who are under the age of five die from easily preventable causes.[3]

Now, take 30,000 children a day who will die and multiply that by 365 days in the year. The product is 10,950,000. That is 10.9 MILLION children. The previous two sentences should have made you sit back in your chair a bit. If they didn't, you might want to consider the possibility that there is something wrong with the way you view the world. Those do seem to be nearly imaginary numbers! Of course, the notion of imaginary numbers is quite mind numbing to most of us. One might even react by suggesting that those numbers can't possibly be correct. You might be right; they may be a tad low.

[3] United Nations Development Programme, *Human Development Report 2001*, (New York: Oxford University Press, 2001) p. 8.

Should Christians see justice differently?

One might ask oneself, should Christians have a different view and understanding of justice than the rest of the world? That is, should we see things differently? Norwood Russell Hanson in his book, *Patterns of Discovery*, raises a very interesting and well-known question from a scenario he created. He writes,

> Let us consider Johannes Kepler: imagine him on a hill watching the dawn. With him is Tycho Brahe. Kepler regarded the sun as fixed: it was the earth that moved. But Tycho followed Ptolemy and Aristotle: the earth was fixed and all other celestial bodies moved around it. *Do Kepler and Tycho see the same thing in the east at dawn?*[4]

Of course, the answer from Hanson's position is "No, they don't see the same thing." To fully appreciate the wit and the profundity of this scenario, one must recognize the utter separation of understanding between the two gifted astronomers. There they are upon the hill. Kepler sees heliocentrically; Brahe sees geocentrically. Yes, of course, they have received the same retinal image through their eyeballs as they looked out at the scene. But as someone has said, and I haven't been able to track down who said it first, "eyeballs are blind." People are able to "see," but a digital camera is blind. The difference between the two observers, Kepler and Brahe, is interpretive; they both have the same visual data, and yet, they see things differently.

The Kepler/Brahe story was originally set in the context of Hanson discussing the notion of observation. He would, later in the book, develop an argument against the idea of what is called theory-free observation. Hanson's point was that there are no theory-neutral observations. We all come to our observations with the baggage of experience, belief, and presupposition. While Kepler and Brahe were looking at the same object, they each came to that experience with their baggage. For Kepler, the sun was coming into view as earth was turning on its axis. Contrarily, Brahe saw the sun as it was starting to make its daily trip around a stationary planet. Thus, for Hanson, "Seeing is not only the having of a visual expe-

[4]N. R. Hanson, *Patterns of Discovery*. (London: Cambridge University Press, 1958) p. 5.

rience; it is also the way in which the visual experience is had."[5]

In his book, Hanson was attacking a two-staged model of seeing. This Two-Staged Theory presumes that seeing involves two distinct things. First, the raw perception or data, i.e. photons hitting rods and cones in the retina. Second, it also involves the *interpretation* of that physical perception. Hanson goes on to argue that there is no seeing apart from interpretation.

I suppose, at this point, one might comment, "While this whole thing is wildly entertaining, what does it have to do with biblical justice?" I have one word for you, "analogy." Just as Kepler and Brahe see things differently in Hanson's little story, so also should Christians see things differently from non-believers. While Christians have the same retinal images as everybody else, we had better *see* differently. For as Hanson so cleverly put it, "There is more to seeing than meets the eyeball." It is the interpretive lens of Scripture that enables us to see in such a way that we not only perceive the photons of injustice upon our retinas, but we are also able to interpret the sight and subsequently initiate behavioral change based on the interpretive model of Christ's Gospel.

A note on why the texts are ordered as they are

Finally, the order of the texts you will be reading presented a small problem that I wrestled with for a minute or two. My initial inclination was to present each text in the order in which they appear in Scripture. Thereby, one would follow the canonical order of the books, e.g. Genesis, Exodus, Leviticus...Matthew, Mark, Luke, etc. Naturally, the ordering of the chapters and the verses would then also be kept sequential. However, I felt that a surprising order might prove to be more shocking to the reader, avoiding any sense of predictability. I thought of the Psalter, and I decided to use that as my model. That is, I decided that the ordering of texts would not be based on any particular criteria. Some texts are occasionally clustered, however, most often, there is no logical structure to the order. This is not unlike the presentation of texts in the Psalter. The Psalter is, in fact, an unpredictable

[5] *Ibid.* p. 15.

array. It leads one from the hilltop to the valley with astonishing rapidity. As Holladay[6] aptly notes concerning the ordering of the individual psalms: "The advantage of the present canonical order is precisely that it is *not* a very 'logical' order— the sequence catches us unawares, forcing us to ponder the sudden actions of God in our lives." In this way, the arbitrary order of these texts is a call to ponder, and it is a call to action. While the texts presented here are clearly thematic, the reader cannot help but be surprised by what comes next.

[6]William Holladay, *The Psalms Through Three Thousand Years.* (Minneapolis: Fortress Press, 1993) p. 356.

PART I:
TEXTS FROM SCRIPTURE

Grinding the face of the poor

Isaiah 3:14-15

<14> The LORD enters into judgment
    with the elders and princes of his people:
It is you who have devoured the vineyard;
    the spoil of the poor is in your houses.
<15> What do you mean by crushing my people,
by grinding the face of the poor? says the Lord GOD of hosts.

Gaining wealth by violence

Habakkuk 2:5-12

<5> Moreover, wealth is treacherous;
    the arrogant do not endure.
They open their throats wide as Sheol;
    like Death they never have enough.
They gather all nations for themselves,
    and collect all peoples as their own.
<6> Shall not everyone taunt such people and, with mocking riddles,
say about them,
"Alas for you who heap up what is not your own!"
    How long will you load yourselves with goods taken in pledge?
<7> Will not your own creditors suddenly rise,
    and those who make you tremble wake up?
    Then you will be booty for them.
<8> Because you have plundered many nations,
    all that survive of the peoples shall plunder you—
because of human bloodshed, and violence to the earth,
    to cities and all who live in them.
<9> "Alas for you who get evil gain for your houses,
    setting your nest on high

to be safe from the reach of harm!"

<10> You have devised shame for your house
      by cutting off many peoples;
      you have forfeited your life.

<11> The very stones will cry out from the wall,
      and the plaster will respond from the woodwork.

<12> "Alas for you who build a town by bloodshed,
      and found a city on iniquity!"

Justice for slaves

Exodus 21:1-11

<21:1> These are the ordinances that you shall set before them:

<2> When you buy a male Hebrew slave, he shall serve six years, but in the seventh he shall go out a free person, without debt.

<3> If he comes in single, he shall go out single; if he comes in married, then his wife shall go out with him.

<4> If his master gives him a wife and she bears him sons or daughters, the wife and her children shall be her master's and he shall go out alone.

<5> But if the slave declares, "I love my master, my wife, and my children; I will not go out a free person,"

<6> then his master shall bring him before God. He shall be brought to the door or the doorpost; and his master shall pierce his ear with an awl; and he shall serve him for life.

<7> When a man sells his daughter as a slave, she shall not go out as the male slaves do.

<8> If she does not please her master, who designated her for himself, then he shall let her be redeemed; he shall have no right to sell her to a foreign people, since he has dealt unfairly with her.

<9> If he designates her for his son, he shall deal with her as with a daughter.

<10> If he takes another wife to himself, he shall not diminish the food, clothing, or marital rights of the first wife.

<11> And if he does not do these three things for her, she shall go out without debt, without payment of money.

The alien, the orphan, and the widow

Deuteronomy 24:10-22

<10> When you make your neighbor a loan of any kind, you shall not go into the house to take the pledge.

<11> You shall wait outside, while the person to whom you are making the loan brings the pledge out to you.

<12> If the person is poor, you shall not sleep in the garment given you as the pledge.

<13> You shall give the pledge back by sunset, so that your neighbor may sleep in the cloak and bless you; and it will be to your credit before the LORD your God.

<14> You shall not withhold the wages of poor and needy laborers, whether other Israelites or aliens who reside in your land in one of your towns.

<15> You shall pay them their wages daily before sunset, because they are poor and their livelihood depends on them; otherwise they might cry to the LORD against you, and you would incur guilt.

<16> Parents shall not be put to death for their children, nor shall children be put to death for their parents; only for their own crimes may persons be put to death.

<17> You shall not deprive a resident alien or an orphan of justice; you shall not take a widow's garment in pledge.

<18> Remember that you were a slave in Egypt and the LORD your God redeemed you from there; therefore I command you to do this.

<19> When you reap your harvest in your field and forget a sheaf in the field, you shall not go back to get it; it shall be left for the alien, the orphan, and the widow, so that the LORD your God may bless you in all your undertakings.

<20> When you beat your olive trees, do not strip what is left; it shall be for the alien, the orphan, and the widow.

<21> When you gather the grapes of your vineyard, do not glean what is left; it shall be for the alien, the orphan, and the widow.

<22> Remember that you were a slave in the land of Egypt; therefore I am commanding you to do this.

Crushing the needy

Amos 4:1-3

<4:1> Hear this word, you cows of Bashan
   who are on Mount Samaria,
who oppress the poor, who crush the needy,
   who say to their husbands, "Bring something to drink!"
<2> The Lord GOD has sworn by his holiness:
   The time is surely coming upon you,
when they shall take you away with hooks,
   even the last of you with fishhooks.
<3> Through breaches in the wall you shall leave,
   each one straight ahead;
and you shall be flung out into Harmon, says the LORD.

The ruler and justice

2 Samuel 23:3-4

<3> The God of Israel has spoken,
   the Rock of Israel has said to me:
One who rules over people justly,
   ruling in the fear of God,
<4> is like the light of morning,
   like the sun rising on a cloudless morning,
gleaming from the rain on the grassy land.

Consequences of doing justice

Proverbs 21:15

<15> When justice is done, it is a joy to the righteous,
   but dismay to evildoers.

Pride in riches

1 John 2:15-17

<15> Do not love the world or the things in the world. The love of the

Father is not in those who love the world;

<16> for all that is in the world—the desire of the flesh, the desire of the eyes, the pride in riches—comes not from the Father but from the world.

<17> And the world and its desire are passing away, but those who do the will of God live forever.

Do not covet

Deuteronomy 5:21

<21> Neither shall you covet your neighbor's wife.
Neither shall you desire your neighbor's house, or field, or male or female slave, or ox, or donkey, or anything that belongs to your neighbor.

Cheating orphans, widows, and foreigners

Ezekiel 22:6-13

<6> The princes of Israel in you, everyone according to his power, have been bent on shedding blood.

<7> Father and mother are treated with contempt in you; the alien residing within you suffers extortion; the orphan and the widow are wronged in you.

<8> You have despised my holy things, and profaned my sabbaths.

<9> In you are those who slander to shed blood, those in you who eat upon the mountains, who commit lewdness in your midst.

<10> In you they uncover their fathers' nakedness; in you they violate women in their menstrual periods.

<11> One commits abomination with his neighbor's wife; another lewdly defiles his daughter-in-law; another in you defiles his sister, his father's daughter.

<12> In you, they take bribes to shed blood; you take both advance interest and accrued interest, and make gain of your neighbors by extortion; and you have forgotten me, says the Lord GOD.

<13> See, I strike my hands together at the dishonest gain you have made, and at the blood that has been shed within you.

Passing up a bribe

Isaiah 33:15-16

\<15\> Those who walk righteously and speak uprightly,
    who despise the gain of oppression,
who wave away a bribe instead of accepting it,
    who stop their ears from hearing of bloodshed
    and shut their eyes from looking on evil,
\<16\> they will live on the heights;
    their refuge will be the fortresses of rocks;
    their food will be supplied, their water assured.

Be doers

James 1:22-24

\<22\> But be doers of the word, and not merely hearers who deceive themselves.

\<23\> For if any are hearers of the word and not doers, they are like those who look at themselves in a mirror;

\<24\> for they look at themselves and, on going away, immediately forget what they were like.

Grieving for the poor

Job 30:25

\<25\> Did I not weep for those whose day was hard? Was not my soul grieved for the poor?

Sell and give

Luke 12:32-34

\<32\> "Do not be afraid, little flock, for it is your Father's good pleasure to give you the kingdom.

\<33\> Sell your possessions, and give alms. Make purses for yourselves that do not wear out, an unfailing treasure in heaven, where no thief comes near and no moth destroys.

\<34\> For where your treasure is, there your heart will be also.

She gave all she had to live on

Mark 12:41-44

12:41 And he sat down opposite the treasury, and watched the multitude putting money into the treasury. Many rich people put in large sums. 12:42 And a poor widow came, and put in two copper coins, which make a penny. 12:43 And he called his disciples to him, and said to them, "Truly, I say to you, this poor widow has put in more than all those who are contributing to the treasury. 12:44 For they all contributed out of their abundance; but she out of her poverty has put in everything she had, her whole living."

When you give to the needy

Matthew 6:1-4

6:1 "Beware of practicing your piety before men in order to be seen by them; for then you will have no reward from your Father who is in heaven. 6:2 "Thus, when you give alms, sound no trumpet before you, as the hypocrites do in the synagogues and in the streets, that they may be praised by men. Truly, I say to you, they have received their reward. 6:3 But when you give alms, do not let your left hand know what your right hand is doing, 6:4 so that your alms may be in secret; and your Father who sees in secret will reward you.

Extending arms to the poor

Proverbs 31:20

<20> She opens her hand to the poor,
and reaches out her hands to the needy.

Don't put a stumbling block in their way

Romans 14:1-12

<14:1> Welcome those who are weak in faith, but not for the purpose of quarreling over opinions.
<2> Some believe in eating anything, while the weak eat only vegetables.
<3> Those who eat must not despise those who abstain, and those

who abstain must not pass judgment on those who eat; for God has welcomed them.

<4> Who are you to pass judgment on servants of another? It is before their own lord that they stand or fall. And they will be upheld, for the Lord is able to make them stand.

<5> Some judge one day to be better than another, while others judge all days to be alike. Let all be fully convinced in their own minds.

<6> Those who observe the day, observe it in honor of the Lord. Also those who eat, eat in honor of the Lord, since they give thanks to God; while those who abstain, abstain in honor of the Lord and give thanks to God.

<7> We do not live to ourselves, and we do not die to ourselves.

<8> If we live, we live to the Lord, and if we die, we die to the Lord; so then, whether we live or whether we die, we are the Lord's.

<9> For to this end Christ died and lived again, so that he might be Lord of both the dead and the living.

<10> Why do you pass judgment on your brother or sister? Or you, why do you despise your brother or sister? For we will all stand before the judgment seat of God.

<11> For it is written,
"As I live, says the Lord, every knee shall bow to me,
and every tongue shall give praise to God."

<12> So then, each of us will be accountable to God.

<13> Let us therefore no longer pass judgment on one another, but resolve instead never to put a stumbling block or hindrance in the way of another.

<14> I know and am persuaded in the Lord Jesus that nothing is unclean in itself; but it is unclean for anyone who thinks it unclean.

Give to the poor

Proverbs 28:27

<27> Whoever gives to the poor will lack nothing,
but one who turns a blind eye will get many a curse.

The baited net

Proverbs 1:10-19

\<10\> My child, if sinners entice you,
> do not consent.

\<11\> If they say, "Come with us, let us lie in wait for blood;
> let us wantonly ambush the innocent;

\<12\> like Sheol let us swallow them alive
> and whole, like those who go down to the Pit.

\<13\> We shall find all kinds of costly things;
> we shall fill our houses with booty.

\<14\> Throw in your lot among us;
> we will all have one purse"—

\<15\> my child, do not walk in their way,
> keep your foot from their paths;

\<16\> for their feet run to evil,
> and they hurry to shed blood.

\<17\> For in vain is the net baited
> while the bird is looking on;

\<18\> yet they lie in wait—to kill themselves!
> and set an ambush—for their own lives!

\<19\> Such is the end of all who are greedy for gain;
> it takes away the life of its possessors.

Give to the one who asks

Matthew 5:42

5:42 Give to him who begs from you, and do not refuse him who would borrow from you.

The year of Jubilee

Leviticus 25:8-17

\<8\> You shall count off seven weeks of years, seven times seven years, so that the period of seven weeks of years gives forty-nine years.

\<9\> Then you shall have the trumpet sounded loud; on the tenth day of the seventh month—on the day of atonement—you shall have the trumpet sounded throughout all your land.

<10> And you shall hallow the fiftieth year and you shall proclaim liberty throughout the land to all its inhabitants. It shall be a jubilee for you: you shall return, every one of you, to your property and every one of you to your family.

<11> That fiftieth year shall be a jubilee for you: you shall not sow, or reap the aftergrowth, or harvest the unpruned vines.

<12> For it is a jubilee; it shall be holy to you: you shall eat only what the field itself produces.

<13> In this year of jubilee you shall return, every one of you, to your property.

<14> When you make a sale to your neighbor or buy from your neighbor, you shall not cheat one another.

<15> When you buy from your neighbor, you shall pay only for the number of years since the jubilee; the seller shall charge you only for the remaining crop years.

<16> If the years are more, you shall increase the price, and if the years are fewer, you shall diminish the price; for it is a certain number of harvests that are being sold to you.

<17> You shall not cheat one another, but you shall fear your God; for I am the LORD your God.

Act with justice

Jeremiah 22:1-5

<22:1> Thus says the LORD: Go down to the house of the king of Judah, and speak there this word,

<2> and say: Hear the word of the LORD, O King of Judah sitting on the throne of David—you, and your servants, and your people who enter these gates.

<3> Thus says the LORD: Act with justice and righteousness, and deliver from the hand of the oppressor anyone who has been robbed. And do no wrong or violence to the alien, the orphan, and the widow, or shed innocent blood in this place.

<4> For if you will indeed obey this word, then through the gates of this house shall enter kings who sit on the throne of David, riding in

chariots and on horses, they, and their servants, and their people.

<5> But if you will not heed these words, I swear by myself, says the LORD, that this house shall become a desolation.

You had compassion

Hebrews 10:32-34

<32> But recall those earlier days when, after you had been enlightened, you endured a hard struggle with sufferings,

<33> sometimes being publicly exposed to abuse and persecution, and sometimes being partners with those so treated.

<34> For you had compassion for those who were in prison, and you cheerfully accepted the plundering of your possessions, knowing that you yourselves possessed something better and more lasting.

Perverting justice

Exodus 23:1-3

<23:1> You shall not spread a false report. You shall not join hands with the wicked to act as a malicious witness.

<2> You shall not follow a majority in wrongdoing; when you bear witness in a lawsuit, you shall not side with the majority so as to pervert justice;

<3> nor shall you be partial to the poor in a lawsuit.

Dishonesty is abhorrent to the Lord

Deuteronomy 25:13-16

<13> You shall not have in your bag two kinds of weights, large and small.

<14> You shall not have in your house two kinds of measures, large and small.

<15> You shall have only a full and honest weight; you shall have only a full and honest measure, so that your days may be long in the land that the LORD your God is giving you.

<16> For all who do such things, all who act dishonestly, are abhorrent to the LORD your God.

Cornelius prayed and gave alms

Acts 10:1-4

<10:1> In Caesarea there was a man named Cornelius, a centurion of the Italian Cohort, as it was called.

<2> He was a devout man who feared God with all his household; he gave alms generously to the people and prayed constantly to God.

<3> One afternoon at about three o'clock he had a vision in which he clearly saw an angel of God coming in and saying to him, "Cornelius."

<4> He stared at him in terror and said, "What is it, Lord?" He answered, "Your prayers and your alms have ascended as a memorial before God.

Having nothing, and yet possessing everything

2 Corinthians 6:3-10

<3> We are putting no obstacle in anyone's way, so that no fault may be found with our ministry,

<4> but as servants of God we have commended ourselves in every way: through great endurance, in afflictions, hardships, calamities,

<5> beatings, imprisonments, riots, labors, sleepless nights, hunger;

<6> by purity, knowledge, patience, kindness, holiness of spirit, genuine love,

<7> truthful speech, and the power of God; with the weapons of righteousness for the right hand and for the left;

<8> in honor and dishonor, in ill repute and good repute. We are treated as impostors, and yet are true;

<9> as unknown, and yet are well known; as dying, and see—we are alive; as punished, and yet not killed;

<10> as sorrowful, yet always rejoicing; as poor, yet making many rich; as having nothing, and yet possessing everything.

Greed is really bad

1 Corinthians 6:9-10

<9> Do you not know that wrongdoers will not inherit the kingdom of God? Do not be deceived! Fornicators, idolaters, adulterers, male

prostitutes, sodomites,

<10> thieves, the greedy, drunkards, revilers, robbers—none of these will inherit the kingdom of God.

Economic Justice: the case of Naboth

1 Kings 21:1-19

<21:1> Later the following events took place: Naboth the Jezreelite had a vineyard in Jezreel, beside the palace of King Ahab of Samaria.

<2> And Ahab said to Naboth, "Give me your vineyard, so that I may have it for a vegetable garden, because it is near my house; I will give you a better vineyard for it; or, if it seems good to you, I will give you its value in money."

<3> But Naboth said to Ahab, "The LORD forbid that I should give you my ancestral inheritance."

<4> Ahab went home resentful and sullen because of what Naboth the Jezreelite had said to him; for he had said, "I will not give you my ancestral inheritance." He lay down on his bed, turned away his face, and would not eat.

<5> His wife Jezebel came to him and said, "Why are you so depressed that you will not eat?"

<6> He said to her, "Because I spoke to Naboth the Jezreelite and said to him, 'Give me your vineyard for money; or else, if you prefer, I will give you another vineyard for it'; but he answered, 'I will not give you my vineyard.'"

<7> His wife Jezebel said to him, "Do you now govern Israel? Get up, eat some food, and be cheerful; I will give you the vineyard of Naboth the Jezreelite."

<8> So she wrote letters in Ahab's name and sealed them with his seal; she sent the letters to the elders and the nobles who lived with Naboth in his city.

<9> She wrote in the letters, "Proclaim a fast, and seat Naboth at the head of the assembly;

<10> seat two scoundrels opposite him, and have them bring a charge against him, saying, 'You have cursed God and the king.' Then take him out, and stone him to death."

<11> The men of his city, the elders and the nobles who lived in his city, did as Jezebel had sent word to them. Just as it was written in the letters that she had sent to them,

<12> they proclaimed a fast and seated Naboth at the head of the assembly.

<13> The two scoundrels came in and sat opposite him; and the scoundrels brought a charge against Naboth, in the presence of the people, saying, "Naboth cursed God and the king." So they took him outside the city, and stoned him to death.

<14> Then they sent to Jezebel, saying, "Naboth has been stoned; he is dead."

<15> As soon as Jezebel heard that Naboth had been stoned and was dead, Jezebel said to Ahab, "Go, take possession of the vineyard of Naboth the Jezreelite, which he refused to give you for money; for Naboth is not alive, but dead."

<16> As soon as Ahab heard that Naboth was dead, Ahab set out to go down to the vineyard of Naboth the Jezreelite, to take possession of it.

<17> Then the word of the LORD came to Elijah the Tishbite, saying:

<18> Go down to meet King Ahab of Israel, who rules in Samaria; he is now in the vineyard of Naboth, where he has gone to take possession.

<19> You shall say to him, "Thus says the LORD: Have you killed, and also taken possession?" You shall say to him, "Thus says the LORD: In the place where dogs licked up the blood of Naboth, dogs will also lick up your blood."

I coveted no one's silver or gold or clothing
Acts 20:32-35

<32> And now I commend you to God and to the message of his grace, a message that is able to build you up and to give you the inheritance among all who are sanctified.

<33> I coveted no one's silver or gold or clothing.

<34> You know for yourselves that I worked with my own hands to support myself and my companions.

<35> In all this I have given you an example that by such work we must support the weak, remembering the words of the Lord Jesus, for he himself said, 'It is more blessed to give than to receive.'"

Justice turned into bitterness

Amos 5:7
7> Ah, you that turn justice to wormwood,
and bring righteousness to the ground!

Pursue justice

Deuteronomy 16:18-20
<18> You shall appoint judges and officials throughout your tribes, in all your towns that the LORD your God is giving you, and they shall render just decisions for the people.
<19> You must not distort justice; you must not show partiality; and you must not accept bribes, for a bribe blinds the eyes of the wise and subverts the cause of those who are in the right.
<20> Justice, and only justice, you shall pursue, so that you may live and occupy the land that the LORD your God is giving you.

So as to share with the needy

Ephesians 4:28
<28> Thieves must give up stealing; rather let them labor and work honestly with their own hands, so as to have something to share with the needy.

A just man feeds the poor

Ezekiel 18:5-9
<5> If a man is righteous and does what is lawful and right—
<6> if he does not eat upon the mountains or lift up his eyes to the idols of the house of Israel, does not defile his neighbor's wife or approach a woman during her menstrual period,

<7> does not oppress anyone, but restores to the debtor his pledge, commits no robbery, gives his bread to the hungry and covers the naked with a garment,

<8> does not take advance or accrued interest, withholds his hand from iniquity, executes true justice between contending parties,

<9> follows my statutes, and is careful to observe my ordinances, acting faithfully—such a one is righteous; he shall surely live, says the Lord GOD.

For the good of all

Galatians 6:9-10

<9> So let us not grow weary in doing what is right, for we will reap at harvest time, if we do not give up.

<10> So then, whenever we have an opportunity, let us work for the good of all, and especially for those of the family of faith.

Rescue the oppressed

Isaiah 1:10-20

<10> Hear the word of the LORD,
  you rulers of Sodom!
Listen to the teaching of our God,
  you people of Gomorrah!
<11> What to me is the multitude of your sacrifices?
  says the LORD;
I have had enough of burnt offerings of rams
  and the fat of fed beasts;
I do not delight in the blood of bulls,
  or of lambs, or of goats.
<12> When you come to appear before me,
  who asked this from your hand?
  Trample my courts no more;
<13> bringing offerings is futile;
  incense is an abomination to me.
New moon and sabbath and calling of convocation—
  I cannot endure solemn assemblies with iniquity.

<14> Your new moons and your appointed festivals
    my soul hates;
they have become a burden to me,
    I am weary of bearing them.
<15> When you stretch out your hands,
    I will hide my eyes from you;
even though you make many prayers,
    I will not listen;
    your hands are full of blood.
<16> Wash yourselves; make yourselves clean;
    remove the evil of your doings
    from before my eyes;
cease to do evil,
<17> learn to do good; seek justice,
    rescue the oppressed,
defend the orphan,
    plead for the widow.
<18> Come now, let us argue it out,
    says the LORD:
though your sins are like scarlet,
    they shall be like snow;
though they are red like crimson,
    they shall become like wool.
<19> If you are willing and obedient,
    you shall eat the good of the land;
<20> but if you refuse and rebel,
    you shall be devoured by the sword;
for the mouth of the LORD has spoken.

A poor person in dirty clothes

James 2:1-9

<2:1> My brothers and sisters, do you with your acts of favoritism really believe in our glorious Lord Jesus Christ?
<2> For if a person with gold rings and in fine clothes comes into your assembly, and if a poor person in dirty clothes also comes in,

<3> and if you take notice of the one wearing the fine clothes and say, "Have a seat here, please," while to the one who is poor you say, "Stand there," or, "Sit at my feet,"

<4> have you not made distinctions among yourselves, and become judges with evil thoughts?

<5> Listen, my beloved brothers and sisters. Has not God chosen the poor in the world to be rich in faith and to be heirs of the kingdom that he has promised to those who love him?

<6> But you have dishonored the poor. Is it not the rich who oppress you? Is it not they who drag you into court?

<7> Is it not they who blaspheme the excellent name that was invoked over you?

<8> You do well if you really fulfill the royal law according to the scripture, "You shall love your neighbor as yourself."

<9> But if you show partiality, you commit sin and are convicted by the law as transgressors.

Exploiting workers

Jeremiah 22:13

<13> Woe to him who builds his house by unrighteousness,
    and his upper rooms by injustice;
who makes his neighbors work for nothing,
    and does not give them their wages;

A father to the needy

Job 29:13-16

<13> The blessing of the wretched came upon me,
    and I caused the widow's heart to sing for joy.

<14> I put on righteousness, and it clothed me;
    my justice was like a robe and a turban.

<15> I was eyes to the blind,
    and feet to the lame.

<16> I was a father to the needy,
and I championed the cause of the stranger.

Being generous

Proverbs 11:25-26

<25> A generous person will be enriched,
   and one who gives water will get water.

<26> The people curse those who hold back grain,
   but a blessing is on the head of those who sell it.

Precepts of justice

Leviticus 19:11-18

<11> You shall not steal; you shall not deal falsely; and you shall not lie to one another.

<12> And you shall not swear falsely by my name, profaning the name of your God: I am the LORD.

<13> You shall not defraud your neighbor; you shall not steal; and you shall not keep for yourself the wages of a laborer until morning.

<14> You shall not revile the deaf or put a stumbling block before the blind; you shall fear your God: I am the LORD.

<15> You shall not render an unjust judgment; you shall not be partial to the poor or defer to the great: with justice you shall judge your neighbor.

<16> You shall not go around as a slanderer among your people, and you shall not profit by the blood of your neighbor: I am the LORD.

<17> You shall not hate in your heart anyone of your kin; you shall reprove your neighbor, or you will incur guilt yourself.

<18> You shall not take vengeance or bear a grudge against any of your people, but you shall love your neighbor as yourself: I am the LORD.

Neglecting justice

Luke 11:42

<42> "But woe to you Pharisees! For you tithe mint and rue and herbs of all kinds, and neglect justice and the love of God; it is these you ought to have practiced, without neglecting the others.

Restore their property to them

Nehemiah 5:1-12

<5:1> Now there was a great outcry of the people and of their wives against their Jewish kin.

<2> For there were those who said, "With our sons and our daughters, we are many; we must get grain, so that we may eat and stay alive."

<3> There were also those who said, "We are having to pledge our fields, our vineyards, and our houses in order to get grain during the famine."

<4> And there were those who said, "We are having to borrow money on our fields and vineyards to pay the king's tax.

<5> Now our flesh is the same as that of our kindred; our children are the same as their children; and yet we are forcing our sons and daughters to be slaves, and some of our daughters have been ravished; we are powerless, and our fields and vineyards now belong to others."

<6> I was very angry when I heard their outcry and these complaints.

<7> After thinking it over, I brought charges against the nobles and the officials; I said to them, "You are all taking interest from your own people." And I called a great assembly to deal with them,

<8> and said to them, "As far as we were able, we have bought back our Jewish kindred who had been sold to other nations; but now you are selling your own kin, who must then be bought back by us!" They were silent, and could not find a word to say.

<9> So I said, "The thing that you are doing is not good. Should you not walk in the fear of our God, to prevent the taunts of the nations our enemies?

<10> Moreover I and my brothers and my servants are lending them money and grain. Let us stop this taking of interest.

<11> Restore to them, this very day, their fields, their vineyards, their olive orchards, and their houses, and the interest on money, grain, wine, and oil that you have been exacting from them."

<12> Then they said, "We will restore everything and demand nothing more from them. We will do as you say." And I called the priests, and made them take an oath to do as they had promised.

Honoring Him

Proverbs 14:31

<31> Those who oppress the poor insult their Maker,
but those who are kind to the needy honor him.

Yahweh's justice includes mercy

Psalm 119:156

<156> Great is your mercy, O LORD;
give me life according to your justice.

The needy groan

Psalm 12:5

<5> "Because the poor are despoiled, because the needy groan,
    I will now rise up," says the LORD;
"I will place them in the safety for which they long."

Protecting those who might be exploited

Deuteronomy 26:12-13

<12> When you have finished paying all the tithe of your produce in
the third year (which is the year of the tithe), giving it to the Levites,
the aliens, the orphans, and the widows, so that they may eat their fill
within your towns,

<13> then you shall say before the LORD your God: "I have removed
the sacred portion from the house, and I have given it to the Levites,
the resident aliens, the orphans, and the widows, in accordance with
your entire commandment that you commanded me; I have neither
transgressed nor forgotten any of your commandments:

Evildoers frustrate the poor

Psalm 14:6

<6> You would confound the plans of the poor,
    but the LORD is their refuge.

Rights of poor

Psalm 82:3

<3> Give justice to the weak and the orphan;
    maintain the right of the lowly and the destitute.

I need nothing

Revelation 3:14-18

<14> "And to the angel of the church in Laodicea write: The words of the Amen, the faithful and true witness, the origin of God's creation:
<15> "I know your works; you are neither cold nor hot. I wish that you were either cold or hot.
<16> So, because you are lukewarm, and neither cold nor hot, I am about to spit you out of my mouth.
<17> For you say, 'I am rich, I have prospered, and I need nothing.' You do not realize that you are wretched, pitiable, poor, blind, and naked.

God hates injustice

Zechariah 8:14-17

<14> For thus says the LORD of hosts: Just as I purposed to bring disaster upon you, when your ancestors provoked me to wrath, and I did not relent, says the LORD of hosts,
<15> so again I have purposed in these days to do good to Jerusalem and to the house of Judah; do not be afraid.
<16> These are the things that you shall do: Speak the truth to one another, render in your gates judgments that are true and make for peace,
<17> do not devise evil in your hearts against one another, and love no false oath; for all these are things that I hate, says the LORD.

Treasure in heaven, not on earth

Matthew 6:19-21

6:19 "Do not lay up for yourselves treasures on earth, where moth and rust consume and where thieves break in and steal, 6:20 but lay up for yourselves treasures in heaven, where neither moth nor rust consumes and where thieves do not break in and steal. 6:21 For where your treasure is, there will your heart be also.

Oppressing the poor to get rich

Proverbs 22:16

<16> Oppressing the poor in order to enrich oneself,
and giving to the rich, will lead only to loss.

Oppression

Micah 2:1-10

<2:1> Alas for those who devise wickedness
and evil deeds on their beds!
When the morning dawns, they perform it,
because it is in their power.
<2> They covet fields, and seize them;
houses, and take them away;
they oppress householder and house,
people and their inheritance.
<3> Therefore thus says the LORD:
Now, I am devising against this family an evil
from which you cannot remove your necks;
and you shall not walk haughtily,
for it will be an evil time.
<4> On that day they shall take up a taunt song against you,
and wail with bitter lamentation,
and say, "We are utterly ruined;
the LORD alters the inheritance of my people;
how he removes it from me!
Among our captors he parcels out our fields."
<5> Therefore you will have no one to cast the line by lot in the assembly of the LORD.
<6> "Do not preach"—thus they preach—

"one should not preach of such things;
            disgrace will not overtake us."
<7> Should this be said, O house of Jacob?
            Is the LORD's patience exhausted?
            Are these his doings?
Do not my words do good
            to one who walks uprightly?
<8> But you rise up against my people as an enemy;
            you strip the robe from the peaceful,
from those who pass by trustingly
            with no thought of war.
<9> The women of my people you drive out
            from their pleasant houses;
from their young children you take away
            my glory forever.
<10> Arise and go;
            for this is no place to rest,
because of uncleanness that destroys with a grievous destruction.

Would you be homeless?

Luke 9:57-58

<9:57> As they were walking along the road, a man said to him, "I will follow you wherever you go."
<9:57> Jesus replied, "Foxes have holes and birds of the air have nests, but the Son of Man has no place to lay his head."

Leaving grain for poor

Leviticus 23:22

<22> When you reap the harvest of your land, you shall not reap to the very edges of your field, or gather the gleanings of your harvest; you shall leave them for the poor and for the alien: I am the LORD your God.

God gives hope to the poor

Job 5:15-16

<15> But he saves the needy from the sword of their mouth,
   from the hand of the mighty.
<16> So the poor have hope,
and injustice shuts its mouth.

He didn't care about the poor

John 12:4-6

<4> But Judas Iscariot, one of his disciples (the one who was about to betray him), said,
<5> "Why was this perfume not sold for three hundred denarii and the money given to the poor?"
<6> (He said this not because he cared about the poor, but because he was a thief; he kept the common purse and used to steal what was put into it.)

Protect the oppressed

Jeremiah 21:12

<12> O house of David! Thus says the LORD:
Execute justice in the morning,
   and deliver from the hand of the oppressor
   anyone who has been robbed,
or else my wrath will go forth like fire,
   and burn, with no one to quench it,
because of your evil doings.

You want something

James 4:1-3

<4:1> Those conflicts and disputes among you, where do they come from? Do they not come from your cravings that are at war within you?
<2> You want something and do not have it; so you commit murder. And you covet something and cannot obtain it; so you engage in dis-

putes and conflicts. You do not have, because you do not ask.
<3> You ask and do not receive, because you ask wrongly, in order to
spend what you get on your pleasures.

Failure to do justice blinds people
Isaiah 59:12-15
12> For our transgressions before you are many,
      and our sins testify against us.
Our transgressions indeed are with us,
      and we know our iniquities:
<13> transgressing, and denying the LORD,
      and turning away from following our God,
talking oppression and revolt,
      conceiving lying words and uttering them from the heart.
<14> Justice is turned back,
      and righteousness stands at a distance;
for truth stumbles in the public square,
      and uprightness cannot enter.
<15> Truth is lacking,
      and whoever turns from evil is despoiled.

A king will reign in righteousness
Isaiah 32:1-3
<32:1> See, a king will reign in righteousness,
      and princes will rule with justice.
<2> Each will be like a hiding place from the wind,
      a covert from the tempest,
like streams of water in a dry place,
      like the shade of a great rock in a weary land.
<3> Then the eyes of those who have sight will not be closed,
      and the ears of those who have hearing will listen.

You push the needy aside

Amos   5:11-12

<11> Therefore because you trample on the poor
    and take from them levies of grain,
you have built houses of hewn stone,
    but you shall not live in them;
you have planted pleasant vineyards,
    but you shall not drink their wine.
<12> For I know how many are your transgressions,
    and how great are your sins—
you who afflict the righteous, who take a bribe,
    and push aside the needy in the gate.

Respecting your neighbor's boundaries

Deuteronomy 27:17

<17> "Cursed be anyone who moves a neighbor's boundary marker."
All the people shall say, "Amen!"

Don't be amazed

Ecclesiastes 5:8

<8> If you see in a province the oppression of the poor and the violation of justice and right, do not be amazed at the matter; for the high official is watched by a higher, and there are yet higher ones over them.

Created for good works

Ephesians 2:10

<10> For we are what he has made us, created in Christ Jesus for good works, which God prepared beforehand to be our way of life.

They were ruthless

Exodus 1:13-14

<13> The Egyptians became ruthless in imposing tasks on the Israelites,

<14> and made their lives bitter with hard service in mortar and brick and in every kind of field labor. They were ruthless in all the tasks that they imposed on them.

Show hospitality to strangers

Hebrews 13:1-3

<13:1> Let mutual love continue.

<2> Do not neglect to show hospitality to strangers, for by doing that some have entertained angels without knowing it.

<3> Remember those who are in prison, as though you were in prison with them; those who are being tortured, as though you yourselves were being tortured.

They asked only one thing

Galatians 2:10

<10> They asked only one thing, that we remember the poor, which was actually what I was eager to do.

My servant will bring forth justice

Isaiah 42:1-3

<42:1> Here is my servant, whom I uphold,
> my chosen, in whom my soul delights;
I have put my spirit upon him;
> he will bring forth justice to the nations.
<2> He will not cry or lift up his voice,
> or make it heard in the street;
<3> a bruised reed he will not break,
> and a dimly burning wick he will not quench;
> he will faithfully bring forth justice.

Yikes! Does this apply to me?

James 4:17

<17> Anyone, then, who knows the right thing to do and fails to do it, commits sin.

We wait for justice

Isaiah 59:9-11

<9> Therefore justice is far from us,
    and righteousness does not reach us;
we wait for light, and lo! there is darkness;
    and for brightness, but we walk in gloom.
<10> We grope like the blind along a wall,
    groping like those who have no eyes;
we stumble at noon as in the twilight,
    among the vigorous as though we were dead.
<11> We all growl like bears;
    like doves we moan mournfully.
We wait for justice, but there is none;
    for salvation, but it is far from us.

Stop oppressing the foreigners, widows, orphans

Jeremiah 7:5-7

<5> For if you truly amend your ways and your doings, if you truly act justly one with another,

<6> if you do not oppress the alien, the orphan, and the widow, or shed innocent blood in this place, and if you do not go after other gods to your own hurt,

<7> then I will dwell with you in this place, in the land that I gave of old to your ancestors forever and ever.

Resources for the poor

Leviticus 19:9-10

<9> When you reap the harvest of your land, you shall not reap to the

very edges of your field, or gather the gleanings of your harvest.
<10> You shall not strip your vineyard bare, or gather the fallen grapes of your vineyard; you shall leave them for the poor and the alien: I am the LORD your God.

Welcoming a child

Luke 9:46-48

<9:46> An argument started among the disciples as to which of them would be the greatest.

<9:47> Jesus, knowing their thoughts, took a little child and had him stand beside him.

<9:48> Then he said to them, "Whoever welcome this little child in my name welcomes me; and whoever welcomes me welcomes the one who sent m. For he who is least among you all – he is the greatest."

Widows, orphans, aliens and poor

Zechariah 7:8-14

<8> The word of the LORD came to Zechariah, saying:

<9> Thus says the LORD of hosts: Render true judgments, show kindness and mercy to one another;

<10> do not oppress the widow, the orphan, the alien, or the poor; and do not devise evil in your hearts against one another.

<11> But they refused to listen, and turned a stubborn shoulder, and stopped their ears in order not to hear.

<12> They made their hearts adamant in order not to hear the law and the words that the LORD of hosts had sent by his spirit through the former prophets. Therefore great wrath came from the LORD of hosts.

<13> Just as, when I called, they would not hear, so, when they called, I would not hear, says the LORD of hosts,

<14> and I scattered them with a whirlwind among all the nations that they had not known. Thus the land they left was desolate, so that no one went to and fro, and a pleasant land was made desolate.

Raising the poor from the dust

Psalm 113:5-8

\<5\> Who is like the LORD our God,
     who is seated on high,
\<6\> who looks far down
     on the heavens and the earth?
\<7\> He raises the poor from the dust,
     and lifts the needy from the ash heap,
\<8\> to make them sit with princes,
with the princes of his people.

Yahweh loves justice

Psalm 37:28

\<28\> For the LORD loves justice;
     he will not forsake his faithful ones.

Know the rights of the poor

Proverbs 29:7

\<7\> The righteous know the rights of the poor;
     the wicked have no such understanding.

Be kind to the poor

Proverbs 14:20-21

\<20\> The poor are disliked even by their neighbors,
     but the rich have many friends.
\<21\> Those who despise their neighbors are sinners,
     but happy are those who are kind to the poor.

Level of righteousness

Matthew 5:20

\<20\> For I tell you that unless your righteousness surpasses that of the Pharisees and the teachers of the law, you will certainly not enter the kingdom of heaven.

Not to be served

Mark 10:35-45

<35> And James and John, the sons of Zeb'edee, came forward to him, and said to him, "Teacher, we want you to do for us whatever we ask of you." <36> And he said to them, "What do you want me to do for you?" <37> And they said to him, "Grant us to sit, one at your right hand and one at your left, in your glory." <38> But Jesus said to them, "You do not know what you are asking. Are you able to drink the cup that I drink, or to be baptized with the baptism with which I am baptized?" <39> And they said to him, "We are able." And Jesus said to them, "The cup that I drink you will drink; and with the baptism with which I am baptized, you will be baptized; <40> but to sit at my right hand or at my left is not mine to grant, but it is for those for whom it has been prepared." <41> And when the ten heard it, they began to be indignant at James and John. <42> And Jesus called them to him and said to them, "You know that those who are supposed to rule over the Gentiles lord it over them, and their great men exercise authority over them. <43> But it shall not be so among you; but whoever would be great among you must be your servant, <44 and whoever would be first among you must be slave of all. <45> For the Son of man also came not to be served but to serve, and to give his life as a ransom for many."

Invite the poor, crippled, lame, and blind

Luke 14:12-14

<12> He said also to the one who had invited him, "When you give a luncheon or a dinner, do not invite your friends or your brothers or your relatives or rich neighbors, in case they may invite you in return, and you would be repaid.

<13> But when you give a banquet, invite the poor, the crippled, the lame, and the blind.

<14> And you will be blessed, because they cannot repay you, for you will be repaid at the resurrection of the righteous.

Open doors

Job 31:32

<32> the stranger has not lodged in the street;
I have opened my doors to the traveler—

A hope for justice

Isaiah 9:6-7

<6> For a child has been born for us,
    a son given to us;
authority rests upon his shoulders;
    and he is named
Wonderful Counselor, Mighty God,
    Everlasting Father, Prince of Peace.
<7> His authority shall grow continually,
    and there shall be endless peace
for the throne of David and his kingdom.
    He will establish and uphold it
with justice and with righteousness
    from this time onward and forevermore.
The zeal of the LORD of hosts will do this.

Just exchange of goods and services

Ezekiel 45:9-12

<9> Thus says the Lord GOD: Enough, O princes of Israel! Put away violence and oppression, and do what is just and right. Cease your evictions of my people, says the Lord GOD.
<10> You shall have honest balances, an honest ephah, and an honest bath.
<11> The ephah and the bath shall be of the same measure, the bath containing one-tenth of a homer, and the ephah one-tenth of a homer; the homer shall be the standard measure.
<12> The shekel shall be twenty gerahs. Twenty shekels, twenty-five shekels, and fifteen shekels shall make a mina for you.

Justice in the wilderness

Isaiah 32:15-17

\<15\> until a spirit from on high is poured out on us,
>and the wilderness becomes a fruitful field,
>and the fruitful field is deemed a forest.

\<16\> Then justice will dwell in the wilderness,
>and righteousness abide in the fruitful field.

\<17\> The effect of righteousness will be peace,
>and the result of righteousness, quietness and trust forever.

That they may eat

Exodus 23:10-11

\<10\> For six years you shall sow your land and gather in its yield;
\<11\> but the seventh year you shall let it rest and lie fallow, so that the poor of your people may eat; and what they leave the wild animals may eat. You shall do the same with your vineyard, and with your olive orchard.

If anyone is in need

Deuteronomy 15:7-18

\<7\> If there is among you anyone in need, a member of your community in any of your towns within the land that the LORD your God is giving you, do not be hard-hearted or tight-fisted toward your needy neighbor.

\<8\> You should rather open your hand, willingly lending enough to meet the need, whatever it may be.

\<9\> Be careful that you do not entertain a mean thought, thinking, "The seventh year, the year of remission, is near," and therefore view your needy neighbor with hostility and give nothing; your neighbor might cry to the LORD against you, and you would incur guilt.

\<10\> Give liberally and be ungrudging when you do so, for on this account the LORD your God will bless you in all your work and in all that you undertake.

\<11\> Since there will never cease to be some in need on the earth, I therefore command you, "Open your hand to the poor and needy neighbor in your land."

<12> If a member of your community, whether a Hebrew man or a Hebrew woman, is sold to you and works for you six years, in the seventh year you shall set that person free.

<13> And when you send a male slave out from you a free person, you shall not send him out empty-handed.

<14> Provide liberally out of your flock, your threshing floor, and your wine press, thus giving to him some of the bounty with which the LORD your God has blessed you.

<15> Remember that you were a slave in the land of Egypt, and the LORD your God redeemed you; for this reason I lay this command upon you today.

<16> But if he says to you, "I will not go out from you," because he loves you and your household, since he is well off with you,

<17> then you shall take an awl and thrust it through his earlobe into the door, and he shall be your slave forever.
You shall do the same with regard to your female slave.

<18> Do not consider it a hardship when you send them out from you free persons, because for six years they have given you services worth the wages of hired laborers; and the LORD your God will bless you in all that you do.

Love of money

Hebrews 13:5

<5> Keep your lives free from the love of money, and be content with what you have; for he has said, "I will never leave you or forsake you."

It was distributed to each as any had need

Acts 4:32-37

<32> Now the whole group of those who believed were of one heart and soul, and no one claimed private ownership of any possessions, but everything they owned was held in common.

<33> With great power the apostles gave their testimony to the resur-

rection of the Lord Jesus, and great grace was upon them all.

<34> There was not a needy person among them, for as many as owned lands or houses sold them and brought the proceeds of what was sold.

<35> They laid it at the apostles' feet, and it was distributed to each as any had need.

<36> There was a Levite, a native of Cyprus, Joseph, to whom the apostles gave the name Barnabas (which means "son of encouragement").

<37> He sold a field that belonged to him, then brought the money, and laid it at the apostles' feet.

Let justice flow like a stream
Amos   5:21-24

<21> I hate, I despise your festivals,
     and I take no delight in your solemn assemblies.
<22> Even though you offer me your burnt offerings and grain offerings,
     I will not accept them;
and the offerings of well-being of your fatted animals
     I will not look upon.
<23> Take away from me the noise of your songs;
     I will not listen to the melody of your harps.
<24> But let justice roll down like waters,
and righteousness like an ever-flowing stream.

Honest measuring
Leviticus 19:32-37

<32> You shall rise before the aged, and defer to the old; and you shall fear your God: I am the LORD.

<33> When an alien resides with you in your land, you shall not oppress the alien.

<34> The alien who resides with you shall be to you as the citizen among you; you shall love the alien as yourself, for you were aliens in

the land of Egypt: I am the LORD your God.

<35> You shall not cheat in measuring length, weight, or quantity.

<36> You shall have honest balances, honest weights, an honest ephah, and an honest hin: I am the LORD your God, who brought you out of the land of Egypt.

<37> You shall keep all my statutes and all my ordinances, and observe them: I am the LORD.

Rulers who abhor justice
Micah 3:9-11

<9> Hear this, you rulers of the house of Jacob
    and chiefs of the house of Israel,
who abhor justice
    and pervert all equity,
<10> who build Zion with blood
    and Jerusalem with wrong!
<11> Its rulers give judgment for a bribe,
        its priests teach for a price,
        its prophets give oracles for money;
yet they lean upon the LORD and say,
        "Surely the LORD is with us!
No harm shall come upon us."

Relation of the ruler and ruled
Proverbs 28:15-16

<15> Like a roaring lion or a charging bear
        is a wicked ruler over a poor people.
<16> A ruler who lacks understanding is a cruel oppressor;
        but one who hates unjust gain will enjoy a long life.

The guy who didn't show kindness to the poor
Psalm 109:1-16

<109:1> Do not be silent, O God of my praise.

<2> For wicked and deceitful mouths are opened against me,
      speaking against me with lying tongues.

<3> They beset me with words of hate,
      and attack me without cause.

<4> In return for my love they accuse me,
      even while I make prayer for them.

<5> So they reward me evil for good,
      and hatred for my love.

<6> They say, "Appoint a wicked man against him;
      let an accuser stand on his right.

<7> When he is tried, let him be found guilty;
      let his prayer be counted as sin.

<8> May his days be few;
      may another seize his position.

<9> May his children be orphans,
      and his wife a widow.

<10> May his children wander about and beg;
      may they be driven out of the ruins they inhabit.

<11> May the creditor seize all that he has;
      may strangers plunder the fruits of his toil.

<12> May there be no one to do him a kindness,
      nor anyone to pity his orphaned children.

<13> May his posterity be cut off;
      may his name be blotted out in the second generation.

<14> May the iniquity of his father be remembered before the LORD,
      and do not let the sin of his mother be blotted out.

<15> Let them be before the LORD continually,
      and may his memory be cut off from the earth.

<16> For he did not remember to show kindness,
      but pursued the poor and needy
      and the brokenhearted to their death.

Those who gained wealth

Revelation 18:11-17

<11> And the merchants of the earth weep and mourn for her, since

no one buys their cargo anymore,

<12> cargo of gold, silver, jewels and pearls, fine linen, purple, silk and scarlet, all kinds of scented wood, all articles of ivory, all articles of costly wood, bronze, iron, and marble,

<13> cinnamon, spice, incense, myrrh, frankincense, wine, olive oil, choice flour and wheat, cattle and sheep, horses and chariots, slaves— and human lives.

<14> "The fruit for which your soul longed
>   has gone from you,
and all your dainties and your splendor
>   are lost to you,
>   never to be found again!"

<15> The merchants of these wares, who gained wealth from her, will stand far off, in fear of her torment, weeping and mourning aloud,

<16> "Alas, alas, the great city,
>   clothed in fine linen,
>   in purple and scarlet,
>   adorned with gold,
>   with jewels, and with pearls!

<17> For in one hour all this wealth has been laid waste!"

The king and the poor

Proverbs 29:14

<14> If a king judges the poor with equity,
>   his throne will be established forever.

What does the Lord require?

Micah 6:8

<8> He has told you, O mortal, what is good;
>   and what does the LORD require of you
but to do justice, and to love kindness,
>   and to walk humbly with your God?

Leading justice to victory

Matthew 12:15-21

<15> Jesus, aware of this, withdrew from there. And many followed him, and he healed them all, <16> and ordered them not to make him known. <17> This was to fulfill what was spoken by the prophet Isaiah:

<18>   "Behold, my servant whom I have chosen,
 my beloved with whom my soul is well pleased.
 I will put my Spirit upon him,
 and he shall proclaim justice to the Gentiles.
<19>   He will not wrangle or cry aloud,
 nor will any one hear his voice in the streets;
<20>   he will not break a bruised reed
 or quench a smoldering wick,
 till he brings justice to victory;
<21>   and in his name will the Gentiles hope."

So men can see your good deeds

Matthew 5:14-16

<14> "You are the light of the world. A city set on a hill cannot be hid. <15> Nor do men light a lamp and put it under a bushel, but on a stand, and it gives light to all in the house. <16> Let your light so shine before men, that they may see your good works and give glory to your Father who is in heaven.

What is prized by human beings

Luke 16:14-15

<14> The Pharisees, who were lovers of money, heard all this, and they ridiculed him.

<15> So he said to them, "You are those who justify yourselves in the sight of others; but God knows your hearts; for what is prized by human beings is an abomination in the sight of God.

Josiah was fair to the poor

Jeremiah 22:15-16

<15> Are you a king
> because you compete in cedar?
Did not your father eat and drink
> and do justice and righteousness?
> Then it was well with him.
<16> He judged the cause of the poor and needy;
> then it was well.
Is not this to know me?
> says the LORD.

Lack of honesty in the courts

Isaiah 59:4

<4> No one brings suit justly,
> no one goes to law honestly;
they rely on empty pleas, they speak lies,
> conceiving mischief and begetting iniquity.

The case of Naaman

2 Kings 5:20-27

<20> Gehazi, the servant of Elisha the man of God, thought, "My master has let that Aramean Naaman off too lightly by not accepting from him what he offered. As the LORD lives, I will run after him and get something out of him."

<21> So Gehazi went after Naaman. When Naaman saw someone running after him, he jumped down from the chariot to meet him and said, "Is everything all right?"

<22> He replied, "Yes, but my master has sent me to say, 'Two members of a company of prophets have just come to me from the hill country of Ephraim; please give them a talent of silver and two changes of clothing.'"

<23> Naaman said, "Please accept two talents." He urged him, and

tied up two talents of silver in two bags, with two changes of clothing, and gave them to two of his servants, who carried them in front of Gehazi.

<24> When he came to the citadel, he took the bags from them, and stored them inside; he dismissed the men, and they left.

<25> He went in and stood before his master; and Elisha said to him, "Where have you been, Gehazi?" He answered, "Your servant has not gone anywhere at all."

<26> But he said to him, "Did I not go with you in spirit when someone left his chariot to meet you? Is this a time to accept money and to accept clothing, olive orchards and vineyards, sheep and oxen, and male and female slaves?

<27> Therefore the leprosy of Naaman shall cling to you, and to your descendants forever." So he left his presence leprous, as white as snow.

Resources for orphans, widow, resident aliens
Deuteronomy 14:27-29

<27> As for the Levites resident in your towns, do not neglect them, because they have no allotment or inheritance with you.

<28> Every third year you shall bring out the full tithe of your produce for that year, and store it within your towns;

<29> the Levites, because they have no allotment or inheritance with you, as well as the resident aliens, the orphans, and the widows in your towns, may come and eat their fill so that the LORD your God may bless you in all the work that you undertake.

You thought you could obtain God's gift with money
Acts 8:18-22

<18> Now when Simon saw that the Spirit was given through the laying on of the apostles' hands, he offered them money,

<19> saying, "Give me also this power so that anyone on whom I lay my hands may receive the Holy Spirit."

<20> But Peter said to him, "May your silver perish with you, because you

thought you could obtain God's gift with money!

<21> You have no part or share in this, for your heart is not right before God.

<22> Repent therefore of this wickedness of yours, and pray to the Lord that, if possible, the intent of your heart may be forgiven you.

Relationship of the ruler and ruled

2 Chronicles 1:7-12

<7> That night God appeared to Solomon, and said to him, "Ask what I should give you."

<8> Solomon said to God, "You have shown great and steadfast love to my father David, and have made me succeed him as king.

<9> O LORD God, let your promise to my father David now be fulfilled, for you have made me king over a people as numerous as the dust of the earth.

<10> Give me now wisdom and knowledge to go out and come in before this people, for who can rule this great people of yours?"

<11> God answered Solomon, "Because this was in your heart, and you have not asked for possessions, wealth, honor, or the life of those who hate you, and have not even asked for long life, but have asked for wisdom and knowledge for yourself that you may rule my people over whom I have made you king,

<12> wisdom and knowledge are granted to you. I will also give you riches, possessions, and honor, such as none of the kings had who were before you, and none after you shall have the like."

Anyone who has the world's goods

1 John 3:17

<17> How does God's love abide in anyone who has the world's goods and sees a brother or sister in need and yet refuses help?

Send presents to the poor

Esther 9:20-33

<20> Mordecai recorded these things, and sent letters to all the Jews who were in all the provinces of King Ahasuerus, both near and far,

<21> enjoining them that they should keep the fourteenth day of the month Adar and also the fifteenth day of the same month, year by year,
<22> as the days on which the Jews gained relief from their enemies, and as the month that had been turned for them from sorrow into gladness and from mourning into a holiday; that they should make them days of feasting and gladness, days for sending gifts of food to one another and presents to the poor.

Maintain justice

Isaiah 56:1-2

<56:1> Thus says the LORD:
Maintain justice, and do what is right,
for soon my salvation will come,
and my deliverance be revealed.
<2> Happy is the mortal who does this,
the one who holds it fast,
who keeps the sabbath, not profaning it,
and refrains from doing any evil.

The golden rule

Matthew 7:12

<12> So whatever you wish that men would do to you, do so to them; for this is the law and the prophets.

Making fun of the poor

Proverbs 17:5

<5> Those who mock the poor insult their Maker;
those who are glad at calamity will not go unpunished.

No payback

Proverbs 24:29

\<29\> Do not say, "I will do to others as they have done to me;
     I will pay them back for what they have done."

God rescues the poor

Psalm 72:12-14

\<12\> For he delivers the needy when they call,
     the poor and those who have no helper.
\<13\> He has pity on the weak and the needy,
     and saves the lives of the needy.
\<14\> From oppression and violence he redeems their life; and precious is their blood in his sight.

Hang out with the lowly

Romans 12:16-17

\<16\> Live in harmony with one another; do not be haughty, but associate with the lowly; do not claim to be wiser than you are.
\<17\> Do not repay anyone evil for evil, but take thought for what is noble in the sight of all.

Greed is pretty bad

1 Corinthians 5:11

\<11\> But now I am writing to you not to associate with anyone who bears the name of brother or sister who is sexually immoral or greedy, or is an idolater, reviler, drunkard, or robber. Do not even eat with such a one.

Be ready to share

1 Timothy 6:17-19

\<17\> As for those who in the present age are rich, command them not to be haughty, or to set their hopes on the uncertainty of riches, but rather on God who richly provides us with everything for our enjoyment.

<18> They are to do good, to be rich in good works, generous, and ready to share,

<19> thus storing up for themselves the treasure of a good foundation for the future, so that they may take hold of the life that really is life.

The good life & lounging

Amos 6:6-7

<6> who drink wine from bowls,
>
> and anoint themselves with the finest oils,
>
> but are not grieved over the ruin of Joseph!

<7> Therefore they shall now be the first to go into exile,
>
> and the revelry of the loungers shall pass away.

Justice will return

Psalm 94:14-15

<14> For the LORD will not forsake his people;
he will not abandon his heritage;
<15> for justice will return to the righteous,
and all the upright in heart will follow it.

Failure to do justice blinds people

Isaiah 59:12-15

12> For our transgressions before you are many,
>
> and our sins testify against us.

Our transgressions indeed are with us,
>
> and we know our iniquities:

<13> transgressing, and denying the LORD,
>
> and turning away from following our God,

talking oppression and revolt,

conceiving lying words and uttering them from the heart.
<14> Justice is turned back,
and righteousness stands at a distance;
for truth stumbles in the public square,
and uprightness cannot enter.
<15> Truth is lacking,
and whoever turns from evil is despoiled.

Widows were being neglected

Acts 6:1-6

<1> Now during those days, when the disciples were increasing in number, the Hellenists complained against the Hebrews because their widows were being neglected in the daily distribution of food.
<2> And the twelve called together the whole community of the disciples and said, "It is not right that we should neglect the word of God in order to wait on tables.
<3> Therefore, friends, select from among yourselves seven men of good standing, full of the Spirit and of wisdom, whom we may appoint to this task,
<4> while we, for our part, will devote ourselves to prayer and to serving the word."
<5> What they said pleased the whole community, and they chose Stephen, a man full of faith and the Holy Spirit, together with Philip, Prochorus, Nicanor, Timon, Parmenas, and Nicolaus, a proselyte of Antioch.
<6> They had these men stand before the apostles, who prayed and laid their hands on them.

Orphans, widows, strangers

Deuteronomy 10:17-19

<17> For the LORD your God is God of gods and Lord of lords, the great God, mighty and awesome, who is not partial and takes no bribe,
<18> who executes justice for the orphan and the widow, and who

loves the strangers, providing them food and clothing.

<19> You shall also love the stranger, for you were strangers in the land of Egypt.

Two men compared

Ezekiel 18:10-17

<10> If he has a son who is violent, a shedder of blood,

<11> who does any of these things (though his father does none of them), who eats upon the mountains, defiles his neighbor's wife,

<12> oppresses the poor and needy, commits robbery, does not restore the pledge, lifts up his eyes to the idols, commits abomination,

<13> takes advance or accrued interest; shall he then live? He shall not. He has done all these abominable things; he shall surely die; his blood shall be upon himself.

<14> But if this man has a son who sees all the sins that his father has done, considers, and does not do likewise,

<15> who does not eat upon the mountains or lift up his eyes to the idols of the house of Israel, does not defile his neighbor's wife,

<16> does not wrong anyone, exacts no pledge, commits no robbery, but gives his bread to the hungry and covers the naked with a garment,

<17> withholds his hand from iniquity, takes no advance or accrued interest, observes my ordinances, and follows my statutes; he shall not die for his father's iniquity; he shall surely live.

Ruining the poor with lies

Isaiah 32:6-8

<6> For fools speak folly,
>
> and their minds plot iniquity:
>
to practice ungodliness,
>
> to utter error concerning the LORD,
>
to leave the craving of the hungry unsatisfied,
>
> and to deprive the thirsty of drink.

<7> The villainies of villains are evil;

they devise wicked devices
to ruin the poor with lying words,
      even when the plea of the needy is right.
<8> But those who are noble plan noble things,
      and by noble things they stand.

Cheating customers

Hosea 12:7-9

<7> A trader, in whose hands are false balances,
      he loves to oppress.
<8> Ephraim has said, "Ah, I am rich,
      I have gained wealth for myself;
in all of my gain
      no offense has been found in me
      that would be sin."
<9> I am the LORD your God
      from the land of Egypt;
I will make you live in tents again,
      as in the days of the appointed festival.

The abundance of possessions

Luke 12:13-21

<13> Someone in the crowd said to him, "Teacher, tell my brother to
divide the family inheritance with me."
<14> But he said to him, "Friend, who set me to be a judge or arbitra-
tor over you?"
<15> And he said to them, "Take care! Be on your guard against all
kinds of greed; for one's life does not consist in the abundance of
possessions."
<16> Then he told them a parable: "The land of a rich man produced
abundantly.
<17> And he thought to himself, 'What should I do, for I have no
place to store my crops?'
<18> Then he said, 'I will do this: I will pull down my barns and build

larger ones, and there I will store all my grain and my goods.
<19> And I will say to my soul, 'Soul, you have ample goods laid up for many years; relax, eat, drink, be merry.'
<20> But God said to him, 'You fool! This very night your life is being demanded of you. And the things you have prepared, whose will they be?'
<21> So it is with those who store up treasures for themselves but are not rich toward God."

Oppressing widows, orphans and foreigners
Malachi 3:5
<5> Then I will draw near to you for judgment; I will be swift to bear witness against the sorcerers, against the adulterers, against those who swear falsely, against those who oppress the hired workers in their wages, the widow and the orphan, against those who thrust aside the alien, and do not fear me, says the LORD of hosts.

Some women who provided for them out of their resources
Luke 8:1-3
<1> Soon afterwards he went on through cities and villages, proclaiming and bringing the good news of the kingdom of God. The twelve were with him,
<2> as well as some women who had been cured of evil spirits and infirmities: Mary, called Magdalene, from whom seven demons had gone out,
<3> and Joanna, the wife of Herod's steward Chuza, and Susanna, and many others, who provided for them out of their resources.

What then should we do?
Luke 3:7-11
<7> John said to the crowds that came out to be baptized by him, "You brood of vipers! Who warned you to flee from the wrath to come?

<8> Bear fruits worthy of repentance. Do not begin to say to yourselves, 'We have Abraham as our ancestor'; for I tell you, God is able from these stones to raise up children to Abraham.
<9> Even now the ax is lying at the root of the trees; every tree therefore that does not bear good fruit is cut down and thrown into the fire."
<10> And the crowds asked him, "What then should we do?"
<11> In reply he said to them, "Whoever has two coats must share with anyone who has none; and whoever has food must do likewise."

Don't provide food at a profit
Leviticus 25:35-37
<35> If any of your kin fall into difficulty and become dependent on you, you shall support them; they shall live with you as though resident aliens.
<36> Do not take interest in advance or otherwise make a profit from them, but fear your God; let them live with you.
<37> You shall not lend them your money at interest taken in advance, or provide them food at a profit.

The king is to help needy
Psalm 72:4
<4> May he defend the cause of the poor of the people,
    give deliverance to the needy,
    and crush the oppressor.

The poor are with you always
Mark 14:3-9
<3> And while he was at Bethany in the house of Simon the leper, as he sat at table, a woman came with an alabaster flask of ointment of pure nard, very costly, and she broke the flask and poured it over his head. <4> But there were some who said to themselves indignantly, "Why was the ointment thus wasted? <5> For this ointment might

have been sold for more than three hundred denarii, and given to the poor." And they reproached her. <6> But Jesus said, "Let her alone; why do you trouble her? She has done a beautiful thing to me. <7> For you always have the poor with you, and whenever you will, you can do good to them; but you will not always have me. <8> She has done what she could; she has anointed my body beforehand for burying. <9> And truly, I say to you, wherever the gospel is preached in the whole world, what she has done will be told in memory of her."

Swept away

Proverbs 13:23
<23> The field of the poor may yield much food,
but it is swept away through injustice.

Distributing to the poor

Psalm 112:9
<9> They have distributed freely, they have given to the poor; their righteousness endures forever; their horn is exalted in honor.

Extend hospitality to strangers

Romans 12:9-15
<9> Let love be genuine; hate what is evil, hold fast to what is good;
<10> love one another with mutual affection; outdo one another in showing honor.
<11> Do not lag in zeal, be ardent in spirit, serve the Lord.
<12> Rejoice in hope, be patient in suffering, persevere in prayer.
<13> Contribute to the needs of the saints; extend hospitality to strangers.
<14> Bless those who persecute you; bless and do not curse them.
<15> Rejoice with those who rejoice, weep with those who weep.

Unless you give up all your possessions

Luke 14:25-33

\<25\> Now large crowds were traveling with him; and he turned and said to them,

\<26\> "Whoever comes to me and does not hate father and mother, wife and children, brothers and sisters, yes, and even life itself, cannot be my disciple.

\<27\> Whoever does not carry the cross and follow me cannot be my disciple.

\<28\> For which of you, intending to build a tower, does not first sit down and estimate the cost, to see whether he has enough to complete it?

\<29\> Otherwise, when he has laid a foundation and is not able to finish, all who see it will begin to ridicule him,

\<30\> saying, 'This fellow began to build and was not able to finish.'

\<31\> Or what king, going out to wage war against another king, will not sit down first and consider whether he is able with ten thousand to oppose the one who comes against him with twenty thousand?

\<32\> If he cannot, then, while the other is still far away, he sends a delegation and asks for the terms of peace.

\<33\> So therefore, none of you can become my disciple if you do not give up all your possessions.

God knows when justice is perverted

Lamentations 3:34-36

\<34\> When all the prisoners of the land
      are crushed under foot,

\<35\> when human rights are perverted
      in the presence of the Most High,

\<36\> when one's case is subverted
—does the Lord not see it?

Oppression under the sun

Ecclesiastes 4:1

<4:1> Again I saw all the oppressions that are practiced under the sun. Look, the tears of the oppressed—with no one to comfort them! On the side of their oppressors there was power—with no one to comfort them.

Each would send relief

Acts 11:27-30

<27> At that time prophets came down from Jerusalem to Antioch. <28> One of them named Agabus stood up and predicted by the Spirit that there would be a severe famine over all the world; and this took place during the reign of Claudius.
<29> The disciples determined that according to their ability, each would send relief to the believers living in Judea;
<30> this they did, sending it to the elders by Barnabas and Saul.

Don't take advantage of the poor

Proverbs 22:22-23

<22> Do not rob the poor because they are poor,
	or crush the afflicted at the gate;
<23> for the LORD pleads their cause
	and despoils of life those who despoil them.

They seize the poor

Psalm 10:8b-14

Their eyes stealthily watch for the helpless;
	<9> they lurk in secret like a lion in its covert;
they lurk that they may seize the poor;
	they seize the poor and drag them off in their net.
<10> They stoop, they crouch,
	and the helpless fall by their might.
<11> They think in their heart, "God has forgotten,

he has hidden his face, he will never see it."
<12> Rise up, O LORD; O God, lift up your hand;
       do not forget the oppressed.
<13> Why do the wicked renounce God,
       and say in their hearts, "You will not call us to account"?
<14> But you do see! Indeed you note trouble and grief,
       that you may take it into your hands;
the helpless commit themselves to you;
       you have been the helper of the orphan.

Conducting your affairs with justice
Psalm 112:5
<5> It is well with those who deal generously and lend,
who conduct their affairs with justice.

God delivers the needy from oppressors
Psalm 35:10
<10> All my bones shall say,
       "O LORD, who is like you?
You deliver the weak
       from those too strong for them,
       the weak and needy from those who despoil them."

They want to bring down the poor
Psalm 37:14
<14> The wicked draw the sword and bend their bows
       to bring down the poor and needy,
       to kill those who walk uprightly;

We have left everything
Matthew 19:27-30
<27> Then Peter said in reply, "Lo, we have left everything and fol-

lowed you. What then shall we have?" <28> Jesus said to them, "Truly, I say to you, in the new world, when the Son of man shall sit on his glorious throne, you who have followed me will also sit on twelve thrones, judging the twelve tribes of Israel. <29> And every one who has left houses or brothers or sisters or father or mother or children or lands, for my name's sake, will receive a hundredfold, and inherit eternal life. <30> But many that are first will be last, and the last first.

So that you may share abundantly
2 Corinthians 9:6-14

<6> The point is this: the one who sows sparingly will also reap sparingly, and the one who sows bountifully will also reap bountifully.

<7> Each of you must give as you have made up your mind, not reluctantly or under compulsion, for God loves a cheerful giver.

<8> And God is able to provide you with every blessing in abundance, so that by always having enough of everything, you may share abundantly in every good work.

<9> As it is written,

"He scatters abroad, he gives to the poor;
            his righteousness endures forever."

<10> He who supplies seed to the sower and bread for food will supply and multiply your seed for sowing and increase the harvest of your righteousness.

<11> You will be enriched in every way for your great generosity, which will produce thanksgiving to God through us;

<12> for the rendering of this ministry not only supplies the needs of the saints but also overflows with many thanksgivings to God.

<13> Through the testing of this ministry you glorify God by your obedience to the confession of the gospel of Christ and by the generosity of your sharing with them and with all others,

<14> while they long for you and pray for you because of the surpassing grace of God that he has given you.

Buying the poor for silver

Amos 8:4-7

<4> Hear this, you that trample on the needy,
    and bring to ruin the poor of the land,
<5> saying, "When will the new moon be over
        so that we may sell grain;
and the sabbath,
        so that we may offer wheat for sale?
We will make the ephah small and the shekel great,
        and practice deceit with false balances,
<6> buying the poor for silver
        and the needy for a pair of sandals,
        and selling the sweepings of the wheat."
<7> The LORD has sworn by the pride of Jacob:
Surely I will never forget any of their deeds.

Lending to the poor

Exodus 22:25-27

<25> If you lend money to my people, to the poor among you, you shall not deal with them as a creditor; you shall not exact interest from them.
<26> If you take your neighbor's cloak in pawn, you shall restore it before the sun goes down;
<27> for it may be your neighbor's only clothing to use as cover; in what else shall that person sleep? And if your neighbor cries out to me, I will listen, for I am compassionate.

Yahweh, lover of justice

Psalm 99:4

<4> Mighty King, lover of justice,
        you have established equity;
you have executed justice
and righteousness in Jacob.

Giving food to the hungry

Psalm 146:5-7

\<5\> Happy are those whose help is the God of Jacob,
  whose hope is in the LORD their God,
\<6\> who made heaven and earth,
  the sea, and all that is in them;
who keeps faith forever;
\<7\> who executes justice for the oppressed;
  who gives food to the hungry.

Use of Money

Psalm 15:5

\<5\> who do not lend money at interest,
  and do not take a bribe against the innocent.

For the love of money

1 Timothy 6:6-10

\<6\> Of course, there is great gain in godliness combined with contentment;
\<7\> for we brought nothing into the world, so that we can take nothing out of it;
\<8\> but if we have food and clothing, we will be content with these.
\<9\> But those who want to be rich fall into temptation and are trapped by many senseless and harmful desires that plunge people into ruin and destruction.
\<10\> For the love of money is a root of all kinds of evil, and in their eagerness to be rich some have wandered away from the faith and pierced themselves with many pains.

Depriving the alien, the orphan, the widow

Deuteronomy 27:19

\<19\> "Cursed be anyone who deprives the alien, the orphan, and the widow of justice." All the people shall say, "Amen!"

Fat and lean sheep

Ezekiel 34:16b-24

<16> I will seek the lost, and I will bring back the strayed, and I will bind up the injured, and I will strengthen the weak, but the fat and the strong I will destroy. I will feed them with justice.

<17> As for you, my flock, thus says the Lord GOD: I shall judge between sheep and sheep, between rams and goats:

<18> Is it not enough for you to feed on the good pasture, but you must tread down with your feet the rest of your pasture? When you drink of clear water, must you foul the rest with your feet?

<19> And must my sheep eat what you have trodden with your feet, and drink what you have fouled with your feet?

<20> Therefore, thus says the Lord GOD to them: I myself will judge between the fat sheep and the lean sheep.

<21> Because you pushed with flank and shoulder, and butted at all the weak animals with your horns until you scattered them far and wide,

<22> I will save my flock, and they shall no longer be ravaged; and I will judge between sheep and sheep.

<23> I will set up over them one shepherd, my servant David, and he shall feed them: he shall feed them and be their shepherd.

<24> And I, the LORD, will be their God, and my servant David shall be prince among them; I, the LORD, have spoken.

Bring in the poor, the crippled, the blind, and the lame

Luke 14:15-23

<15> One of the dinner guests, on hearing this, said to him, "Blessed is anyone who will eat bread in the kingdom of God!"

<16> Then Jesus said to him, "Someone gave a great dinner and invited many.

<17> At the time for the dinner he sent his slave to say to those who had been invited, 'Come; for everything is ready now.'

<18> But they all alike began to make excuses. The first said to him, 'I

have bought a piece of land, and I must go out and see it; please accept my regrets.'

<19> Another said, 'I have bought five yoke of oxen, and I am going to try them out; please accept my regrets.'

<20> Another said, 'I have just been married, and therefore I cannot come.'

<21> So the slave returned and reported this to his master. Then the owner of the house became angry and said to his slave, 'Go out at once into the streets and lanes of the town and bring in the poor, the crippled, the blind, and the lame.'

<22> And the slave said, 'Sir, what you ordered has been done, and there is still room.'

<23> Then the master said to the slave, 'Go out into the roads and lanes, and compel people to come in, so that my house may be filled.

There was a rich man

Luke 16:19-31

<19> "There was a rich man who was dressed in purple and fine linen and who feasted sumptuously every day.

<20> And at his gate lay a poor man named Lazarus, covered with sores,

<21> who longed to satisfy his hunger with what fell from the rich man's table; even the dogs would come and lick his sores.

<22> The poor man died and was carried away by the angels to be with Abraham. The rich man also died and was buried.

<23> In Hades, where he was being tormented, he looked up and saw Abraham far away with Lazarus by his side.

<24> He called out, 'Father Abraham, have mercy on me, and send Lazarus to dip the tip of his finger in water and cool my tongue; for I am in agony in these flames.'

<25> But Abraham said, 'Child, remember that during your lifetime you received your good things, and Lazarus in like manner evil things; but now he is comforted here, and you are in agony.

<26> Besides all this, between you and us a great chasm has been fixed, so that those who might want to pass from here to you cannot

do so, and no one can cross from there to us.'

<27> He said, 'Then, father, I beg you to send him to my father's house—

<28> for I have five brothers—that he may warn them, so that they will not also come into this place of torment.'

<29> Abraham replied, 'They have Moses and the prophets; they should listen to them.'

<30> He said, 'No, father Abraham; but if someone goes to them from the dead, they will repent.'

<31> He said to him, 'If they do not listen to Moses and the prophets, neither will they be convinced even if someone rises from the dead.'"

The land is mine

Leviticus 25:23

<23> The land shall not be sold in perpetuity, for the land is mine; with me you are but aliens and tenants.

Relation of the ruler and ruled

Proverbs 20:28

<28> Loyalty and faithfulness preserve the king,
     and his throne is upheld by righteousness.

He loves righteousness and justice

Psalm 33:4-5

For the word of the LORD is upright,
     and all his work is done in faithfulness.

<5> He loves righteousness and justice;
     the earth is full of the steadfast love of the LORD.

Reject partiality

Proverbs 24:23-25

<23> These also are sayings of the wise:

Partiality in judging is not good.

<24> Whoever says to the wicked, "You are innocent,"
      will be cursed by peoples, abhorred by nations;
<25> but those who rebuke the wicked will have delight,
      and a good blessing will come upon them.

Food that I need

Proverbs 30:8-9

<8> Remove far from me falsehood and lying;
      give me neither poverty nor riches;
      feed me with the food that I need,
<9> or I shall be full, and deny you,
      and say, "Who is the LORD?"
or I shall be poor, and steal,
      and profane the name of my God.

God's interest in providing for the needy

Psalm 68:9-10

<9> Rain in abundance, O God, you showered abroad;
      you restored your heritage when it languished;
<10> your flock found a dwelling in it;
      in your goodness, O God, you provided for the needy.

Concerning the collection for the saints

1 Corinthians 16:1-3

<1> Now concerning the collection for the saints: you should follow the directions I gave to the churches of Galatia.

<2> On the first day of every week, each of you is to put aside and save whatever extra you earn, so that collections need not be taken when I come.

<3> And when I arrive, I will send any whom you approve with letters to take your gift to Jerusalem.

Acts of charity

Acts 9:36

<36> Now in Joppa there was a disciple whose name was Tabitha, which in Greek is Dorcas. She was devoted to good works and acts of charity.

The rich will disappear

James 1:9-11

<9> Let the believer who is lowly boast in being raised up, <10> and the rich in being brought low, because the rich will disappear like a flower in the field.

<11> For the sun rises with its scorching heat and withers the field; its flower falls, and its beauty perishes. It is the same way with the rich; in the midst of a busy life, they will wither away.

He will decide with equity

Isaiah 11:1-4

<11:1> A shoot shall come out from the stump of Jesse,
    and a branch shall grow out of his roots.
<2> The spirit of the LORD shall rest on him,
    the spirit of wisdom and understanding,
    the spirit of counsel and might,
    the spirit of knowledge and the fear of the LORD.
<3> His delight shall be in the fear of the LORD.
He shall not judge by what his eyes see,
    or decide by what his ears hear;
<4> but with righteousness he shall judge the poor,
    and decide with equity for the meek of the earth;

Pushing the needy off the road

Job 24

<24:1> "Why are times not kept by the Almighty,
    and why do those who know him never see his days?

<2> The wicked remove landmarks;
>> they seize flocks and pasture them.
<3> They drive away the donkey of the orphan;
>> they take the widow's ox for a pledge.
<4> They thrust the needy off the road;
>> the poor of the earth all hide themselves.
<5> Like wild asses in the desert
>> they go out to their toil,
scavenging in the wasteland
>> food for their young.
<6> They reap in a field not their own
>> and they glean in the vineyard of the wicked.
<7> They lie all night naked, without clothing,
>> and have no covering in the cold.
<8> They are wet with the rain of the mountains,
>> and cling to the rock for want of shelter.
<9> "There are those who snatch the orphan child from the breast,
>> and take as a pledge the infant of the poor.
<10> They go about naked, without clothing;
>> though hungry, they carry the sheaves;
<11> between their terraces they press out oil;
>> they tread the wine presses, but suffer thirst.
<12> From the city the dying groan,
>> and the throat of the wounded cries for help;
>> yet God pays no attention to their prayer.
<13> "There are those who rebel against the light,
>> who are not acquainted with its ways,
>> and do not stay in its paths.
<14> The murderer rises at dusk
>> to kill the poor and needy,
>> and in the night is like a thief.
<15> The eye of the adulterer also waits for the twilight,
>> saying, 'No eye will see me';
>> and he disguises his face.
<16> In the dark they dig through houses;
>> by day they shut themselves up;

they do not know the light.

<17> For deep darkness is morning to all of them;
   for they are friends with the terrors of deep darkness.

<18> "Swift are they on the face of the waters;
   their portion in the land is cursed;
   no treader turns toward their vineyards.

<19> Drought and heat snatch away the snow waters;
   so does Sheol those who have sinned.

<20> The womb forgets them;
   the worm finds them sweet;
they are no longer remembered;
   so wickedness is broken like a tree.

<21> "They harm the childless woman,
   and do no good to the widow.

<22> Yet God prolongs the life of the mighty by his power;
   they rise up when they despair of life.

<23> He gives them security, and they are supported;
   his eyes are upon their ways.

<24> They are exalted a little while, and then are gone;
   they wither and fade like the mallow;
   they are cut off like the heads of grain.

<25> If it is not so, who will prove me a liar,
   and show that there is nothing in what I say?"

Unjust economic gain

Jeremiah 17:11

<11> Like the partridge hatching what it did not lay,
   so are all who amass wealth unjustly;
in mid-life it will leave them,
   and at their end they will prove to be fools.

Don't curse the rich

Ecclesiastes 10:20

<20> Do not curse the king, even in your thoughts,

or curse the rich, even in your bedroom;
for a bird of the air may carry your voice,
or some winged creature tell the matter.

A cup of cold water

Matthew 10:42

<42> "And whoever gives to one of these little ones even a cup of cold water because he is a disciple, truly, I say to you, he shall not lose his reward."

Riches by dishonesty

Proverbs 21:6-7

<6> The getting of treasures by a lying tongue
is a fleeting vapor and a snare of death.
<7> The violence of the wicked will sweep them away,
because they refuse to do what is just.

Taking economic advantage of people

Proverbs 28:8

<8> One who augments wealth by exorbitant interest
gathers it for another who is kind to the poor.

Those who observe justice

Psalm 106:3

<3> Happy are those who observe justice,
who do righteousness at all times.

A rich young man

Matthew 19:16-26

<16> And behold, one came up to him, saying, "Teacher, what good

deed must I do, to have eternal life?"

<17> And he said to him, "Why do you ask me about what is good? One there is who is good. If you would enter life, keep the commandments."

<18> He said to him, "Which?" And Jesus said, "You shall not kill, You shall not commit adultery, You shall not steal, You shall not bear false witness,

<19> Honor your father and mother, and, You shall love your neighbor as yourself."

<20> The young man said to him, "All these I have observed; what do I still lack?"

<21> Jesus said to him, "If you would be perfect, go, sell what you possess and give to the poor, and you will have treasure in heaven; and come, follow me."

<22> When the young man heard this he went away sorrowful; for he had great possessions.

<23> And Jesus said to his disciples, "Truly, I say to you, it will be hard for a rich man to enter the kingdom of heaven.

<24> Again I tell you, it is easier for a camel to go through the eye of a needle than for a rich man to enter the kingdom of God."

<25> When the disciples heard this they were greatly astonished, saying, "Who then can be saved?"

<26> But Jesus looked at them and said to them, "With men this is impossible, but with God all things are possible."

Economic justice

Proverbs 16:11

<11> Honest balances and scales are the LORD's;
　　all the weights in the bag are his work.

Pleased to share their resources with the poor

Romans 15:25-29

<25> At present, however, I am going to Jerusalem in a ministry to the

saints;

<26> for Macedonia and Achaia have been pleased to share their resources with the poor among the saints at Jerusalem.

<27> They were pleased to do this, and indeed they owe it to them; for if the Gentiles have come to share in their spiritual blessings, they ought also to be of service to them in material things.

<28> So, when I have completed this, and have delivered to them what has been collected, I will set out by way of you to Spain;

<29> and I know that when I come to you, I will come in the fullness of the blessing of Christ.

The orphan and the oppressed
Psalm 10:17-18

<17> O LORD, you will hear the desire of the meek;

you will strengthen their heart, you will incline your ear

<18> to do justice for the orphan and the oppressed,

so that those from earth may strike terror no more.

Deceitfulness of wealth
Matthew 13:22

<22> As for what was sown among thorns, this is he who hears the word, but the cares of the world and the delight in riches choke the word, and it proves unfruitful.

Examples of oppression
Job 22:5-9

<5> Is not your wickedness great?

There is no end to your iniquities.

<6> For you have exacted pledges from your family for no reason,

and stripped the naked of their clothing.

<7> You have given no water to the weary to drink,

and you have withheld bread from the hungry.

<8> The powerful possess the land,

and the favored live in it.

<9> You have sent widows away empty-handed,

and the arms of the orphans you have crushed.

Domestic justice

Leviticus 25:39-55

<39> If any who are dependent on you become so impoverished that they sell themselves to you, you shall not make them serve as slaves.

<40> They shall remain with you as hired or bound laborers. They shall serve with you until the year of the jubilee.

<41> Then they and their children with them shall be free from your authority; they shall go back to their own family and return to their ancestral property.

<42> For they are my servants, whom I brought out of the land of Egypt; they shall not be sold as slaves are sold.

<43> You shall not rule over them with harshness, but shall fear your God.

<44> As for the male and female slaves whom you may have, it is from the nations around you that you may acquire male and female slaves.

<45> You may also acquire them from among the aliens residing with you, and from their families that are with you, who have been born in your land; and they may be your property.

<46> You may keep them as a possession for your children after you, for them to inherit as property. These you may treat as slaves, but as for your fellow Israelites, no one shall rule over the other with harshness.

<47> If resident aliens among you prosper, and if any of your kin fall into difficulty with one of them and sell themselves to an alien, or to a branch of the alien's family,

<48> after they have sold themselves they shall have the right of redemption; one of their brothers may redeem them,

<49> or their uncle or their uncle's son may redeem them, or anyone of their family who is of their own flesh may redeem them; or if they prosper they may redeem themselves.

<50> They shall compute with the purchaser the total from the year

when they sold themselves to the alien until the jubilee year; the price of the sale shall be applied to the number of years: the time they were with the owner shall be rated as the time of a hired laborer.

<51> If many years remain, they shall pay for their redemption in proportion to the purchase price;

<52> and if few years remain until the jubilee year, they shall compute thus: according to the years involved they shall make payment for their redemption.

<53> As a laborer hired by the year they shall be under the alien's authority, who shall not, however, rule with harshness over them in your sight.

<54> And if they have not been redeemed in any of these ways, they and their children with them shall go free in the jubilee year.

<55> For to me the people of Israel are servants; they are my servants whom I brought out from the land of Egypt: I am the LORD your God.

Contributing out of abundance is not so admirable
Luke 21:1-4

<1> He looked up and saw rich people putting their gifts into the treasury;

<2> he also saw a poor widow put in two small copper coins.

<3> He said, "Truly I tell you, this poor widow has put in more than all of them;

<4> for all of them have contributed out of their abundance, but she out of her poverty has put in all she had to live on."

Dishonest weights

Proverbs 20:10

<10> Diverse weights and diverse measures
> are both alike an abomination to the LORD.

Don't take the property of orphans
Proverbs 23:10-11
<10> Do not remove an ancient landmark
or encroach on the fields of orphans,
<11> for their redeemer is strong;
he will plead their cause against you.

The poor praising Yahweh
Psalm 72:20-21
<20> Have regard for your covenant,
for the dark places of the land are full of the haunts of violence.
<21> Do not let the downtrodden be put to shame;
let the poor and needy praise your name.

Looking out for your neighbor's best interest
Deuteronomy 22:1-4
<1> You shall not watch your neighbor's ox or sheep straying away and ignore them; you shall take them back to their owner.
<2> If the owner does not reside near you or you do not know who the owner is, you shall bring it to your own house, and it shall remain with you until the owner claims it; then you shall return it.
<3> You shall do the same with a neighbor's donkey; you shall do the same with a neighbor's garment; and you shall do the same with anything else that your neighbor loses and you find. You may not withhold your help.
<4> You shall not see your neighbor's donkey or ox fallen on the road and ignore it; you shall help to lift it up.

Partner to a thug
Proverbs 28:24
<24> Anyone who robs father or mother

and says, "That is no crime,"
is partner to a thug.

When you give to the needy
Matthew 6:1-4
<1> "Beware of practicing your piety before men in order to be seen by them; for then you will have no reward from your Father who is in heaven.
<2> "Thus, when you give alms, sound no trumpet before you, as the hypocrites do in the synagogues and in the streets, that they may be praised by men. Truly, I say to you, they have received their reward.
<3> But when you give alms, do not let your left hand know what your right hand is doing,
<4> so that your alms may be in secret; and your Father who sees in secret will reward you.

Share food with the poor
Proverbs 22:9
<9> Those who are generous are blessed,
 for they share their bread with the poor.

Justice as a foundation
Psalm 97:2
<97:1> The LORD is king! Let the earth rejoice;
 let the many coastlands be glad!
<2> Clouds and thick darkness are all around him;
 righteousness and justice are the foundation of his throne.

The cause of the needy
Psalm 140:12
<12> I know that the LORD maintains the cause of the needy,
 and executes justice for the poor.

False scales

Proverbs 20:23

<23> Differing weights are an abomination to the LORD,
    and false scales are not good.

I was hungry and you fed me

Matthew 25:31-46

<31> "When the Son of man comes in his glory, and all the angels with him, then he will sit on his glorious throne.

<32> Before him will be gathered all the nations, and he will separate them one from another as a shepherd separates the sheep from the goats,

<33> and he will place the sheep at his right hand, but the goats at the left.

<34> Then the King will say to those at his right hand, 'Come, O blessed of my Father, inherit the kingdom prepared for you from the foundation of the world;

<35> for I was hungry and you gave me food, I was thirsty and you gave me drink, I was a stranger and you welcomed me,

<36> I was naked and you clothed me, I was sick and you visited me, I was in prison and you came to me.'

<37> Then the righteous will answer him, 'Lord, when did we see thee hungry and feed thee, or thirsty and give thee drink?

<38> And when did we see thee a stranger and welcome thee, or naked and clothe thee?

<39> And when did we see thee sick or in prison and visit thee?'

<40> And the King will answer them, 'Truly, I say to you, as you did it to one of the least of these my brethren, you did it to me.'

<41> Then he will say to those at his left hand, 'Depart from me, you cursed, into the eternal fire prepared for the devil and his angels;

<42> for I was hungry and you gave me no food, I was thirsty and you gave me no drink,

<43> I was a stranger and you did not welcome me, naked and you did not clothe me, sick and in prison and you did not visit me.'

<44> Then they also will answer, 'Lord, when did we see thee hungry

or thirsty or a stranger or naked or sick or in prison, and did not minister to thee?'

<45> Then he will answer them, 'Truly, I say to you, as you did it not to one of the least of these, you did it not to me.'

<46> And they will go away into eternal punishment, but the righteous into eternal life."

Rescue the poor

Job 29:11-12

<11> When the ear heard, it commended me,
     and when the eye saw, it approved;
<12> because I delivered the poor who cried,
     and the orphan who had no helper.

The poor have good news brought to them

Luke 7:18-23

<18> The disciples of John reported all these things to him. So John summoned two of his disciples

<19> and sent them to the Lord to ask, "Are you the one who is to come, or are we to wait for another?"

<20> When the men had come to him, they said, "John the Baptist has sent us to you to ask, 'Are you the one who is to come, or are we to wait for another?'"

<21> Jesus had just then cured many people of diseases, plagues, and evil spirits, and had given sight to many who were blind.

<22> And he answered them, "Go and tell John what you have seen and heard: the blind receive their sight, the lame walk, the lepers are cleansed, the deaf hear, the dead are raised, the poor have good news brought to them.

<23> And blessed is anyone who takes no offense at me."

We have left everything

Mark 10:28-31

<28> Peter began to say to him, "Lo, we have left everything and followed you."

<29> Jesus said, "Truly, I say to you, there is no one who has left house or brothers or sisters or mother or father or children or lands, for my sake and for the gospel,

<30> who will not receive a hundredfold now in this time, houses and brothers and sisters and mothers and children and lands, with persecutions, and in the age to come eternal life.

<31> But many that are first will be last, and the last first."

Stealing

Exodus 20:15

<15> You shall not steal.

Listen to cry of the poor

Proverbs 21:13

<13> If you close your ear to the cry of the poor,
you will cry out and not be heard.

Justice against oppression

Psalm 103:6-7

<6> The LORD works vindication
    and justice for all who are oppressed.
<7> He made known his ways to Moses,
    his acts to the people of Israel.

A hope of the poor

Psalm 9:9-12

<9> The LORD is a stronghold for the oppressed,

a stronghold in times of trouble.
<10> And those who know your name put their trust in you,
　　　for you, O LORD, have not forsaken those who seek you.
<11> Sing praises to the LORD, who dwells in Zion.
　　　Declare his deeds among the peoples.
<12> For he who avenges blood is mindful of them;
　　　he does not forget the cry of the afflicted.

Nathan's parable

2 Samuel 12:1-6

<12:1> and the LORD sent Nathan to David. He came to him, and said to him, "There were two men in a certain city, the one rich and the other poor.
<2> The rich man had very many flocks and herds;
<3> but the poor man had nothing but one little ewe lamb, which he had bought. He brought it up, and it grew up with him and with his children; it used to eat of his meager fare, and drink from his cup, and lie in his bosom, and it was like a daughter to him.
<4> Now there came a traveler to the rich man, and he was loath to take one of his own flock or herd to prepare for the wayfarer who had come to him, but he took the poor man's lamb, and prepared that for the guest who had come to him."
<5> Then David's anger was greatly kindled against the man. He said to Nathan, "As the LORD lives, the man who has done this deserves to die;
<6> he shall restore the lamb fourfold, because he did this thing, and because he had no pity."

Usury and interest

Deuteronomy 23:19

<19> You shall not charge interest on loans to another Israelite, interest on money, interest on provisions, interest on anything that is lent.

Not greedy for money

1 Timothy 3:8

<8> Deacons likewise must be serious, not double-tongued, not indulging in much wine, not greedy for money;

Give it to them now

Proverbs 3:27-30

<27> Do not withhold good from those to whom it is due,
　　　when it is in your power to do it.
<28> Do not say to your neighbor, "Go, and come again,
tomorrow I will give it"—when you have it with you.
<29> Do not plan harm against your neighbor
　　　who lives trustingly beside you.
<30> Do not quarrel with anyone without cause,
　　　when no harm has been done to you.

At the right hand of the needy

Psalm 109:30-31

<30> With my mouth I will give great thanks to the LORD;
　　　I will praise him in the midst of the throng.
<31> For he stands at the right hand of the needy,
　　　to save them from those who would condemn them to death.

Give them bread

Proverbs 25:21

<21> If your enemies are hungry, give them bread to eat;
　　　and if they are thirsty, give them water to drink;

Feed four thousand

Mark 8:1-9

<1 > In those days, when again a great crowd had gathered, and they

had nothing to eat, he called his disciples to him, and said to them,
<2> "I have compassion on the crowd, because they have been with me now three days, and have nothing to eat;
<3> and if I send them away hungry to their homes, they will faint on the way; and some of them have come a long way."
<4> And his disciples answered him, "How can one feed these men with bread here in the desert?"
<5> And he asked them, "How many loaves have you?" They said, "Seven."
<6> And he commanded the crowd to sit down on the ground; and he took the seven loaves, and having given thanks he broke them and gave them to his disciples to set before the people; and they set them before the crowd.
<7> And they had a few small fish; and having blessed them, he commanded that these also should be set before them.
<8> And they ate, and were satisfied; and they took up the broken pieces left over, seven baskets full.
<9> And there were about four thousand people.

Your clothes are moth-eaten

James 5:1-6

<1> Come now, you rich people, weep and wail for the miseries that are coming to you.
<2> Your riches have rotted, and your clothes are moth-eaten.
<3> Your gold and silver have rusted, and their rust will be evidence against you, and it will eat your flesh like fire. You have laid up treasure for the last days.
<4> Listen! The wages of the laborers who mowed your fields, which you kept back by fraud, cry out, and the cries of the harvesters have reached the ears of the Lord of hosts.
<5> You have lived on the earth in luxury and in pleasure; you have fattened your hearts in a day of slaughter.
<6> You have condemned and murdered the righteous one, who does not resist you.

Pour yourself out for the poor

Isaiah 58:6-11

<6> Is not this the fast that I choose:
>   to loose the bonds of injustice,
>   to undo the thongs of the yoke,
to let the oppressed go free,
>   and to break every yoke?

<7> Is it not to share your bread with the hungry,
>   and bring the homeless poor into your house;
when you see the naked, to cover them,
>   and not to hide yourself from your own kin?

<8> Then your light shall break forth like the dawn,
>   and your healing shall spring up quickly;
your vindicator shall go before you,
>   the glory of the LORD shall be your rear guard.

<9> Then you shall call, and the LORD will answer;
>   you shall cry for help, and he will say, Here I am.
If you remove the yoke from among you,
>   the pointing of the finger, the speaking of evil,

<10> if you offer your food to the hungry
>   and satisfy the needs of the afflicted,
then your light shall rise in the darkness
>   and your gloom be like the noonday.

<11> The LORD will guide you continually,
>   and satisfy your needs in parched places,
>   and make your bones strong;
and you shall be like a watered garden,
>   like a spring of water,
>   whose waters never fail.

He discussed justice

Acts 24:24-25

<24> Some days later when Felix came with his wife Drusilla, who was Jewish, he sent for Paul and heard him speak concerning faith in Christ Jesus.

<25> And as he discussed justice, self-control, and the coming judgment, Felix became frightened and said, "Go away for the present; when I have an opportunity, I will send for you."

They voluntarily gave

2 Corinthians 8:1-9

<1> We want you to know, brothers and sisters, about the grace of God that has been granted to the churches of Macedonia;

<2> for during a severe ordeal of affliction, their abundant joy and their extreme poverty have overflowed in a wealth of generosity on their part.

<3> For, as I can testify, they voluntarily gave according to their means, and even beyond their means,

<4> begging us earnestly for the privilege of sharing in this ministry to the saints—

<5> and this, not merely as we expected; they gave themselves first to the Lord and, by the will of God, to us,

<6> so that we might urge Titus that, as he had already made a beginning, so he should also complete this generous undertaking among you.

<7> Now as you excel in everything—in faith, in speech, in knowledge, in utmost eagerness, and in our love for you—so we want you to excel also in this generous undertaking.

<8> I do not say this as a command, but I am testing the genuineness of your love against the earnestness of others.

<9> For you know the generous act of our Lord Jesus Christ, that though he was rich, yet for your sakes he became poor, so that by his poverty you might become rich.

A model of socio-economic domination

1 Samuel 8:10-20

<10> So Samuel reported all the words of the LORD to the people who were asking him for a king.

<11> He said, "These will be the ways of the king who will reign over

you: he will take your sons and appoint them to his chariots and to be his horsemen, and to run before his chariots;

<12> and he will appoint for himself commanders of thousands and commanders of fifties, and some to plow his ground and to reap his harvest, and to make his implements of war and the equipment of his chariots.

<13> He will take your daughters to be perfumers and cooks and bakers.

<14> He will take the best of your fields and vineyards and olive orchards and give them to his courtiers.

<15> He will take one-tenth of your grain and of your vineyards and give it to his officers and his courtiers.

<16> He will take your male and female slaves, and the best of your cattle and donkeys, and put them to his work.

<17> He will take one-tenth of your flocks, and you shall be his slaves.

<18> And in that day you will cry out because of your king, whom you have chosen for yourselves; but the LORD will not answer you in that day."

<19> But the people refused to listen to the voice of Samuel; they said, "No! but we are determined to have a king over us,

<20> so that we also may be like other nations, and that our king may govern us and go out before us and fight our battles."

The king and justice

Proverbs 29:4

<4> By justice a king gives stability to the land,
    but one who makes heavy exactions ruins it.

Persecuting the Poor

Psalm 10:2

<2> In arrogance the wicked persecute the poor—
let them be caught in the schemes they have devised.

Judging the poor

Psalm 72:2

\<2\> May he judge your people with righteousness,
  and your poor with justice.

A beating rain

Proverbs28:3

\<3\> A ruler who oppresses the poor
  is a beating rain that leaves no food.

The lure of all the kingdoms

Matthew 4:8-11

\<8\> Again, the devil took him to a very high mountain, and showed him all the kingdoms of the world and the glory of them;
\<9\> and he said to him, "All these I will give you, if you will fall down and worship me."
\<10\> Then Jesus said to him, "Be gone, Satan! for it is written, 'You shall worship the Lord your God and him only shall you serve.'"
\<11\> Then the devil left him, and behold, angels came and ministered to him.

The wealthy are full of violence

Micah 6:9-12

\<9\> The voice of the LORD cries to the city
  (it is sound wisdom to fear your name):
Hear, O tribe and assembly of the city!
  \<10\> Can I forget the treasures of wickedness in the house of the wicked,
  and the scant measure that is accursed?
\<11\> Can I tolerate wicked scales
  and a bag of dishonest weights?
\<12\> Your wealthy are full of violence;

your inhabitants speak lies,
with tongues of deceit in their mouths.

A righteous branch will execute justice
Jeremiah 33:14-15

<14> The days are surely coming, says the LORD, when I will fulfill the promise I made to the house of Israel and the house of Judah.
<15> In those days and at that time I will cause a righteous Branch to spring up for David; and he shall execute justice and righteousness in the land.

If someone lacks daily food
James 2:14-17

<14> What good is it, my brothers and sisters, if you say you have faith but do not have works? Can faith save you?
<15> If a brother or sister is naked and lacks daily food,
<16> and one of you says to them, "Go in peace; keep warm and eat your fill," and yet you do not supply their bodily needs, what is the good of that?
<17> So faith by itself, if it has no works, is dead.

Job's testimony
Job 31:16-23

<16> "If I have withheld anything that the poor desired,
    or have caused the eyes of the widow to fail,
<17> or have eaten my morsel alone,
    and the orphan has not eaten from it—
<18> for from my youth I reared the orphan like a
father, and from my mother's womb I guided the widow—
<19> if I have seen anyone perish for lack of clothing,
    or a poor person without covering,
<20> whose loins have not blessed me,
    and who was not warmed with the fleece of my sheep;

<21> if I have raised my hand against the orphan,
>   because I saw I had supporters at the gate;
<22> then let my shoulder blade fall from my shoulder,
>   and let my arm be broken from its socket.
<23> For I was in terror of calamity from God,
>   and I could not have faced his majesty.

Giving alms from within

Luke 11:37-41

<37> While he was speaking, a Pharisee invited him to dine with him; so he went in and took his place at the table.

<38> The Pharisee was amazed to see that he did not first wash before dinner.

<39> Then the Lord said to him, "Now you Pharisees clean the outside of the cup and of the dish, but inside you are full of greed and wickedness.

<40> You fools! Did not the one who made the outside make the inside also?

<41> So give for alms those things that are within; and see, everything will be clean for you.

They trample the poor

Amos 2:6-8

<6> Thus says the LORD:
For three transgressions of Israel,
>   and for four, I will not revoke the punishment;
because they sell the righteous for silver,
>   and the needy for a pair of sandals—
<7> they who trample the head of the poor into the dust of the earth,
>   and push the afflicted out of the way;
father and son go in to the same girl,
>   so that my holy name is profaned;
<8> they lay themselves down beside every altar
>   on garments taken in pledge;

and in the house of their God they drink
wine bought with fines they imposed.

They would sell their possessions
Acts 2:41-47

<44> All who believed were together and had all things in common;
<45> they would sell their possessions and goods and distribute the
proceeds to all, as any had need.
<46> Day by day, as they spent much time together in the temple, they
broke bread at home and ate their food with glad and generous
hearts,
<47> praising God and having the goodwill of all the people. And day
by day the Lord added to their number those who were being saved.

An accurate weight
Proverbs 11:1

<11:1> A false balance is an abomination to the LORD,
but an accurate weight is his delight.

They devour widows' houses
Luke 20:45-47

<40> For they no longer dared to ask him another question.
<41> Then he said to them, "How can they say that the Messiah is
David's son?
<42> For David himself says in the book of Psalms,
'The Lord said to my Lord,
"Sit at my right hand,
<43> until I make your enemies your footstool."'
<44> David thus calls him Lord; so how can he be his son?"
<45> In the hearing of all the people he said to the disciples,
<46> "Beware of the scribes, who like to walk around in long robes,
and love to be greeted with respect in the marketplaces, and to have
the best seats in the synagogues and places of honor at banquets.

<47> They devour widows' houses and for the sake of appearance say long prayers. They will receive the greater condemnation."

Speak up for the poor

Proverbs 31:8-9

<8> Speak out for those who cannot speak,
     for the rights of all the destitute.
<9> Speak out, judge righteously,
     defend the rights of the poor and needy.

God Protects orphans and widows

Psalm 68:5-6

<5> Father of orphans and protector of widows
     is God in his holy habitation.
<6> God gives the desolate a home to live in;
     he leads out the prisoners to prosperity,
     but the rebellious live in a parched land.

He kept back some of the proceeds

Acts 5:1-10

<5:1> But a man named Ananias, with the consent of his wife Sapphira, sold a piece of property;
<2> with his wife's knowledge, he kept back some of the proceeds, and brought only a part and laid it at the apostles' feet.
<3> "Ananias," Peter asked, "why has Satan filled your heart to lie to the Holy Spirit and to keep back part of the proceeds of the land?
<4> While it remained unsold, did it not remain your own? And after it was sold, were not the proceeds at your disposal? How is it that you have contrived this deed in your heart? You did not lie to us but to God!"
<5> Now when Ananias heard these words, he fell down and died. And great fear seized all who heard of it.
<6> The young men came and wrapped up his body, then carried him out and buried him.

<7> After an interval of about three hours his wife came in, not knowing what had happened.

<8> Peter said to her, "Tell me whether you and your husband sold the land for such and such a price." And she said, "Yes, that was the price."

<9> Then Peter said to her, "How is it that you have agreed together to put the Spirit of the Lord to the test? Look, the feet of those who have buried your husband are at the door, and they will carry you out."

<10> Immediately she fell down at his feet and died. When the young men came in they found her dead, so they carried her out and buried her beside her husband.

Helping your enemy

Exodus 23:4-6

<4> When you come upon your enemy's ox or donkey going astray, you shall bring it back.

<5> When you see the donkey of one who hates you lying under its burden and you would hold back from setting it free, you must help to set it free.

<6> You shall not pervert the justice due to your poor in their lawsuits.

Oppressing the poor and needy

Ezekiel 22:25-29

<25> Its princes within it are like a roaring lion tearing the prey; they have devoured human lives; they have taken treasure and precious things; they have made many widows within it.

<26> Its priests have done violence to my teaching and have profaned my holy things; they have made no distinction between the holy and the common, neither have they taught the difference between the unclean and the clean, and they have disregarded my sabbaths, so that I am profaned among them.

<27> Its officials within it are like wolves tearing the prey, shedding

blood, destroying lives to get dishonest gain.

<28> Its prophets have smeared whitewash on their behalf, seeing false visions and divining lies for them, saying, "Thus says the Lord GOD," when the LORD has not spoken.

<29> The people of the land have practiced extortion and committed robbery; they have oppressed the poor and needy, and have extorted from the alien without redress.

They don't defend the rights of the needy
Jeremiah 5:21-29

<21> Hear this, O foolish and senseless people,
    who have eyes, but do not see,
    who have ears, but do not hear.

<22> Do you not fear me? says the LORD;
    Do you not tremble before me?
I placed the sand as a boundary for the sea,
    a perpetual barrier that it cannot pass;
though the waves toss, they cannot prevail,
    though they roar, they cannot pass over it.

<23> But this people has a stubborn and rebellious heart;
    they have turned aside and gone away.

<24> They do not say in their hearts,
    "Let us fear the LORD our God,
who gives the rain in its season,
    the autumn rain and the spring rain,
and keeps for us
    the weeks appointed for the harvest."

<25> Your iniquities have turned these away,
    and your sins have deprived you of good.

<26> For scoundrels are found among my people;
    they take over the goods of others.
Like fowlers they set a trap;
    they catch human beings.

<27> Like a cage full of birds,
    their houses are full of treachery;

therefore they have become great and rich,
       <28> they have grown fat and sleek.
They know no limits in deeds of wickedness;
       they do not judge with justice
the cause of the orphan, to make it prosper,
       and they do not defend the rights of the needy.
<29> Shall I not punish them for these things? says the LORD,
       and shall I not bring retribution
       on a nation such as this?

He sent the rich away empty

Luke 1:46-55

<46> And Mary said,
"My soul magnifies the Lord,
       <47> and my spirit rejoices in God my Savior,
<48> for he has looked with favor on the lowliness of his servant.
       Surely, from now on all generations will call me blessed;
<49> for the Mighty One has done great things for me,
       and holy is his name.
<50> His mercy is for those who fear him
       from generation to generation.
<51> He has shown strength with his arm;
       he has scattered the proud in the thoughts of their hearts.
<52> He has brought down the powerful from their thrones,
       and lifted up the lowly;
<53> he has filled the hungry with good things,
       and sent the rich away empty.
<54> He has helped his servant Israel,
       in remembrance of his mercy,
<55> according to the promise he made to our ancestors,
       to Abraham and to his descendants forever."

Beatitudes

Matthew 5:1-12

<5:1> Seeing the crowds, he went up on the mountain, and when he sat down his disciples came to him. <2> And he opened his mouth and taught them, saying: <3> "Blessed are the poor in spirit, for theirs is the kingdom of heaven. <4> "Blessed are those who mourn, for they shall be comforted. <5> "Blessed are the meek, for they shall inherit the earth. <6> "Blessed are those who hunger and thirst for righteousness, for they shall be satisfied. <7> "Blessed are the merciful, for they shall obtain mercy. <8> "Blessed are the pure in heart, for they shall see God. <9 "Blessed are the peacemakers, for they shall be called sons of God. <10> "Blessed are those who are persecuted for righteousness' sake, for theirs is the kingdom of heaven.

<11> "Blessed are you when men revile you and persecute you and utter all kinds of evil against you falsely on my account. <12> Rejoice and be glad, for your reward is great in heaven, for so men persecuted the prophets who were before you.

Sowing injustice

Proverbs 22:7-8

<7> The rich rules over the poor,
     and the borrower is the slave of the lender.
<8> Whoever sows injustice will reap calamity,
     and the rod of anger will fail.

Concern for the poor

Psalm 41:1-2

<41:1> Happy are those who consider the poor;
     the LORD delivers them in the day of trouble.
<2> The LORD protects them and keeps them alive;
     they are called happy in the land.
     You do not give them up to the will of their enemies.

Justice makes a government strong

Proverbs 16:12

<12> It is an abomination to kings to do evil,
>   for the throne is established by righteousness.

He has anointed me to bring good news to the poor

Luke 4:16-21

<16> When he came to Nazareth, where he had been brought up, he went to the synagogue on the sabbath day, as was his custom. He stood up to read,

<17> and the scroll of the prophet Isaiah was given to him. He unrolled the scroll and found the place where it was written:

<18> "The Spirit of the Lord is upon me,
>   because he has anointed me
>   to bring good news to the poor.

He has sent me to proclaim release to the captives
>   and recovery of sight to the blind,
>   to let the oppressed go free,

<19> to proclaim the year of the Lord's favor."

<20> And he rolled up the scroll, gave it back to the attendant, and sat down. The eyes of all in the synagogue were fixed on him.

<21> Then he began to say to them, "Today this scripture has been fulfilled in your hearing."

Neglecting justice

Matthew 23:23

<23> "Woe to you, scribes and Pharisees, hypocrites! for you tithe mint and dill and cummin, and have neglected the weightier matters of the law, justice and mercy and faith; these you ought to have done, without neglecting the others.

The land mourns

Hosea 4:1-3

<4:1> Hear the word of the LORD, O people of Israel;

for the LORD has an indictment against the inhabitants of
the land.

There is no faithfulness or loyalty,

and no knowledge of God in the land.

<2> Swearing, lying, and murder,

and stealing and adultery break out;

bloodshed follows bloodshed.

<3> Therefore the land mourns,

and all who live in it languish;

together with the wild animals

and the birds of the air,

even the fish of the sea are perishing.

Adding field to field

Isaiah 5:8-10

<8> Ah, you who join house to house,

who add field to field,

until there is room for no one but you,

and you are left to live alone

in the midst of the land!

<9> The LORD of hosts has sworn in my hearing:

Surely many houses shall be desolate,

large and beautiful houses, without inhabitant.

<10> For ten acres of vineyard shall yield but one bath,

and a homer of seed shall yield a mere ephah.

Abusing a widow or orphan

Exodus 22:21-24

<22> You shall not abuse any widow or orphan.

<23> If you do abuse them, when they cry out to me, I will surely
heed their cry;

<24> my wrath will burn, and I will kill you with the sword, and your wives shall become widows and your children orphans.

Good news to the poor

Isaiah 61:1-11
<1> The spirit of the Lord GOD is upon me,
    because the LORD has anointed me;
he has sent me to bring good news to the oppressed,
    to bind up the brokenhearted,
to proclaim liberty to the captives,
    and release to the prisoners;
<2> to proclaim the year of the LORD's favor,
    and the day of vengeance of our God;
    to comfort all who mourn;
<3> to provide for those who mourn in Zion—
    to give them a garland instead of ashes,
the oil of gladness instead of mourning,
    the mantle of praise instead of a faint spirit.
They will be called oaks of righteousness,
    the planting of the LORD, to display his glory.
<4> They shall build up the ancient ruins,
    they shall raise up the former devastations;
they shall repair the ruined cities,
    the devastations of many generations.

<5> Strangers shall stand and feed your flocks,
    foreigners shall till your land and dress your vines;
<6> but you shall be called priests of the LORD,
    you shall be named ministers of our God;
you shall enjoy the wealth of the nations,
    and in their riches you shall glory.
<7> Because their shame was double,
    and dishonor was proclaimed as their lot,
therefore they shall possess a double portion;
    everlasting joy shall be theirs.

<8> For I the LORD love justice,
　　I hate robbery and wrongdoing;
I will faithfully give them their recompense,
　　and I will make an everlasting covenant with them.
<9> Their descendants shall be known among the nations,
　　and their offspring among the peoples;
all who see them shall acknowledge
　　that they are a people whom the LORD has blessed.
<10> I will greatly rejoice in the LORD,
　　my whole being shall exult in my God;
for he has clothed me with the garments of salvation,
　　he has covered me with the robe of righteousness,
as a bridegroom decks himself with a garland,
　　and as a bride adorns herself with her jewels.
<11> For as the earth brings forth its shoots,
　　and as a garden causes what is sown in it to spring up,
so the Lord GOD will cause righteousness and praise
　　to spring up before all the nations.

Oppressive statutes

Isaiah 10:1-4

<10:1> Ah, you who make iniquitous decrees,
　　who write oppressive statutes,
<2> to turn aside the needy from justice
　　and to rob the poor of my people of their right,
that widows may be your spoil,
　　and that you may make the orphans your prey!
<3> What will you do on the day of punishment,
　　in the calamity that will come from far away?
To whom will you flee for help,
　　and where will you leave your wealth,
<4> so as not to crouch among the prisoners
　　or fall among the slain?
For all this his anger has not turned away;
　　his hand is stretched out still.

But woe to you who are rich

Luke 6:20-25

<20> Then he looked up at his disciples and said:
"Blessed are you who are poor,
> for yours is the kingdom of God.

<21> "Blessed are you who are hungry now,
> for you will be filled.

"Blessed are you who weep now,
> for you will laugh.

<22> "Blessed are you when people hate you, and when they exclude you, revile you, and defame you on account of the Son of Man.

<23> Rejoice in that day and leap for joy, for surely your reward is great in heaven; for that is what their ancestors did to the prophets.

<24> "But woe to you who are rich,
> for you have received your consolation.

<25> "Woe to you who are full now,
> for you will be hungry.

Half of my possessions

Luke 19:1-10

<19:1> He entered Jericho and was passing through it.

<2> A man was there named Zacchaeus; he was a chief tax collector and was rich.

<3> He was trying to see who Jesus was, but on account of the crowd he could not, because he was short in stature.

<4> So he ran ahead and climbed a sycamore tree to see him, because he was going to pass that way.

<5> When Jesus came to the place, he looked up and said to him, "Zacchaeus, hurry and come down; for I must stay at your house today."

<6> So he hurried down and was happy to welcome him.

<7> All who saw it began to grumble and said, "He has gone to be the guest of one who is a sinner."

<8> Zacchaeus stood there and said to the Lord, "Look, half of my possessions, Lord, I will give to the poor; and if I have defrauded any-

one of anything, I will pay back four times as much."

<9> Then Jesus said to him, "Today salvation has come to this house, because he too is a son of Abraham.

<10> For the Son of Man came to seek out and to save the lost."

Shouldn't you know about justice?

Micah 3:1-3

<3:1> And I said:
Listen, you heads of Jacob
     and rulers of the house of Israel!
Should you not know justice?—
     <2> you who hate the good and love the evil,
who tear the skin off my people,
     and the flesh off their bones;
<3> who eat the flesh of my people,
     flay their skin off them,
break their bones in pieces,
     and chop them up like meat in a kettle,
     like flesh in a caldron.

More than sacrifice

Proverbs 21:3

<3> To do righteousness and justice
     is more acceptable to the LORD than sacrifice.

PART II:
TEXTS FROM THE APOCRYPHA

They give none to the poor
Epistle of Jeremiah 6:28

<28> The priests sell the sacrifices that are offered to these gods and use the money themselves. Likewise their wives preserve some of the meat with salt, but give none to the poor or helpless.

Speaking of the Babylonian gods
Epistle of Jeremiah 6:35-38

<35> Likewise they are not able to give either wealth or money; if one makes a vow to them and does not keep it, they will not require it.
<36> They cannot save anyone from death or rescue the weak from the strong.
<37> They cannot restore sight to the blind; they cannot rescue one who is in distress.
<38> They cannot take pity on a widow or do good to an orphan.

Bring a poor person to dinner
Tobit 2:1-6

<2:1> Then during the reign of Esar-haddon I returned home, and my wife Anna and my son Tobias were restored to me. At our festival of Pentecost, which is the sacred festival of weeks, a good dinner was prepared for me and I reclined to eat.
<2> When the table was set for me and an abundance of food placed before me, I said to my son Tobias, "Go, my child, and bring whatever poor person you may find of our people among the exiles in Nineveh, who is wholeheartedly mindful of God,
 and he shall eat together with me. I will wait for you, until you come back."
<3> So Tobias went to look for some poor person of our people.

97

When he had returned he said, "Father!" And I replied, "Here I am, my child." Then he went on to say, "Look, father, one of our own people has been murdered and thrown into the market place, and now he lies there strangled."

<4> Then I sprang up, left the dinner before even tasting it, and removed the body from the square and laid it in one of the rooms until sunset when I might bury it.

<5> When I returned, I washed myself and ate my food in sorrow.

<6> Then I remembered the prophecy of Amos, how he said against Bethel,

> "Your festivals shall be turned into mourning,
> and all your songs into lamentation."

And I wept.

Don't turn your face from the poor
Tobit 4:5-11

<5> "Revere the Lord all your days, my son, and refuse to sin or to transgress his commandments. Live uprightly all the days of your life, and do not walk in the ways of wrongdoing;

<6> for those who act in accordance with truth will prosper in all their activities. To all those who practice righteousness

<7> give alms from your possessions, and do not let your eye begrudge the gift when you make it. Do not turn your face away from anyone who is poor, and the face of God will not be turned away from you.

<8> If you have many possessions, make your gift from them in proportion; if few, do not be afraid to give according to the little you have.

<9> So you will be laying up a good treasure for yourself against the day of necessity.

<10> For almsgiving delivers from death and keeps you from going into the Darkness.

<11> Indeed, almsgiving, for all who practice it, is an excellent offering in the presence of the Most High.

Let's oppress the poor guy

Wisdom of Solomon 2:6-11

\<6\> "Come, therefore, let us enjoy the good things that exist,
and make use of the creation to the full as in youth.

\<7\> Let us take our fill of costly wine and perfumes,
and let no flower of spring pass us by.

\<8\> Let us crown ourselves with rosebuds before they wither.

\<9\> Let none of us fail to share in our revelry;
everywhere let us leave signs of enjoyment,
because this is our portion, and this our lot.

\<10\> Let us oppress the righteous poor man;
let us not spare the widow
or regard the gray hairs of the aged.

\<11\> But let our might be our law of right,
for what is weak proves itself to be useless.

Don't grieve the hungry

Wisdom of Sirach 4:1-6

\<4:1\> My child, do not cheat the poor of their living,
and do not keep needy eyes waiting.

\<2\> Do not grieve the hungry,
or anger one in need.

\<3\> Do not add to the troubles of the desperate,
or delay giving to the needy.

\<4\> Do not reject a suppliant in distress,
or turn your face away from the poor.

\<5\> Do not avert your eye from the needy,
and give no one reason to curse you;

\<6\> for if in bitterness of soul some should curse you,
their Creator will hear their prayer.

Rescue the oppressed

Wisdom of Sirach 4:8-10

<8> Give a hearing to the poor,

> and return their greeting politely.

<9> Rescue the oppressed from the oppressor;

> and do not be hesitant in giving a verdict.

<10> Be a father to orphans,

> and be like a husband to their mother;

you will then be like a son of the Most High,

> and he will love you more than does your mother.

Visit the sick

Wisdom of Sirach 7:32-35

<32> Stretch out your hand to the poor,

> so that your blessing may be complete.

<33> Give graciously to all the living;

> do not withhold kindness even from the dead.

<34> Do not avoid those who weep,

> but mourn with those who mourn.

<35> Do not hesitate to visit the sick,

> because for such deeds you will be loved.

Injustice is outrageous

Wisdom of Sirach 10:7-8

<7> Arrogance is hateful to the Lord and to mortals,

> and injustice is outrageous to both.

<8> Sovereignty passes from nation to nation

> on account of injustice and insolence and wealth.

Intelligent but poor

Wisdom of Sirach 10:23

<23> It is not right to despise one who is intelligent but poor,

> and it is not proper to honor one who is sinful.

Good looks

Wisdom of Sirach 11:2

<2> Do not praise individuals for their good looks,
      or loathe anyone because of appearance alone.

If you come from a wealth culture

Wisdom of Sirach 11:24-26

<24> Do not say, "I have enough,
      and what harm can come to me now?"

<25> In the day of prosperity, adversity is forgotten,
      and in the day of adversity, prosperity is not remembered.

<26> For it is easy for the Lord on the day of death
      to reward individuals according to their conduct.

If you don't give alms

Wisdom of Sirach 12:3

<3> No good comes to one who persists in evil
      or to one who does not give alms.

The ungodly think poverty is evil

Wisdom of Sirach 13:17-24

<17> What does a wolf have in common with a lamb?
      No more has a sinner with the devout.

<18> What peace is there between a hyena and a dog?
      And what peace between the rich and the poor?

<19> Wild asses in the wilderness are the prey of lions;
      likewise the poor are feeding grounds for the rich.

<20> Humility is an abomination to the proud;
      likewise the poor are an abomination to the rich.

<21> When the rich person totters, he is supported by friends,
      but when the humble falls, he is pushed away even by friends.

<22> If the rich person slips, many come to the rescue;
      he speaks unseemly words, but they justify him.

If the humble person slips, they even criticize him;
      he talks sense, but is not given a hearing.

<23> The rich person speaks and all are silent;
      they extol to the clouds what he says.
The poor person speaks and they say, "Who is this fellow?"
      And should he stumble, they even push him down.
<24> Riches are good if they are free from sin;
      poverty is evil only in the opinion of the ungodly.

Injustice withers the soul

Wisdom of Sirach 14:9

<9> The eye of the greedy person is not satisfied with his share;
      greedy injustice withers the soul.

Pursuing justice

Wisdom of Sirach 27:8

<8> If you pursue justice, you will attain it
      and wear it like a glorious robe.

Help the poor

Wisdom of Sirach 29:8-13

<8> Nevertheless, be patient with someone in humble circumstances,
      and do not keep him waiting for your alms.
<9> Help the poor for the commandment's sake,
      and in their need do not send them away empty-handed.
<10> Lose your silver for the sake of a brother or a friend,
      and do not let it rust under a stone and be lost.
<11> Lay up your treasure according to the commandments of the Most High,
      and it will profit you more than gold.
<12> Store up almsgiving in your treasury,
      and it will rescue you from every disaster;
<13> better than a stout shield and a sturdy spear,
      it will fight for you against the enemy.

Like killing a son before his father's eyes
Wisdom of Sirach 34:24-26

<24> Like one who kills a son before his father's eyes
is the person who offers a sacrifice from the property of the
poor.

<25> The bread of the needy is the life of the poor;
whoever deprives them of it is a murderer.

<26> To take away a neighbor's living is to commit murder;
<27> to deprive an employee of wages is to shed blood.

A generous person
Wisdom of Sirach 40:12-14

<12> All bribery and injustice will be blotted out,
but good faith will last forever.

<13> The wealth of the unjust will dry up like a river,
and crash like a loud clap of thunder in a storm.

<14> As a generous person has cause to rejoice,
so lawbreakers will utterly fail.

Almsgiving rescues
Wisdom of Sirach 40:24

<24> Kindred and helpers are for a time of trouble,
but almsgiving rescues better than either.

Let the blind have a vision
II Esdras 2:20-22

<20> "Guard the rights of the widow, secure justice for the ward, give
to the needy, defend the orphan, clothe the naked,

<21> care for the injured and the weak, do not ridicule the lame, pro-
tect the maimed, and let the blind have a vision of my splendor.

<22> Protect the old and the young within your walls.

APPENDIX A
JUSTICE IN ST. THOMAS AQUINAS'
THE SUMMA THEOLOGIA

St. Thomas Aquinas
The Summa Theologica
(Benziger Dominican Province)

Question 58
OF JUSTICE (TWELVE ARTICLES)

We must now consider justice. Under this head there are twelve points of inquiry:

   (1)   What is justice?
   (2)   Whether justice is always towards another?
   (3)   Whether it is a virtue?
   (4)   Whether it is in the will as its subject?
   (5)   Whether it is a general virtue?
   (6)   Whether, as a general virtue, it is essentially the same as every virtue?
   (7)   Whether there is a particular justice?
   (8)   Whether particular justice has a matter of its own?
   (9)   Whether it is about passions, or about operations only?
  (10)   Whether the mean of justice is the real mean?
  (11)   Whether the act of justice is to render to everyone his own?
  (12)   Whether justice is the chief of the moral virtues?

Article: 1

Whether justice is fittingly defined as being the perpetual and constant will to render to each one his right?

Objection 1: It would seem that lawyers have unfittingly defined justice as being "the perpetual and constant will to render to each one his right" [*Digest.* i, 1; *De Just. et Jure* 10]. For, according to the Philosopher (*Ethic.* v, 1), justice is a habit which makes a man "capable of doing what is just, and of being just in action and in intention." Now "will" denotes a power, or also an act. Therefore justice is unfittingly defined as being a will.

Objection 2: Further, rectitude of the will is not the will; else if the will were its own rectitude, it would follow that no will is unrighteous. Yet, according to Anselm (*De Veritate* xii), justice is rectitude. Therefore justice is not the will.

Objection 3: Further, no will is perpetual save God's. If therefore justice is a perpetual will, in God alone will there be justice.

Objection 4: Further, whatever is perpetual is constant, since it is unchangeable. Therefore it is needless in defining justice, to say that it is both "perpetual" and "constant."

Objection 5: Further, it belongs to the sovereign to give each one his right. Therefore, if justice gives each one his right, it follows that it is in none but the sovereign: which is absurd.

Objection 6: Further, Augustine says (*De Moribus* Eccl. xv) that "justice is love serving God alone." Therefore it does not render to each one his right.

I answer that, The aforesaid definition of justice is fitting if understood aright. For since every virtue is a habit that is the principle of a good act, a virtue must needs be defined by means of the good act bearing on the matter proper to that virtue. Now the proper matter of justice consists of those things that belong to our intercourse with other men, as shall be shown further on (Article [2]). Hence the act of justice in relation to its proper matter and object is indicated in the words, "Rendering to each one his right," since, as Isidore says (*Etym.* x), "a man is said to be just because he respects the rights [jus] of others."

Now in order that an act bearing upon any matter whatever be virtuous, it requires to be voluntary, stable, and firm, because the Philosopher says (*Ethic.* ii, 4) that in order for an act to be virtuous it needs first of all to be done "knowingly," secondly to be done "by choice," and "for a due end," thirdly to be done "immovably." Now the first of these is included in the second, since "what is done through ignorance is involuntary" (*Ethic.* iii, 1). Hence the definition of justice mentions first the "will," in order to show that the act of justice must be voluntary; and mention is made afterwards of its "constancy" and "perpetuity" in order to indicate the firmness of the act.

Accordingly, this is a complete definition of justice; save that the act is mentioned instead of the habit, which takes its species from that act, because habit implies relation to act. And if anyone would reduce it to the proper form of a definition, he might say that "justice is a habit whereby a man renders to each one his due by a constant and perpetual will": and this is about the same definition as that given by the Philosopher (*Ethic.* v, 5) who says that "justice is a habit whereby a man is said to be capable of doing just actions in accordance with his choice."

Reply to Objection 1: Will here denotes the act, not the power: and it is customary among writers to define habits by their acts: thus Augustine says (*Tract. in Joan.* xl) that "faith is to believe what one sees not."

Reply to Objection 2: Justice is the same as rectitude, not essentially but causally; for it is a habit which rectifies the deed and the will.

Reply to Objection 3: The will may be called perpetual in two ways. First on the part of the will's act which endures for ever, and thus God's will alone is perpetual. Secondly on the part of the subject, because, to wit, a man wills to do a certain thing always. and this is a necessary condition of justice. For it does not satisfy the conditions of justice that one wish to observe justice in some particular matter for the time being, because one could scarcely find a man willing to act unjustly in every case; and it is requisite that one should have the will to observe justice at all times and in all cases.

Reply to Objection 4: Since "perpetual" does not imply perpetuity of the act of the will, it is not superfluous to add "constant": for while the "perpetual will" denotes the purpose of observing justice always, "constant" signifies a firm perseverance in this purpose.

Reply to Objection 5: A judge renders to each one what belongs to him, by way of command and direction, because a judge is the "personification of justice," and "the sovereign is its guardian" (*Ethic.* v, 4). On the other hand, the subjects render to each one what belongs to him, by way of execution.

Reply to Objection 6: Just as love of God includes love of our neighbor, as stated above (Question [25], Article [1]), so too the service of God includes rendering to each one his due.

Article: 2
Whether justice is always towards one another?

Objection 1: It would seem that justice is not always towards another. For the Apostle says (Rm. 3:22) that "the justice of God is by faith of Jesus Christ." Now faith does not concern the dealings of one man with another. Neither therefore does justice.

Objection 2: Further, according to Augustine (De Moribus Eccl. xv), "it belongs to justice that man should direct to the service of God his authority over the things that are subject to him." Now the sensitive appetite is subject to man, according to Gn. 4:7, where it is written: "The lust thereof," viz. of sin, "shall be under thee, and thou shalt have dominion over it." Therefore it belongs to justice to have dominion over one's own appetite: so that justice is towards oneself.

Objection 3: Further, the justice of God is eternal. But nothing else is co-eternal with God. Therefore justice is not essentially towards another.

Objection 4: Further, man's dealings with himself need to be rectified no less than his dealings with another. Now man's dealings are rectified by justice, according to Prov. 11:5, "The justice of the upright shall make his way prosperous." Therefore justice is about our dealings not only with others, but also with ourselves.

On the contrary, Tully says (De Officiis i, 7) that "the object of justice is to keep men together in society and mutual intercourse." Now this implies relationship of one man to another. Therefore justice is concerned only about our dealings with others.

I answer that, As stated above (Question [57], Article [1]) since justice by its name implies equality, it denotes essentially relation to another, for a thing is equal, not to itself, but to another. And forasmuch as it belongs to justice to rectify human acts, as stated above (Question [57], Article [1]; FS, Question [113], Article [1]) this otherness which justice demands must needs be between beings capable of action. Now actions belong to supposits [*Cf. FP, Question [29], Article [2]] and wholes and, properly speaking, not to parts and forms or powers, for we do not say properly that the hand strikes, but a man with his hand, nor that heat makes a thing hot, but fire by heat, although such expressions may be employed metaphorically. Hence, justice properly speaking demands a distinction of supposits, and consequently is only in one man towards another. Nevertheless in one and the same man we may speak metaphorically of his various principles of action such as the reason, the irascible, and the concupiscible, as though they were so many agents: so that metaphorically in one and the same man there is said to be justice in so far as the reason commands the irascible and concupiscible, and these obey reason; and in general in so far as to each part of man is ascribed what is becoming to it. Hence the Philosopher (*Ethic.* v, 11) calls this "metaphorical justice."

Reply to Objection 1: The justice which faith works in us, is that whereby the ungodly is justified it consists in the due coordination of the parts of the soul, as stated above (FS, Question [113], Article [1]) where we were treating of the justification of the ungodly. Now this belongs to metaphorical justice, which may be found even in a man who lives all by himself.

This suffices for the Reply to the Second Objection.

Reply to Objection 3: God's justice is from eternity in respect of the eternal will and purpose (and it is chiefly in this that justice consists); although it is not eternal as regards its effect, since nothing is co-eternal with God.

Reply to Objection 4: Man's dealings with himself are sufficiently rectified by the rectification of the passions by the other moral virtues. But his dealings with others need a special rectification, not only in relation to the agent, but also in relation to the person to whom they are directed. Hence about such dealings there is a special virtue, and this is justice.

Article: 3
Whether justice is a virtue?

Objection 1: It would seem that justice is not a virtue. For it is written (Lk. 17:10): "When you shall have done all these things that are commanded you, say: We are unprofitable servants; we have done that which we ought to do." Now it is not unprofitable to do a virtuous deed: for Ambrose says (De Officiis ii, 6): "We look to a profit that is estimated not by pecuniary gain but by the acquisition of godliness." Therefore to do what one ought to do, is not a virtuous deed. And yet it is an act of justice. Therefore justice is not a virtue.

Objection 2: Further, that which is done of necessity, is not meritorious. But to render to a man what belongs to him, as justice requires, is of necessity. Therefore it is not meritorious. Yet it is by virtuous actions that we gain merit. Therefore justice is not a virtue.

Objection 3: Further, every moral virtue is about matters of action. Now those things which are wrought externally are not things concerning behavior but concerning handicraft, according to the Philosopher (Metaph. ix) [*Didot ed., viii, 8]. Therefore since it belongs to justice to produce externally a deed that is just in itself, it seems that justice is not a moral virtue.

On the contrary, Gregory says (Moral. ii, 49) that "the entire structure of good works is built on four virtues," viz. temperance, prudence, fortitude and justice

I answer that, A human virtue is one "which renders a human act and man himself good" [*Ethic*. ii, 6], and this can be applied to justice. For a man's act is made good through attaining the rule of reason, which is the rule whereby human acts are regulated. Hence, since justice regulates human operations, it is evident that it renders man's operations good, and, as Tully declares (De Officiis i, 7), good men are so called chiefly from their justice, wherefore, as he says again (De Officiis i, 7) "the luster of virtue appears above all in justice."

Reply to Objection 1: When a man does what he ought, he brings no gain to the person to whom he does what he ought, but only abstains from doing him a harm. He does however profit himself, in so far as he does what he ought, spontaneously and readily, and this is to act virtuously. Hence it is written (Wis. 8:7) that Divine wisdom "teacheth temperance, and prudence, and justice, and fortitude, which are such things as men (i.e. virtuous men) can have nothing more profitable in life."

Reply to Objection 2: Necessity is twofold. One arises from "constraint," and this removes merit, since it runs counter to the will. The other arises from the obligation of a "command," or from the necessity of obtaining an end, when, to wit, a man is unable to achieve the end of virtue without doing some particular thing. The latter necessity does not remove merit, when a man does voluntarily that which is necessary in this way. It does however exclude the credit of supererogation, according to 1 Cor. 9:16, "If I preach the Gospel, it is no glory to me, for a necessity lieth upon me."

Reply to Objection 3: Justice is concerned about external things, not by making them, which pertains to art, but by using them in our dealings with other men.

Article: 4
Whether justice is in the will as its subject?

Objection 1: It would seem that justice is not in the will as its subject. For justice is sometimes called truth. But truth is not in the will, but in the intellect. Therefore justice is not in the will as its subject.

Objection 2: Further, justice is about our dealings with others. Now it belongs to the reason to direct one thing in relation to another. Therefore justice is not in the will as its subject but in the reason.

Objection 3: Further, justice is not an intellectual virtue, since it is not directed to knowledge; wherefore it follows that it is a moral virtue. Now the subject of moral virtue is the faculty which is "rational by participation," viz. the irascible and the concupiscible, as the Philosopher declares (*Ethic.* i, 13). Therefore justice is not in the will as its subject, but in the irascible and concupiscible.

On the contrary, Anselm says (De Verit. xii) that "justice is rectitude of the will observed for its own sake."

I answer that, The subject of a virtue is the power whose act that virtue aims at rectifying. Now justice does not aim at directing an act of the cognitive power, for we are not said to be just through knowing something aright. Hence the subject of justice is not the intellect or reason which is a cognitive power. But since we are said to be just through doing something aright, and because the proximate principle of action is the appetitive power, justice must needs be in some appetitive power as its subject.

Now the appetite is twofold; namely, the will which is in the reason and the sensitive appetite which follows on sensitive apprehension, and is divided into the irascible and the concupiscible, as stated in the FP, Question [81], Article [2]. Again the act of rendering his due to each man cannot proceed from the sensitive appetite, because sensitive apprehension does not go so far as to be able to consider the relation of one thing to another; but this is proper to the reason. Therefore justice cannot be in the irascible or concupiscible as its subject, but only in the will: hence the Philosopher (*Ethic.* v, 1) defines justice by an act of the will, as may be seen above (Article [1]).

Reply to Objection 1: Since the will is the rational appetite, when the rectitude of the reason which is called truth is imprinted on the will on account of its nighness to the reason, this imprint retains the name of truth; and hence it is that justice sometimes goes by the name of truth.

Reply to Objection 2: The will is borne towards its object consequently on the apprehension of reason: wherefore, since the reason directs one thing in relation to another, the will can will one thing in relation to another, and this belongs to justice.

Reply to Objection 3: Not only the irascible and concupiscible parts are "rational by participation," but the entire "appetitive" faculty, as stated in *Ethic.* i, 13, because all appetite is subject to reason. Now the will is contained in the appetitive faculty, wherefore it can be the subject of moral virtue.

Article: 5
Whether justice is a general virtue?

Objection 1: It would seem that justice is not a general virtue. For justice is specified with the other virtues, according to Wis. 8:7, "She teacheth temperance and prudence, and justice, and fortitude." Now the "general" is not specified or reckoned together with the species contained under the same "general." Therefore justice is not a general virtue.

Objection 2: Further, as justice is accounted a cardinal virtue, so are temperance and fortitude. Now neither temperance nor fortitude is reckoned to be a general virtue. Therefore neither should justice in any way be reckoned a general virtue.

Objection 3: Further, justice is always towards others, as stated above (Article [2]). But a sin committed against one's neighbor cannot be a general sin, because it is condivided with sin committed against oneself. Therefore neither is justice a general virtue.

On the contrary, The Philosopher says (*Ethic.* v, 1) that "justice is every virtue."

I answer that, Justice, as stated above (Article [2]) directs man in his relations with other men. Now this may happen in two ways: first as regards his relation with individuals, secondly as regards his relations with others in general, in so far as a man who serves a community, serves all those who are included in that community. Accordingly justice in its proper acceptation can be directed to another in both these senses. Now it is evident that all who are included in a community, stand in relation to that community as parts to a whole; while a part, as such, belongs to a whole, so that whatever is the good of a part can be directed to the good of the whole. It follows therefore that the good of any virtue, whether such virtue direct man in relation to himself, or in relation to certain other individual persons, is referable to the common good, to which justice directs: so that all acts of virtue can pertain to justice, in so far as it directs man to the common good. It is in this sense that justice is called a general virtue. And since it belongs to the law to direct to the common good, as stated above (FS, Question [90], Article [2]), it follows that the justice which is in this way styled general, is called "legal justice," because thereby man is in harmony with the law which directs the acts of all the virtues to the common good.

Reply to Objection 1: Justice is specified or enumerated with the other virtues, not as a general but as a special virtue, as we shall state further on (Articles [7],12).

Reply to Objection 2: Temperance and fortitude are in the sensitive appetite, viz. in the concupiscible and irascible. Now these powers are appetitive of certain particular goods, even as the senses are cognitive of particulars. On the other hand justice is in the intellective appetite as its subject, which can have the universal good as its object, knowledge whereof belongs to the intellect. Hence justice can be a general virtue rather than temperance or fortitude.

Reply to Objection 3: Things referable to oneself are referable to another, especially in regard to the common good. Wherefore legal justice, in so far as it directs to the common good, may be called a general virtue: and in like manner injustice may be called a general sin; hence it is written (1 Jn. 3:4) that all "sin is iniquity."

Article: 6
Whether justice, as a general virtue, is essentially the same as all virtue?

Objection 1: It would seem that justice, as a general virtue, is essentially the same as all virtue. For the Philosopher says (*Ethic.* v, 1) that "virtue and legal justice are the same as all virtue, but differ in their mode of being." Now things that differ merely in their mode of being or logically do not differ essentially. Therefore justice is essentially the same as every virtue.

Objection 2: Further, every virtue that is not essentially the same as all virtue is a part of virtue. Now the aforesaid justice, according to the Philosopher (*Ethic.* v. 1) "is not a part but the whole of virtue." Therefore the aforesaid justice is essentially the same as all virtue.

Objection 3: Further, the essence of a virtue does not change through that virtue directing its act to some higher end even as the habit of temperance remains essentially the same even though its act be directed to a Divine good. Now it belongs to legal justice that the acts

115

of all the virtues are directed to a higher end, namely the common good of the multitude, which transcends the good of one single individual. Therefore it seems that legal justice is essentially all virtue.

Objection 4: Further, every good of a part can be directed to the good of the whole, so that if it be not thus directed it would seem without use or purpose. But that which is in accordance with virtue cannot be so. Therefore it seems that there can be no act of any virtue, that does not belong to general justice, which directs to the common good; and so it seems that general justice is essentially the same as all virtue.

On the contrary, The Philosopher says (*Ethic.* v, 1) that "many are able to be virtuous in matters affecting themselves, but are unable to be virtuous in matters relating to others," and (Polit. iii, 2) that "the virtue of the good man is not strictly the same as the virtue of the good citizen." Now the virtue of a good citizen is general justice, whereby a man Is directed to the common good. Therefore general justice is not the same as virtue in general, and it is possible to have one without the other.

I answer that, A thing is said to be "general" in two ways. First, by "predication": thus "animal" is general in relation to man and horse and the like: and in this sense that which is general must needs be essentially the same as the things in relation to which it is general, for the reason that the genus belongs to the essence of the species, and forms part of its definition. Secondly a thing is said to be general "virtually"; thus a universal cause is general in relation to all its effects, the sun, for instance, in relation to all bodies that are illumined, or transmuted by its power; and in this sense there is no need for that which is "general" to be essentially the same as those things in relation to which it is general, since cause and effect are not essentially the same. Now it is in the latter sense that, according to what has been said (Article [5]), legal justice is said to be a general virtue, in as much, to wit, as it directs the acts of the other virtues to its own end, and this is to move all the other virtues by its command; for just as charity may be called a general virtue in so far as it directs the acts of all the virtues to the Divine good, so too is legal justice, in so far as it directs the acts of all the virtues to the common good. Accordingly, just as charity which regards the Divine good as its proper object, is a special virtue in respect of its essence, so too legal justice is a special virtue in respect of its essence, in so far as it regards the common good as its proper object. And thus it is in the sovereign principally and by way of a mastercraft, while it is secondarily and administratively in his subjects.

However the name of legal justice can be given to every virtue, in so far as every virtue is directed to the common good by the aforesaid legal justice, which though special essentially is nevertheless virtually general. Speaking in this way, legal justice is essentially the same as all virtue, but differs therefrom logically: and it is in this sense that the Philosopher speaks.

Wherefore the Replies to the First and Second Objections are manifest.

Reply to Objection 3: This argument again takes legal justice for the virtue commanded by legal justice.

Reply to Objection 4: Every virtue strictly speaking directs its act to that virtue's proper end: that it should happen to be directed to a further end either always or sometimes, does not belong to that virtue considered strictly, for it needs some higher virtue to direct it to that end. Consequently there must be one supreme virtue essentially distinct from every other virtue, which directs all the virtues to the common good; and this virtue is legal justice.

Article: 7
Whether there is a particular besides a general justice?

Objection 1: It would seem that there is not a particular besides a general justice. For there is nothing superfluous in the virtues, as neither is there in nature. Now general justice directs man sufficiently in all his relations with other men. Therefore there is no need for a particular justice.

Objection 2: Further, the species of a virtue does not vary according to "one" and "many." But legal justice directs one man to another in matters relating to the multitude, as shown above (Articles [5],6). Therefore there is not another species of justice directing one man to another in matters relating to the individual.

Objection 3: Further, between the individual and the general public stands the household community. Consequently, if in addition to general justice there is a particular justice corresponding to the individual, for the same reason there should be a domestic justice directing man to the common good of a household: and yet this is not the case. Therefore neither should there be a particular besides a legal justice.

On the contrary, Chrysostom in his commentary on Mt. 5:6, "Blessed are they that hunger and thirst after justice," says (Hom. xv in Matth.): "By justice He signifies either the general virtue, or the particular virtue which is opposed to covetousness."

I answer that, As stated above (Article [6]), legal justice is not essentially the same as every virtue, and besides legal justice which directs man immediately to the common good, there is a need for other virtues to direct him immediately in matters relating to particular goods: and these virtues may be relative to himself or to another individual person. Accordingly, just as in addition to legal justice there is a need for particular virtues to direct man in relation to himself, such as temperance and fortitude, so too besides legal justice there is need for particular justice to direct man in his relations to other individuals.

Reply to Objection 1: Legal justice does indeed direct man sufficiently in his relations towards others. As regards the common good it does so immediately, but as to the good of the individual, it does so mediately. Wherefore there is need for particular justice to direct a man immediately to the good of another individual.

Reply to Objection 2: The common good of the realm and the particular good of the individual differ not only in respect of the "many" and the "few," but also under a formal aspect. For the aspect of the "common" good differs from the aspect of the "individual" good, even as the aspect of "whole" differs from that of "part." Wherefore the Philosopher says (Polit. i, 1) that "they are wrong who maintain that the State and the home and the like differ only as many and few and not specifically."

Reply to Objection 3: The household community, according to the Philosopher (Polit. i, 2), differs in respect of a threefold fellowship; namely "of husband and wife, father and son, master and slave," in each of which one person is, as it were, part of the other. Wherefore between such persons there is not justice simply, but a species of justice, viz. "domestic" justice, as stated in *Ethic.* v, 6.

Article: 8
Whether particular justice has a special matter?

Objection 1: It would seem that particular justice has no special matter. Because a gloss on Gn. 2:14, "The fourth river is Euphrates," says: "Euphrates signifies 'fruitful'; nor is it stated through what country it flows, because justice pertains to all the parts of the soul." Now this would not be the case, if justice had a special matter, since every special matter belongs to a special power. Therefore particular justice has no special matter.

Objection 2: Further, Augustine says (Questions. lxxxiii, qu. 61) that "the soul has four virtues whereby, in this life, it lives spiritually, viz. temperance, prudence, fortitude and justice;" and he says that "the fourth is justice, which pervades all the virtues." Therefore particular justice, which is one of the four cardinal virtues, has no special matter.

Objection 3: Further, justice directs man sufficiently in matters relating to others. Now a man can be directed to others in all matters relating to this life. Therefore the matter of justice is general and not special.

On the contrary, The Philosopher reckons (*Ethic.* v, 2) particular justice to be specially about those things which belong to social life.

I answer that, Whatever can be rectified by reason is the matter of moral virtue, for this is defined in reference to right reason, according to the Philosopher (*Ethic.* ii, 6). Now the reason can rectify not only the internal passions of the soul, but also external actions, and also those external things of which man can make use. And yet it is in respect of external actions and external things by means of which men can communicate with one another, that the relation of one man to another is to be considered; whereas it is in respect of internal passions that we consider man's rectitude in himself. Consequently, since justice is directed to others, it is not about the entire matter of moral virtue, but only about external actions and things, under a certain special aspect of the object, in so far as one man is related to another through them.

Reply to Objection 1: It is true that justice belongs essentially to one part of the soul, where it resides as in its subject; and this is the will which moves by its command all the other parts of the soul; and accordingly justice belongs to all the parts of the soul, not directly but by a kind of diffusion.

Reply to Objection 2: As stated above (FS, Question [61], Articles [3],4), the cardinal virtues may be taken in two ways: first as special virtues, each having a determinate matter; secondly, as certain general modes of virtue. In this latter sense Augustine speaks in the passage quoted: for he says that "prudence is knowledge of what we should seek and avoid, temperance is the curb on the lust for fleeting pleasures, fortitude is strength of mind in bearing with passing trials, justice is the love of God and our neighbor which pervades the other virtues, that is to say, is the common principle of the entire order between one man and another."

Reply to Objection 3: A man's internal passions which are a part of moral matter, are not in themselves directed to another man, which belongs to the specific nature of justice; yet their effects, i.e. external

120

actions, are capable of being directed to another man. Consequently it does not follow that the matter of justice is general.

Article: 9
Whether justice is about the passions?

Objection 1: It would seem that justice is about the passions. For the Philosopher says (*Ethic.* ii, 3) that "moral virtue is about pleasure and pain." Now pleasure or delight, and pain are passions, as stated above [*FS, Question [23], Article [4]; FS, Question [31], Article [1]; FS, Question [35], Article [1]] when we were treating of the passions. Therefore justice, being a moral virtue, is about the passions.

Objection 2: Further, justice is the means of rectifying a man's operations in relation to another man. Now such like operations cannot be rectified unless the passions be rectified, because it is owing to disorder of the passions that there is disorder in the aforesaid operations: thus sexual lust leads to adultery, and overmuch love of money leads to theft. Therefore justice must needs be about the passions.

Objection 3: Further, even as particular justice is towards another person so is legal justice. Now legal justice is about the passions, else it would not extend to all the virtues, some of which are evidently about the passions. Therefore justice is about the passions.

On the contrary, The Philosopher says (*Ethic.* v, 1) that justice is about operations.

I answer that, The true answer to this question may be gathered from a twofold source. First from the subject of justice, i.e. from the will, whose movements or acts are not passions, as stated above (FS, Question [22], Article [3]; FS, Question [59], Article [4]), for it is only the sensitive appetite whose movements are called passions. Hence justice is not about the passions, as are temperance and fortitude, which are in the irascible and concupiscible parts. Secondly, on he part of the matter, because justice is about man's relations with another, and we are not directed immediately to another by the internal passions. Therefore justice is not about the passions.

Reply to Objection 1: Not every moral virtue is about pleasure and pain as its proper matter, since fortitude is about fear and daring: but every moral virtue is directed to pleasure and pain, as to ends to be acquired, for, as the Philosopher says (*Ethic.* vii, 11), "pleasure and pain are the principal end in respect of which we say that this is an evil, and that a good": and in this way too they belong to justice, since "a man is not just unless he rejoice in just actions" (*Ethic.* i, 8).

Reply to Objection 2: External operations are as it were between external things, which are their matter, and internal passions, which are their origin. Now it happens sometimes that there is a defect in one of these, without there being a defect in the other. Thus a man may steal another's property, not through the desire to have the thing, but through the will to hurt the man; or vice versa, a man may covet another's property without wishing to steal it. Accordingly the directing of operations in so far as they tend towards external things, belongs to justice, but in so far as they arise from the passions, it belongs to the other moral virtues which are about the passions. Hence justice hinders theft of another's property, in so far as stealing is contrary to the, equality that should be maintained in external things, while liberality hinders it as resulting from an immoderate desire for wealth. Since, however, external operations take their species, not from the internal passions but from external things as being their objects, it follows that, external operations are essentially the matter of justice rather than of the other moral virtues.

Reply to Objection 3: The common good is the end of each individual member of a community, just as the good of the whole is the end of each part. On the other hand the good of one individual is not the end of another individual: wherefore legal justice which is directed to the common good, is more capable of extending to the internal passions whereby man is disposed in some way or other in himself, than particular justice which is directed to the good of another individual:

although legal justice extends chiefly to other virtues in the point of their external operations, in so far, to wit, as "the law commands us to perform the actions of a courageous person . . . the actions of a temperate person . . . and the actions of a gentle person" (*Ethic.* v, 5).

Article: 10
Whether the mean of justice is the real mean?

Objection 1: It would seem that the mean of justice is not the real mean. For the generic nature remains entire in each species. Now moral virtue is defined (*Ethic.* ii, 6) to be "an elective habit which observes the mean fixed, in our regard, by reason." Therefore justice observes the rational and not the real mean.

Objection 2: Further, in things that are good simply, there is neither excess nor defect, and consequently neither is there a mean; as is clearly the case with the virtues, according to *Ethic.* ii, 6. Now justice is about things that are good simply, as stated in *Ethic.* v. Therefore justice does not observe the real mean.

Objection 3: Further, the reason why the other virtues are said to observe the rational and not the real mean, is because in their case the mean varies according to different persons, since what is too much for one is too little for another (*Ethic.* ii, 6). Now this is also the case in justice: for one who strikes a prince does not receive the same punishment as one who strikes a private individual. Therefore justice also observes, not the real, but the rational mean.

On the contrary, The Philosopher says (*Ethic.* ii, 6; v, 4) that the mean of justice is to be taken according to "arithmetical" proportion, so that it is the real mean.

I answer that, As stated above (Article [9]; FS, Question [59], Article [4]), the other moral virtues are chiefly concerned with the passions, the regulation of which is gauged entirely by a comparison with the very man who is the subject of those passions, in so far as his anger

123

and desire are vested with their various due circumstances. Hence the mean in such like virtues is measured not by the proportion of one thing to another, but merely by comparison with the virtuous man himself, so that with them the mean is only that which is fixed by reason in our regard.

On the other hand, the matter of justice is external operation, in so far as an operation or the thing used in that operation is duly proportionate to another person, wherefore the mean of justice consists in a certain proportion of equality between the external thing and the external person. Now equality is the real mean between greater and less, as stated in Metaph. x [*Didot ed., ix, 5; Cf. *Ethic.* v, 4]: wherefore justice observes the real mean.

Reply to Objection 1: This real mean is also the rational mean, wherefore justice satisfies the conditions of a moral virtue.

Reply to Objection 2: We may speak of a thing being good simply in two ways. First a thing may be good in every way: thus the virtues are good; and there is neither mean nor extremes in things that are good simply in this sense. Secondly a thing is said to be good simply through being good absolutely i.e. in its nature, although it may become evil through being abused. Such are riches and honors; and in the like it is possible to find excess, deficiency and mean, as regards men who can use them well or ill: and it is in this sense that justice is about things that are good simply.

Reply to Objection 3: The injury inflicted bears a different proportion to a prince from that which it bears to a private person: wherefore each injury requires to be equalized by vengeance in a different way: and this implies a real and not merely a rational diversity.

Article: 11
Whether the act of justice is to render to each one his own?

Objection 1: It would seem that the act of justice is not to render to each one his own. For Augustine (De Trin. xiv, 9) ascribes to justice the act of succoring the needy. Now in succoring the needy we give them what is not theirs but ours. Therefore the act of justice does not consist in rendering to each one his own.

Objection 2: Further, Tully says (De Offic. i, 7) that "beneficence which we may call kindness or liberality, belongs to justice." Now it pertains to liberality to give to another of one's own, not of what is his. Therefore the act of justice does not consist in rendering to each one his own.

Objection 3: Further, it belongs to justice not only to distribute things duly, but also to repress injurious actions, such as murder, adultery and so forth. But the rendering to each one of what is his seems to belong solely to the distribution of things. Therefore the act of justice is not sufficiently described by saying that it consists in rendering to each one his own.

On the contrary, Ambrose says (De Offic. i, 24): "It is justice that renders to each one what is his, and claims not another's property; it disregards its own profit in order to preserve the common equity."

I answer that, As stated above (Articles [8],10), the matter of justice is an external operation in so far as either it or the thing we use by it is made proportionate to some other person to whom we are related by justice. Now each man's own is that which is due to him according to equality of proportion. Therefore the proper act of justice is nothing else than to render to each one his own.

Reply to Objection 1: Since justice is a cardinal virtue, other secondary virtues, such as mercy, liberality and the like are connected with it, as we shall state further on (Question [80], Article [1]). Wherefore to succor the needy, which belongs to mercy or pity, and to be liberally beneficent, which pertains to liberality, are by a kind of reduction ascribed to justice as to their principal virtue.

This suffices for the Reply to the Second Objection.

Reply to Objection 3: As the Philosopher states (*Ethic.* v, 4), in matters of justice, the name of "profit" is extended to whatever is excessive, and whatever is deficient is called "loss." The reason for this is that justice is first of all and more commonly exercised in voluntary interchanges of things, such as buying and selling, wherein those expressions are properly employed; and yet they are transferred to all other matters of justice. The same applies to the rendering to each one of what is his own.

Article: 12
Whether justice stands foremost among all moral virtues?

Objection 1: It would seem that justice does not stand foremost among all the moral virtues. Because it belongs to justice to render to each one what is his, whereas it belongs to liberality to give of one's own, and this is more virtuous. Therefore liberality is a greater virtue than justice.

Objection 2: Further, nothing is adorned by a less excellent thing than itself. Now magnanimity is the ornament both of justice and of all the virtues, according to *Ethic.* iv, 3. Therefore magnanimity is more excellent than justice.

Objection 3: Further, virtue is about that which is "difficult" and "good," as stated in *Ethic.* ii, 3. But fortitude is about more difficult things than justice is, since it is about dangers of death, according to *Ethic.* iii, 6. Therefore fortitude is more excellent than justice.

On the contrary, Tully says (De Offic. i, 7): "Justice is the most resplendent of the virtues, and gives its name to a good man."

I answer that, If we speak of legal justice, it is evident that it stands foremost among all the moral virtues, for as much as the common good transcends the individual good of one person. In this sense the

Philosopher declares (*Ethic.* v, 1) that "the most excellent of the virtues would seem to be justice, and more glorious than either the evening or the morning star." But, even if we speak of particular justice, it excels the other moral virtues for two reasons. The first reason may be taken from the subject, because justice is in the more excellent part of the soul, viz. the rational appetite or will, whereas the other moral virtues are in the sensitive appetite, whereunto appertain the passions which are the matter of the other moral virtues. The second reason is taken from the object, because the other virtues are commendable in respect of the sole good of the virtuous person himself, whereas justice is praiseworthy in respect of the virtuous person being well disposed towards another, so that justice is somewhat the good of another person, as stated in *Ethic.* v, 1. Hence the Philosopher says (Rhet. i, 9): "The greatest virtues must needs be those which are most profitable to other persons, because virtue is a faculty of doing good to others. For this reason the greatest honors are accorded the brave and the just, since bravery is useful to others in warfare, and justice is useful to others both in warfare and in time of peace."

Reply to Objection 1: Although the liberal man gives of his own, yet he does so in so far as he takes into consideration the good of his own virtue, while the just man gives to another what is his, through consideration of the common good. Moreover justice is observed towards all, whereas liberality cannot extend to all. Again liberality which gives of a man's own is based on justice, whereby one renders to each man what is his.

Reply to Objection 2: When magnanimity is added to justice it increases the latter's goodness; and yet without justice it would not even be a virtue.

Reply to Objection 3: Although fortitude is about the most difficult things, it is not about the best, for it is only useful in warfare, whereas justice is useful both in war and in peace, as stated above.

Question 59

OF INJUSTICE (FOUR ARTICLES)

We must now consider injustice, under which head there are four points of inquiry:

(1) Whether injustice is a special vice?
(2) Whether it is proper to the unjust man to do unjust deeds?
(3) Whether one can suffer injustice willingly?
(4) Whether injustice is a mortal sin according to its genus?

Article: 1
Whether injustice is a special virtue?

Objection 1: It would seem that injustice is not a special vice. For it is written (1 Jn. 3:4): "All sin is iniquity [*Vulg.: 'Whosoever committeth sin, committeth also iniquity; and sin is iniquity']." Now iniquity would seem to be the same as injustice, because justice is a kind of equality, so that injustice is apparently the same as inequality or iniquity. Therefore injustice is not a special sin.

Objection 2: Further, no special sin is contrary to all the virtues. But injustice is contrary to all the virtues: for as regards adultery it is opposed to chastity, as regards murder it is opposed to meekness, and in like manner as regards the other sins. Therefore injustice is not a special sin.

Objection 3: Further, injustice is opposed to justice which is in the will. But every sin is in the will, as Augustine declares (De Duabus Anim. x). Therefore injustice is not a special sin.

On the contrary, Injustice is contrary to justice. But justice is a special virtue. Therefore injustice is a special vice.

I answer that, Injustice is twofold. First there is illegal injustice which is opposed to legal justice: and this is essentially a special vice, in so far as it regards a special object, namely the common good which it contemns; and yet it is a general vice, as regards the intention, since contempt of the common good may lead to all kinds of sin. Thus too all vices, as being repugnant to the common good, have the character of injustice, as though they arose from injustice, in accord with what has been said above about justice (Question [58], Articles [5],6). Secondly we speak of injustice in reference to an inequality between one person and another, when one man wishes to have more goods, riches for example, or honors, and less evils, such as toil and losses, and thus injustice has a special matter and is a particular vice opposed to particular justice.

Reply to Objection 1: Even as legal justice is referred to human common good, so Divine justice is referred to the Divine good, to which all sin is repugnant, and in this sense all sin is said to be iniquity.

Reply to Objection 2: Even particular justice is indirectly opposed to all the virtues; in so far, to wit, as even external acts pertain both to justice and to the other moral virtues, although in different ways as stated above (Question [58], Article [9], ad 2).

Reply to Objection 3: The will, like the reason, extends to all moral matters, i.e. passions and those external operations that relate to another person. On the other hand justice perfects the will solely in the point of its extending to operations that relate to another: and the same applies to injustice.

Article: 2
Whether a man is called unjust through doing an unjust thing?

Objection 1: It would seem that a man is called unjust through doing an unjust thing. For habits are specified by their objects, as stated above (FS, Question [54], Article [2]). Now the proper object of justice is the just, and the proper object of injustice is the unjust. Therefore a man should be called just through doing a just thing, and unjust through doing an unjust thing.

Objection 2: Further, the Philosopher declares (*Ethic.* v, 9) that they hold a false opinion who maintain that it is in a man's power to do suddenly an unjust thing, and that a just man is no less capable of doing what is unjust than an unjust man. But this opinion would not be false unless it were proper to the unjust man to do what is unjust. Therefore a man is to be deemed unjust from the fact that he does an unjust thing.

Objection 3: Further, every virtue bears the same relation to its proper act, and the same applies to the contrary vices. But whoever does what is intemperate, is said to be intemperate. Therefore whoever does an unjust thing, is said to be unjust.

On the contrary, The Philosopher says (*Ethic.* v, 6) that "a man may do an unjust thing without being unjust."

I answer that, Even as the object of justice is something equal in external things, so too the object of injustice is something unequal, through more or less being assigned to some person than is due to him. To this object the habit of injustice is compared by means of its proper act which is called an injustice. Accordingly it may happen in two ways that a man who does an unjust thing, is not unjust: first, on account of a lack of correspondence between the operation and its proper object. For the operation takes its species and name from its direct and not from its indirect object: and in things directed to an end the direct is that which is intended, and the indirect is what is beside the intention. Hence if a man do that which is unjust, without intending to do an unjust thing, for instance if he do it through ignorance, being unaware that it is unjust, properly speaking he does an unjust thing, not directly, but only indirectly, and, as it were, doing materially that which is unjust: hence such an operation is not called an injustice. Secondly, this may happen on account of a lack of proportion between the operation and the habit. For an injustice may sometimes arise from a passion, for instance, anger or desire, and sometimes from choice, for instance when the injustice itself is the direct object of one's complacency. In the latter case properly speaking it arises from a habit, because whenever a man has a habit, whatever befits that habit is, of itself, pleasant to him.

Accordingly, to do what is unjust intentionally and by choice is proper to the unjust man, in which sense the unjust man is one who has the habit of injustice: but a man may do what is unjust, unintentionally or through passion, without having the habit of injustice.

Reply to Objection 1: A habit is specified by its object in its direct and formal acceptation, not in its material and indirect acceptation.

Reply to Objection 2: It is not easy for any man to do an unjust thing from choice, as though it were pleasing for its own sake and not for the sake of something else: this is proper to one who has the habit, as the Philosopher declares (*Ethic.* v, 9).

Reply to Objection 3: The object of temperance is not something established externally, as is the object of justice: the object of temperance, i.e. the temperate thing, depends entirely on proportion to the man himself. Consequently what is accidental and unintentional cannot be said to be temperate either materially or formally. In like manner neither can it be called intemperate: and in this respect there is dissimilarity between justice and the other moral virtues; but as regards the proportion between operation and habit, there is similarity in all respects.

Article: 3
Whether we can suffer injustice willingly?

Objection 1: It would seem that one can suffer injustice willingly. For injustice is inequality, as stated above (Article [2]). Now a man by injuring himself, departs from equality, even as by injuring another. Therefore a man can do an injustice to himself, even as to another. But whoever does himself an injustice, does so involuntarily. Therefore a man can voluntarily suffer injustice especially if it be inflicted by himself.

Objection 2: Further, no man is punished by the civil law, except for having committed some injustice. Now suicides were formerly punished according to the law of the state by being deprived of an honorable burial, as the Philosopher declares (*Ethic.* v, 11). Therefore a man can do himself an injustice, and consequently it may happen that a man suffers injustice voluntarily.

Objection 3: Further, no man does an injustice save to one who suffers that injustice. But it may happen that a man does an injustice to one who wishes it, for instance if he sell him a thing for more than it is worth. Therefore a man may happen to suffer an injustice voluntarily.

On the contrary, To suffer an injustice and to do an injustice are contraries. Now no man does an injustice against his will. Therefore on the other hand no man suffers an injustice except against his will.

I answer that, Action by its very nature proceeds from an agent, whereas passion as such is from another: wherefore the same thing in the same respect cannot be both agent and patient, as stated in Phys. iii, 1; viii, 5. Now the proper principle of action in man is the will, wherefore man does properly and essentially what he does voluntarily, and on the other hand a man suffers properly what he suffers against his will, since in so far as he is willing, he is a principle in himself, and so, considered thus, he is active rather than passive. Accordingly we must conclude that properly and strictly speaking no man can do an injustice except voluntarily, nor suffer an injustice save involuntarily; but that accidentally and materially so to speak, it is possible for that which is unjust in itself either to be done involuntarily (as when a man does anything unintentionally), or to be suffered voluntarily (as when a man voluntarily gives to another more than he owes him).

Reply to Objection 1: When one man gives voluntarily to another that which he does not owe him, he causes neither injustice nor inequality. For a man's ownership depends on his will, so there is no disproportion if he forfeit something of his own free-will, either by his own or by another's action.

Reply to Objection 2: An individual person may be considered in two ways. First, with regard to himself; and thus, if he inflict an injury on himself, it may come under the head of some other kind of sin, intemperance for instance or imprudence, but not injustice; because injustice no less than justice, is always referred to another person. Secondly, this or that man may be considered as belonging to the State as part thereof, or as belonging to God, as His creature and image; and thus a man who kills himself, does an injury not indeed to himself, but to the State and to God. Wherefore he is punished in accordance with both Divine and human law, even as the Apostle declares in respect of the fornicator (1 Cor. 3:17): "If any man violate the temple of God, him shall God destroy."

Reply to Objection 3: Suffering is the effect of external action. Now in the point of doing and suffering injustice, the material element is that which is done externally, considered in itself, as stated above (Article [2]), and the formal and essential element is on the part of the will of agent and patient, as stated above (Article [2]). Accordingly we must reply that injustice suffered by one man and injustice done by another man always accompany one another, in the material sense. But if we speak in the formal sense a man can do an injustice with the intention of doing an injustice, and yet the other man does not suffer an injustice, because he suffers voluntarily; and on the other hand a man can suffer an injustice if he suffer an injustice against his will, while the man who does the injury unknowingly, does an injustice, not formally but only materially.

Article: 4
Whether whoever does an injustice sins mortally?

Objection 1: It would seem that not everyone who does an injustice sins mortally. For venial sin is opposed to mortal sin. Now it is sometimes a venial sin to do an injury: for the Philosopher says (*Ethic.* v, 8) in reference to those who act unjustly: "Whatever they do not merely in ignorance but through ignorance is a venial matter." Therefore not everyone that does an injustice sins mortally.

Objection 2: Further, he who does an injustice in a small matter, departs but slightly from the mean. Now this seems to be insignificant and should be accounted among the least of evils, as the Philosopher declares (*Ethic.* ii, 9). Therefore not everyone that does an injustice sins mortally.

Objection 3: Further, charity is the "mother of all the virtues" [*Peter Lombard, Sent. iii, D. 23], and it is through being contrary thereto that a sin is called mortal. But not all the sins contrary to the other virtues are mortal. Therefore neither is it always a mortal sin to do an injustice.

On the contrary, Whatever is contrary to the law of God is a mortal sin. Now whoever does an injustice does that which is contrary to the law of God, since it amounts either to theft, or to adultery, or to murder, or to something of the kind, as will be shown further on (Question [64], seqq.). Therefore whoever does an injustice sins mortally.

I answer that, As stated above (FS, Question [12], Article [5]), when we were treating of the distinction of sins, a mortal sin is one that is contrary to charity which gives life to the soul. Now every injury inflicted on another person is of itself contrary to charity, which moves us to will the good of another. And so since injustice always consists in an injury inflicted on another person, it is evident that to do an injustice is a mortal sin according to its genus.

Reply to Objection 1: This saying of the Philosopher is to be understood as referring to ignorance of fact, which he calls "ignorance of particular circumstances" [*Ethic.* iii, 1], and which deserves pardon, and not to ignorance of the law which does not excuse: and he who does an injustice through ignorance, does no injustice except accidentally, as stated above (Article [2])

Reply to Objection 2: He who does an injustice in small matters falls short of the perfection on an unjust deed, in so far as what he does may be deemed not altogether contrary to the will of the person who suffers therefrom: for instance, if a man take an apple or some such thing from another man, in which case it is probable that the latter is not hurt or displeased.

Reply to Objection 3: The sins which are contrary to the other virtues are not always hurtful to another person, but imply a disorder affecting human passions; hence there is no comparison.

Question 61
OF THE PARTS OF JUSTICE (FOUR ARTICLES)

We must now consider the parts of justice; (1) the subjective parts, which are the species of justice, i.e. distributive and commutative justice; (2) the quasi-integral parts; (3) the quasi-potential parts, i.e. the virtues connected with justice. The first consideration will be twofold: (1) The parts of justice; (2) their opposite vices. And since restitution would seem to be an act of commutative justice, we must consider (1) the distinction between commutative and distributive justice; (2) restitution.

Under the first head there are four points of inquiry:

(1) Whether there are two species of justice, viz. distributive and commutative?
(2) Whether in either case the mean is take in the same way?
(3) Whether their matter is uniform or manifold?
(4) Whether in any of these species the just is the same as counter-passion?

Article: 1
Whether two species of justice are suitably assigned, viz. commutative and distributive?

Objection 1: It would seem that the two species of justice are unsuitably assigned, viz. distributive and commutative. That which is hurtful to the many cannot be a species of justice, since justice is directed to the common good. Now it is hurtful to the common good of the many, if the goods of the community are distributed among many, both because the goods of the community would be exhausted, and because the morals of men would be corrupted. For Tully says (De Offic. ii, 15): "He who receives becomes worse, and the more ready to expect that he will receive again." Therefore distribution does not belong to any species of justice.

Objection 2: Further, the act of justice is to render to each one what is his own, as stated above (Question [58], Article [2]). But when things are distributed, a man does not receive what was his, but becomes possessed of something which belonged to the community. Therefore this does not pertain to justice.

Objection 3: Further, justice is not only in the sovereign, but also in the subject, as stated above (Question [58], Article [6]). But it belongs exclusively to the sovereign to distribute. Therefore distribution does not always belong to justice.

Objection 4: Further, "Distributive justice regards common goods" (*Ethic.* v, 4). Now matters regarding the community pertain to legal justice. Therefore distributive justice is a part, not of particular, but of legal justice.

Objection 5: Further, unity or multitude do not change the species of a virtue. Now commutative justice consists in rendering something to one person, while distributive justice consists in giving something to many. Therefore they are not different species of justice.

On the contrary, The Philosopher assigns two parts to justice and says (*Ethic.* v, 2) that "one directs distributions, the other, commutations."

I answer that, As stated above (Question [58], Articles [7],8), particular justice is directed to the private individual, who is compared to the community as a part to the whole. Now a twofold order may be considered in relation to a part. In the first place there is the order of one part to another, to which corresponds the order of one private individual to another. This order is directed by commutative justice, which is concerned about the mutual dealings between two persons. In the second place there is the order of the whole towards the parts, to which corresponds the order of that which belongs to the community in relation to each single person. This order is directed by distributive justice, which distributes common goods proportionately. Hence there are two species of justice, distributive and commutative.

Reply to Objection 1: Just as a private individual is praised for moderation in his bounty, and blamed for excess therein, so too ought moderation to be observed in the distribution of common goods, wherein distributive justice directs.

Reply to Objection 2: Even as part and whole are somewhat the same, so too that which pertains to the whole, pertains somewhat to the part also: so that when the goods of the community are distributed among a number of individuals each one receives that which, in a way, is his own.

Reply to Objection 3: The act of distributing the goods of the community, belongs to none but those who exercise authority over those goods; and yet distributive justice is also in the subjects to whom those goods are distributed in so far as they are contented by a just distribution. Moreover distribution of common goods is sometimes made not to the state but to the members of a family, and such distribution can be made by authority of a private individual.

Reply to Objection 4: Movement takes its species from the term "whereunto." Hence it belongs to legal justice to direct to the common good those matters which concern private individuals: whereas on the contrary it belongs to particular justice to direct the common good to particular individuals by way of distribution.

Reply to Objection 5: Distributive and commutative justice differ not only in respect of unity and multitude, but also in respect of different kinds of due: because common property is due to an individual in one way, and his personal property in another way.

Article: 2
Whether the mean is to be observed in the same way in distributive as in commutative justice?

Objection 1: It would seem that the mean in distributive justice is to be observed in the same way as in commutative justice. For each of these is a kind of particular justice, as stated above (Article [1]). Now the mean is taken in the same way in all the parts of temperance or fortitude. Therefore the mean should also be observed in the same way in both distributive and commutative justice.

Objection 2: Further, the form of a moral virtue consists in observing the mean which is determined in accordance with reason. Since, then, one virtue has one form, it seems that the mean for both should be the same.

Objection 3: Further, in order to observe the mean in distributive justice we have to consider the various deserts of persons. Now a person's deserts are considered also in commutative justice, for instance, in punishments; thus a man who strikes a prince is punished more than one who strikes a private individual. Therefore the mean is observed in the same way in both kinds of justice.

On the contrary, The Philosopher says (*Ethic.* v, 3,4) that the mean in distributive justice is observed according to "geometrical proportion," whereas in commutative justice it follows "arithmetical proportion."

I answer that, As stated above (Article [1]), in distributive justice something is given to a private individual, in so far as what belongs to the whole is due to the part, and in a quantity that is proportionate to the importance of the position of that part in respect of the whole. Consequently in distributive justice a person receives all the more of the common goods, according as he holds a more prominent position in the community. This prominence in an aristocratic community is gauged according to virtue, in an oligarchy according to wealth, in a democracy according to liberty, and in various ways according to various forms of community. Hence in distributive justice the mean is observed, not according to equality between thing and thing, but according to proportion between things and persons: in such a way that even as one person surpasses another, so that which is given to one person surpasses that which is allotted to another. Hence the Philosopher says (*Ethic.* v, 3,4) that the mean in the latter case follows "geometrical proportion," wherein equality depends not on quantity but on proportion. For example we say that 6 is to 4 as 3 is to 2, because in either case the proportion equals 1-1/2; since the greater number is the sum of the lesser plus its half: whereas the equality of excess is not one of quantity, because 6 exceeds 4 by 2, while 3 exceeds 2 by 1.

On the other hand in commutations something is paid to an individual on account of something of his that has been received, as may be seen chiefly in selling and buying, where the notion of commutation is found primarily. Hence it is necessary to equalize thing with thing, so that the one person should pay back to the other just so much as he has become richer out of that which belonged to the other. The result of this will be equality according to the "arithmetical mean" which is gauged according to equal excess in quantity. Thus 5 is the mean between 6 and 4, since it exceeds the latter and is exceeded by the former, by 1. Accordingly if, at the start, both persons have 5, and one of them receives 1 out of the other's belongings, the one that is the receiver, will have 6, and the other will be left with 4: and so there will be justice if both be brought back to the mean, 1 being taken from him that has 6, and given to him that has 4, for then both will have 5 which is the mean.

Reply to Objection 1: In the other moral virtues the rational, not the real mean, is to be followed: but justice follows the real mean; wherefore the mean, in justice, depends on the diversity of things.

Reply to Objection 2: Equality is the general form of justice, wherein distributive and commutative justice agree: but in one we find equality of geometrical proportion, whereas in the other we find equality of arithmetical proportion.

Reply to Objection 3: In actions and passions a person's station affects the quantity of a thing: for it is a greater injury to strike a prince than a private person. Hence in distributive justice a person's station is considered in itself, whereas in commutative justice it is considered in so far as it causes a diversity of things.

Article: 3
Whether there is a different matter for both kinds of justice?

Objection 1: It would seem that there is not a different matter for both kinds of justice. Diversity of matter causes diversity of virtue, as in the case of fortitude and temperance. Therefore, if distributive and commutative justice have different matters, it would seem that they are not comprised under the same virtue, viz. justice.

Objection 2: Further, the distribution that has to do with distributive justice is one of "wealth or of honors, or of whatever can be distributed among the members of the community" (*Ethic.* v, 2), which very things are the subject matter of commutations between one person and another, and this belongs to commutative justice. Therefore the matters of distributive and commutative justice are not distinct.

Objection 3: Further, if the matter of distributive justice differs from that of commutative justice, for the reason that they differ specifically, where there is no specific difference, there ought to be no diversity of matter. Now the Philosopher (*Ethic.* v, 2) reckons commutative justice as one species, and yet this has many kinds of matter. Therefore the matter of these species of justice is, seemingly, not of many kinds.

On the contrary, It is stated in *Ethic.* v, 2 that "one kind of justice directs distributions, and another commutations."

I answer that, As stated above (Question [51], Articles [8],10), justice is about certain external operations, namely distribution and commutation. These consist in the use of certain externals, whether things, persons or even works: of things, as when one man takes from or restores to another that which is his; of persons, as when a man does an injury to the very person of another, for instance by striking or insulting him, or even by showing respect for him; and of works, as when a man justly exacts a work of another, or does a work for him. Accordingly, if we take for the matter of each kind of justice the things themselves of which the operations are the use, the matter of distributive and commutative justice is the same, since things can be distributed out of the common property to individuals, and be the subject of commutation between one person and another; and again there is a certain distribution and payment of laborious works.

If, however, we take for the matter of both kinds of justice the principal actions themselves, whereby we make use of persons, things, and works, there is then a difference of matter between them. For distributive justice directs distributions, while commutative justice directs commutations that can take place between two persons. of these some are involuntary, some voluntary. They are involuntary when anyone uses another man's chattel, person, or work against his will, and this may be done secretly by fraud, or openly by violence. In either case the offense may be committed against the other man's chattel or person, or against a person connected with him. If the offense is against his chattel and this be taken secretly, it is called "theft," if openly, it is called "robbery." If it be against another man's person, it may affect either the very substance of his person, or his dignity. If it be against the substance of his person, a man is injured secretly if he is treacherously slain, struck or poisoned, and openly, if he is publicly slain, imprisoned, struck or maimed. If it be against his personal dignity, a man is injured secretly by false witness, detractions and so forth, whereby he is deprived of his good name, and openly, by being accused in a court of law, or by public insult. If it be against a personal connection, a man is injured in the person of his wife, secretly (for the most part) by adultery, in the person of his slave, if the latter be induced to leave his master: which things

141

can also be done openly. The same applies to other personal connections, and whatever injury may be committed against the principal, may be committed against them also. Adultery, however, and inducing a slave to leave his master are properly injuries against the person; yet the latter, since a slave is his master's chattel, is referred to theft. Voluntary commutations are when a man voluntarily transfers his chattel to another person. And if he transfer it simply so that the recipient incurs no debt, as in the case of gifts, it is an act, not of justice but of liberality. A voluntary transfer belongs to justice in so far as it includes the notion of debt, and this may occur in many ways. First when one man simply transfers his thing to another in exchange for another thing, as happens in selling and buying. Secondly when a man transfers his thing to another, that the latter may have the use of it with the obligation of returning it to its owner. If he grant the use of a thing gratuitously, it is called "usufruct" in things that bear fruit; and simply "borrowing" on "loan" in things that bear no fruit, such as money, pottery, etc.; but if not even the use is granted gratis, it is called "letting" or "hiring." Thirdly, a man transfers his thing with the intention of recovering it, not for the purpose of its use, but that it may be kept safe, as in a "deposit," or under some obligation, as when a man pledges his property, or when one man stands security for another. In all these actions, whether voluntary or involuntary, the mean is taken in the same way according to the equality of repayment. Hence all these actions belong to the one same species of justice, namely commutative justice. And this suffices for the Replies to the Objections.

Article: 4
Whether the just is absolutely the same as retaliation?

Objection 1: It would seem that the just is absolutely the same as retaliation. For the judgment of God is absolutely just. Now the judgment of God is such that a man has to suffer in proportion with his deeds, according to Mt. 7:2: "With what measure you judge, you shall be judged: and with what measure you mete, it shall be measured to you again." Therefore the just is absolutely the same as retaliation.

Objection 2: Further, in either kind of justice something is given to someone according to a kind of equality. In distributive justice this equality regards personal dignity, which would seem to depend chiefly on what a person has done for the good of the community; while in commutative justice it regards the thing in which a person has suffered loss. Now in respect of either equality there is retaliation in respect of the deed committed. Therefore it would seem that the just is absolutely the same as retaliation.

Objection 3: Further, the chief argument against retaliation is based on the difference between the voluntary and the involuntary; for he who does an injury involuntarily is less severely punished. Now voluntary and involuntary taken in relation to ourselves, do not diversify the mean of justice since this is the real mean and does not depend on us. Therefore it would seem that the just is absolutely the same as retaliation.

On the contrary, The Philosopher proves (*Ethic.* v, 5) that the just is not always the same as retaliation.

I answer that, Retaliation [contrapassum] denotes equal passion repaid for previous action; and the expression applies most properly to injurious passions and actions, whereby a man harms the person of his neighbor; for instance if a man strike, that he be struck back. This kind of just is laid down in the Law (Ex. 21:23,24): "He shall render life for life, eye for eye," etc. And since also to take away what belongs to another is to do an unjust thing, it follows that secondly retaliation consists in this also, that whosoever causes loss to another, should suffer loss in his belongings. This just loss is also found in the Law (Ex. 22:1): "If any man steal an ox or a sheep, and kill or sell it, he shall restore five oxen for one ox and four sheep for one sheep." Thirdly retaliation is transferred to voluntary commutations, where action and passion are on both sides, although voluntariness detracts from the nature of passion, as stated above (Question [59], Article [3]).

In all these cases, however, repayment must be made on a basis of equality according to the requirements of commutative justice, namely that the need of passion be equal to the action. Now there would not always be equality if passion were in the same species as the action. Because, in the first place, when a person injures the person of one who is greater, the action surpasses any passion of the same species that he might undergo, wherefore he that strikes a prince, is not only struck back, but is much more severely punished. In like manner when a man despoils another of his property against the latter's will, the action surpasses the passion if he be merely deprived of that thing, because the man who caused another's loss, himself would lose nothing, and so he is punished by making restitution several times over, because not only did he injure a private individual, but also the common weal, the security of whose protection he has infringed. Nor again would there be equality of passion in voluntary commutations, were one always to exchange one's chattel for another man's, because it might happen that the other man's chattel is much greater than our own: so that it becomes necessary to equalize passion and action in commutations according to a certain proportionate commensuration, for which purpose money was invented. Hence retaliation is in accordance with commutative justice: but there is no place for it in distributive justice, because in distributive justice we do not consider the equality between thing and thing or between passion and action (whence the expression 'contrapassum'), but according to proportion between things and persons, as stated above (Article [2]).

Reply to Objection 1: This form of the Divine judgment is in accordance with the conditions of commutative justice, in so far as rewards are apportioned to merits, and punishments to sins.

Reply to Objection 2: When a man who has served the community is paid for his services, this is to be referred to commutative, not distributive, justice. Because distributive justice considers the equality, not between the thing received and the thing done, but between the thing received by one person and the thing received by another according to the respective conditions of those persons.

Reply to Objection 3: When the injurious action is voluntary, the injury is aggravated and consequently is considered as a greater thing. Hence it requires a greater punishment in repayment, by reason of a difference, not on part, but on the part of the thing.

APPENDIX B

ECONOMIC JUSTICE FOR ALL PASTORAL LETTER BY THE U.S.CATHOLIC BISHOPS

The following are selected paragraphs from the 1986 pastoral letter entitled, Economic Justice For All composed by the U.S. Catholic Bishops.

A Pastoral Message

Brothers and Sisters in Christ:

1. We are believers called to follow Our Lord Jesus Christ and proclaim his Gospel in the midst of a complex and powerful economy. This reality poses both opportunities and responsibilities for Catholics in the United States. Our faith calls us to measure this economy, not by what it produces but also by how it touches human life and whether it protects or undermines the dignity of the human person. Economic decisions have human consequences and moral content; they help or hurt people, strengthen or weaken family life, advance or diminish the quality of justice in our land.

4. We write to share our teaching, to raise questions, to challenge one another to live our faith in the world. We write as heirs of the biblical prophets who summon us "to do right, and to love goodness, and to walk humbly with your God" (Mi. 6:8). We write as followers of Jesus who told us in the Sermon on the Mount: "Blessed are the poor in spirit .... Blessed are the meek .... Blessed are they who hunger and thirst for righteousness .... You are the salt of the earth .... You are the light of the world" (Mt 5:1-6, 13-14). These words challenge us not only as believers but also as consumers, citizens, workers, and owners. In the parable of the Last Judgment, Jesus said, "For I was hungry and you gave me food, I was thirsty and you gave me drink .... As often as you

147

did it for one of my least brothers, you did it for me" (Mt. 25:35-40). The challenge for us is to discover in our own place and time what it means to be "poor in spirit" and "the salt of the earth" and what it means to serve "the least among us" and to "hunger and thirst for righteousness."

Principal Themes of the Pastoral Letter

12. The pastoral letter is not a blueprint for the American economy. It does not embrace any particular theory of how the economy works, nor does it attempt to resolve disputes between different schools of economic thought. Instead, our letter turns to Scripture and to the social teaching of the Church. There, we discover what our economic life must serve, what standards it must meet. Let us examine some of these basic moral principles.

13. Every economic decision and institution must be judged in light of whether it protects or undermines the dignity of the human person. The pastoral letter begins with the human person. We believe the person is sacred – the clearest reflection of God among us. Human dignity comes from God, not from nationality, race, sex, economic status, or any human accomplishment. We judge any economic system by what it does *for* and *to* people and by how it permits all to *participate* in it. The economy should serve people, not the other way around.

14. Human dignity can be realized and protected only in community. In our teaching, the human person is not only sacred but social. How we organize our society – in economics and politics, in law and policy – directly affects human dignity and the capacity of individuals to grow in community. The obligation to "love our neighbor" has an individual dimension, but it also requires a broader social commitment to the common good. We have many partial ways to measure and debate the health of our economy: Gross National Product, per capita income, stock market prices, and so forth. The Christian vision of economic life looks beyond them all and asks, Does economic life enhance or threaten our life together as a community?

15. All people have a right to participate in the economic life of society. Basic justice demands that people be assured a minimum level of participation in the economy. It is wrong for a person or a group to

be excluded unfairly or to be unable to participate or contribute to the economy. For example, people who are both able and willing, but cannot get a job are deprived of the participation that is so vital to human development. For, it is through employment that most individuals and families meet their material needs, exercise their talents, and have an opportunity to contribute to the larger community. Such participation has a special significance in our tradition because we believe that it is a means by which we join in carrying forward God's creative activity.

16. All members of society have a special obligation to the poor and vulnerable. From the Scriptures and church teaching, we learn that the justice of a society is tested by the treatment of the poor. The justice that was the sign of God's covenant with Israel was measured by how the poor and unprotected – the widow, the orphan, and the stranger – were treated. The kingdom that Jesus proclaimed in his word and ministry excludes no one. Throughout Israel's history and in early Christianity, the poor are agents of God's transforming power. "The Spirit of the Lord is upon me, therefore he has anointed me. He has sent me to bring glad tidings to the poor" (Lk. 4:18). This was Jesus' first public utterance. Jesus takes the side of those most in need. In the Last Judgment, so dramatically described in St. Matthew's Gospel, we are told that we will be judged according to how we respond to the hungry, the thirsty, the naked, the stranger. As followers of Christ, we are challenged to make a fundamental "option for the poor" – to speak for the voiceless, to defend the defenseless, to assess life styles, policies, and social institutions in terms of their impact on the poor. This "option for the poor" does not mean pitting one group against another, but rather, strengthening the whole community by assisting those who are the most vulnerable. As Christians, we are called to respond to the needs of *all* our brothers and sisters, but those with the greatest needs require the greatest response.

27. The pursuit of economic justice takes believers into the public arena, testing the policies of government by the principles of our teaching. We ask you to become more informed and active citizens, using your voices and votes to speak for the voiceless, to defend the poor and the vulnerable and to advance the common good. We are called to

shape a constituency of conscience, measuring every policy by how it touches the least, the lost, and the left-out among us. This letter calls us to conversion and common action, to new forms of stewardship, service, and citizenship.

Chapter I
The Church and the Future of the U.S. Economy

24. The quality of the national discussion about our economic future will affect the poor most of all, in this country and throughout the world. The life and dignity of millions of men, women and children hang in the balance. Decisions must be judged in light of what they do *for* the poor, what they do to the poor, and what they enable the poor to do *for themselves*. The fundamental moral criterion for all economic decisions, policies, and institutions is this: They must be at the service of *all people, especially the poor*.

Chapter II
The Christian Vision of Economic Life

28. The basis for all that the Church believes about the moral dimensions of economic life is its vision of the transcendent worth – the sacredness – of human beings. *The dignity of the human person, realized in community with others, is the criterion against which all aspects of economic life must be measured* [1]. All human beings, therefore, are ends to be served by the institutions that make up the economy, not means to be exploited for more narrowly defined goals. Human personhood must be respected with a reverence that is religious. When we deal with each other, we should do so with the sense of awe that arises in the presence of something holy and sacred. For that is what human beings are: we are created in the image of God (Gn 1:27). Similarly, all economic institutions must support the bonds of community and solidarity that are essential to the dignity of a person. Wherever our economic arrangements fail to conform to the demands of human dignity lived in community, they must be questioned and transformed. These convictions have a biblical basis. They are also supported by a long tradition of the-

ological and philosophical reflection and through the reasoned analysis of human experience by contemporary men and women.

29. In presenting the Christian moral vision, we turn first to the Scriptures for guidance. Though our comments are necessarily selective, we hope that pastors and other church members will become personally engaged with the biblical texts. The Scriptures contain many passages that speak directly of economic life. We must also attend to the Bible's deeper vision of God, of the purpose of creation, and of the dignity of human life in society. Along with other churches and ecclesial communities who are "strengthened by the grace of Baptism and the hearing of God's Word," we strive to become faithful hearers and doers of the word [2]. We also claim the Hebrew Scriptures as common heritage with our Jewish brothers and sisters, and we join with them in the quest for an economic life worthy of the divine revelation we share.

37. When the people turn away from the living God to serve idols and no longer heed the commands of the covenant, God sends prophets to recall his saving deeds and to summon them to return to the one who betrothed them "in right and in justice, in love and in mercy" (Hos 2:21). The substance of prophetic faith is proclaimed by Micah: "to do justice, and to love kindness, and to walk humbly with your God" (Mi 6:8, RSV). Biblical faith in general, and prophetic faith especially, insist that fidelity to the covenant joins obedience to God with reverence and concern for the neighbor. The biblical terms which best summarize this double dimension of Israel's faith are sedaqah, justice (also translated as righteousness), and mishpat (right judgment or justice embodied in a concrete act or deed). The biblical understanding of justice gives a fundamental perspective to our reflections on social and economic justice [7].

38. God is described as a "God of justice" (Is 30:18) who loves justice (Is 61:8, cf. Ps 11:7; 33:5; 37:28; 99:4) and delights in it (Jer 9:23). God demands justice from the whole people (Dt 16:20) and executes justice for the needy (Ps 140:13). Central to the biblical presentation of justice is that the justice of a community is measured by its treatment

of the powerless in society, most often described as the widow, the orphan, the poor, and the stranger (non-Israelite) in the land. The Law, the Prophets, and the Wisdom literature of the Old Testament all show deep concern for the proper treatment of such people [8]. What these groups of people have in common is their vulnerability and lack of power. They are often alone and have no protector or advocate. Therefore, it is God who hears their cries (Ps 109:21; 113:7), and the king who is God's anointed is commanded to have special concern for them.

39. Justice has many nuances [9]. Fundamentally, it suggests a sense of what is right or of what should happen. For example, paths are just when they bring you to your destination (Gn 24:48; Ps 23:3), and laws are just when they create harmony within the community, as Isaiah says: "Justice will bring about peace; right will produce calm and security" (Is 32:17). God is "just" by acting as God should, coming to the people's aid and summoning them to conversion when they stray. People are summoned to be "just," that is, to be in a proper relation to God, by observing God's laws which form them into a faithful community. Biblical justice is more comprehensive than subsequent philosophical definitions. It is not concerned with a strict definition of rights and duties, but with the rightness of the human condition before God and within society. Nor is justice opposed to love; rather, it is both a manifestation of love and a condition for love to grow [10]. Because God loves Israel, he rescues them from oppression and summons them to be a people that "does justice" and loves kindness. The quest for justice arises from loving gratitude for the saving acts of God and manifests itself in wholehearted love of God and neighbor.

40. These perspectives provide the foundation for a biblical vision of economic justice. Every human person is created as an image of God, and the denial of dignity to a person is a blot on this image. Creation is a gift to all men and women, not to be appropriated for the benefit of a few; its beauty is an object of joy and reverence. The same God who came to the aid of an oppressed people and formed them into a covenant community continues to hear the cries of the oppressed and

to create communities which are responsive to God's word. God's love and life are present when people can live in a community of faith and hope. These cardinal points of faith of Israel also furnish the religious context for understanding the saving action of God in the life and teachings of Jesus.

3. The Reign of God and Justice

41. Jesus enters human history as God's anointed son who announces the nearness of the reign of God (Mk 1:9-14). This proclamation summons us to acknowledge God as creator and covenant partner and challenges us to seek ways in which God's revelation of the dignity and destiny of all creation might become incarnate in history. It is not simply the promise of the future victory of God over sin and evil, but that this victory has already begun – in the life and teaching of Jesus.

42. What Jesus proclaims by word, he enacts in his ministry. He resists temptations of power and prestige, follows his Father's will, and teaches us to pray that it be accomplished on earth. He warns against attempts to "lay up treasures on earth" (Mt 6:19) and exhorts his followers not to be anxious about material goods but rather to seek first God's reign and God's justice (Mt 6:25-33). His mighty works symbolize that the reign of God is more powerful than evil, sickness, and the hardness of the human heart. He offers God's loving mercy to sinners (Mk 2:17), takes up the cause of those who suffered religious and social discrimination (Lk 7:36-50; 15:1-2), and attacks the use of religion to avoid the demands of charity and justice (Mk 7:9-13; Mt 23:23).

43. When asked what was the greatest commandment, Jesus quoted the age-old Jewish affirmation of faith that God alone is One and to be loved with the whole heart, mind, and soul (Dt 6:4-5) and immediately adds: "You shall love your neighbor as yourself" (Lv 19:18, Mk 12:28-34). This dual command of love that is at the basis of all Christian morality is illustrated in the Gospel of Luke by the parable of a Samaritan who interrupts his journey to come to the aid of a dying man

(Lk 10:29-37). Unlike the other wayfarers who look on the man and pass by, the Samaritan "was moved with compassion at the sight"; he stops, tends the wounded man, and takes him to a place of safety. In this parable compassion is the bridge between mere seeing and action: love is made real through effective action [11].

44. Near the end of his life, Jesus offers a vivid picture of the last judgment (Mt 25:31-46). All the nations of the world will be assembled and will be divided into those blessed who are welcomed into God's kingdom or those cursed who are sent to eternal punishment. The blessed are those who fed the hungry, gave drink to the thirsty, welcomed the stranger, clothed the naked, and visited the sick and imprisoned; the cursed are those who neglected these works of mercy and love. Neither the blessed nor the cursed are astounded that they are judged by the Son of Man, nor that the judgment is rendered according to the works of charity. The shock comes when they find that in neglecting the poor, the outcast, and the oppressed, they were rejecting Jesus himself. Jesus who came as "Emmanuel" (God with us, Mt 1:23) and who promises to be with his people until the end of the age (Mt 28:20) is hidden in those most in need; to reject them is to reject God made manifest in history.

5. Poverty, Riches, and the Challenge of Discipleship

48. The pattern of Christian life as presented in the Gospel of Luke has special relevance today. In her Magnificat, Mary rejoices in a God who scatters the proud, brings down the mighty, and raises up the poor and lowly (Lk 1:51-53). The first public utterance of Jesus is "The Spirit of the Lord is upon me, because he has anointed me to preach good news to the poor" (Lk 4:18 cf. Is 61:1-2). Jesus adds to the blessing on the poor a warning, "Woe to you who are rich, for you have received your consolation" (Lk 6:24). He warns his followers against greed and reliance on abundant possessions and underscores this by the parable of the man whose life is snatched away at the very moment he tries to secure his wealth (Lk 12:13-21). In Luke alone, Jesus tells the parable of the rich man who does not see the poor and suffering

Lazarus at his gate (Lk 16:19-31). When the rich man finally "sees" Lazarus, it is from the place of torment and the opportunity for conversion has passed. Pope John Paul II has often recalled this parable to warn the prosperous not to be blind to the great poverty that exists beside great wealth [13].

49. Jesus, especially in Luke, lives as a poor man, like the prophets takes the side of the poor, and warns of the dangers of wealth [14]. The terms used for the poor, while primarily describing lack of material goods, also suggest dependence and powerlessness. The poor are also an exiled and oppressed people whom God will rescue (Is 51:21-23) as well as a faithful remnant who will take refuge in God (Zep 3:12-13). Throughout the Bible, material poverty is a misfortune and a cause of sadness. A constant biblical refrain is that the poor must be cared for and protected and that when they are exploited, God hears their cries (Prv 22:22-23). Conversely, even though the goods of the earth are to be enjoyed and people are to thank God for material blessings, wealth is a constant danger. The rich are wise in their own eyes (Prv 28:11), and are prone to apostasy and idolatry (Am 5:4-13; Is 2:6-8), as well as to violence and oppression (Jas 2:6-7) [15]. Since they are neither blinded by wealth nor make it into an idol, the poor can be open to God's presence; throughout Israel's history and in early Christianity the poor are agents of God's transforming power.

50. The poor are often related to the lowly (Mt 5:3, 5) to whom God reveals what was hidden from the wise (Mt 11:25-30). When Jesus calls the poor "blessed", he is not praising their condition of poverty, but their openness to God. When he states that the reign of God is theirs, he voices God's special concern for them, and promises that they are to be the beneficiaries of God's mercy, and justice. When he summons disciples to leave all and follow him, he is calling them to share his own radical trust in the Father and his freedom from care and anxiety (cf. Mt 6:25-34). The practice of evangelical poverty in the Church has always been a living witness to the power of that trust and to the joy that comes with that freedom.

51. Early Christianity saw the poor as an object of God's special love, but it neither canonized material poverty nor accepted deprivation as an inevitable fact of life. Though few early Christians possessed wealth or power (1 Cor 1:26-28; Jas 2:5), their communities had well-off members (Acts 16:14; 18:8). Jesus' concern for the poor was continued in different forms in the early Church. The early community at Jerusalem distributed its possessions so that "there was no needy person among them," and held "all things in common" – a phrase that suggests not only shared material possessions, but more fundamentally, friendship and mutual concern among all its members (Acts 4:32-34; 2:44). While recognizing the dangers of wealth, the early Church proposed the proper use of possessions to alleviate need and suffering, rather than universal dispossession. Beginning in the first century, and throughout history, Christian communities have developed varied structures to support and sustain the weak and powerless in societies that were often brutally unconcerned about human suffering.

52. Such perspectives provide a basis today for what is called the "preferential option for the poor" [16]. Though the Gospels and in the New Testament as a whole the offer of salvation is extended to all peoples, Jesus takes the side of the most in need, physically and spiritually. The example of Jesus poses a number of challenges to the contemporary Church. It imposes a prophetic mandate to speak for those who have no one to speak for them, to be a defender of the defenseless, who in biblical terms are the poor. It also demands a compassionate vision that enables the Church to see things from the side of the poor and powerless and to assess lifestyle, policies, and social institutions in terms of their impact on the poor. It summons the Church also to be an instrument in assisting people to experience the liberating power of God in their own lives so that they may respond to the Gospel in freedom and in dignity. Finally, and most radically, it calls for an emptying of self, both individually and corporately, that allows the Church to experience the power of God in the midst of poverty and powerlessness.

b. Justice and Participation
68. Biblical justice is the goal we strive for. This rich biblical

understanding portrays a just society as one marked by the fullness of love, compassion, holiness, and peace. On their path through history, however, sinful human beings need more specific guidance on how to move toward the realization of this great vision of God's Kingdom. This guidance is contained in the norms of basic or minimal justice. These norms state the minimum levels of mutual care and respect that all persons owe to each other in an imperfect world [23]. Catholic social teaching, like must philosophical reflection, distinguishes three dimensions of basic justice: commutative justice, distributive justice, and social justice [24].

69. *Commutative justice calls for fundamental fairness in all agreements and exchanges between individuals or private social groups.* It demands respect for the equal human dignity of all persons in economic transactions, contracts, or promises. For example, workers owe their employers diligent work in exchange for their wages. Employers are obligated to treat their employees as persons, paying them fair wages in exchange for the work done and establishing conditions and patterns of work that are truly human [25].

70. *Distributive justice requires that the allocation of income, wealth, and power in society be evaluated in light of its effects on persons whose basic material needs are unmet.* The Second Vatican Council stated: "The right to have a share of earthly goods sufficient for oneself and one's family belongs to everyone. The fathers and doctors of the Church held this view, teaching that we are obliged to come to the relief of the poor and to do so not merely out of our superfluous goods" [26]. Minimum material resources are an absolute necessity for human life. If persons are to be recognized as members of the human community, then the community has an obligation to help fulfill these basic needs unless an absolute scarcity of resources makes this strictly impossible. No such scarcity exists in the United States today.

71. Justice also has implications for the way the larger social, economic, and political institutions of society are organized. *Social justice implies that persons have an obligation to be active and productive participants*

in the life of society and that society has a duty to enable them to participate in this way. This form of justice can also be called "contributive," for it stresses the duty of all who are able to help create the goods, services, and other nonmaterial or spiritual values necessary for the welfare of the whole community. In the words of Pius XI, "It is of the very essence of social justice to demand from each individual all that is necessary for the common good" [27]. Productivity is essential if the community is to have the resources to serve the well-being of all. Productivity, however, cannot be measured solely by its output in goods and services. Patterns of production must also be measured in light of their impact on the fulfillment of basic needs, employment levels, patterns of discrimination, environmental quality, and sense of community.

75. This means that all of us must examine our way of living in the light of the needs of the poor. Christian faith and the norms of justice impose distinct limits on what we consume and how we view material goods. The great wealth of the United States can easily blind us to the poverty that exists in this nation and the destitution of hundreds of millions of people in other parts of the world. Americans are challenged today as never before to develop the inner freedom to resist the temptation constantly to seek more. Only in this way will the nation avoid what Paul VI called "the most evident form of moral underdevelopment," namely greed [31].

86. *The obligation to provide justice for all means that the poor have the single most urgent economic claim on the conscience of the nation.* Poverty can take many forms, spiritual as well as material. All people face struggles of the spirit as they ask deep questions about their purpose in life. Many have serious problems in marriage and family life at some time in their lives, and all of us face the certain reality of sickness and death. The Gospel of Christ proclaims that God's love is stronger than all these forms of diminishment. material deprivation, however, seriously compounds such sufferings of the spirit and heart. To see a loved one sick is bad enough, but to have no possibility of obtaining health care is worse. To face family problems, such as death of a spouse or a divorce, can be devastating, but to have these lead to the loss of one's home and

end with living on the streets is something no one should have to endure in a country as rich as ours. In developing countries these human problems are even more greatly intensified by extreme material deprivation. This form of human suffering can be reduced if our own country, so rich in resources, chooses to increase its assistance.

87. As individuals and as a nation, therefore, we are called to make a fundamental "option for the poor" [44]. The obligation to evaluate social and economic activity from the viewpoint of the poor and the powerless arises from the radical command to love one's neighbor as one's self. Those who are marginalized and whose rights are denied have privileged claims if society is to provide justice for *all*. This obligation is deeply rooted in Christian belief. As Paul VI stated:

"In teaching us charity, the Gospel instructs us in the preferential respect due to the poor and the special situation they have in society: the more fortunate should renounce some of their rights so as to place their goods more generously at the service of others" [45].

John Paul II has described this special obligation to the poor as "a call to have a special openness with the small and the weak, those that suffer and weep, those that are humiliated and left on the margin of society, so as to help them win their dignity as human persons and children of God" [46].

88. The primary purpose of this special commitment to the poor is to enable them to become active participants in the life of society. It is to enable all persons to share in and contribute to the common good [47]. The "option for the poor," therefore, is not an adversarial slogan that pits one group or class against another. Rather it states that the deprivation and powerlessness of the poor wounds the whole community. The extent of their suffering is a measure of how far we are from being a true community of persons. These wounds will be healed only by greater solidarity with the poor and among the poor themselves.

89. In summary, the norms of love, basic justice, and human rights imply that personal decisions, social policies, and economic institutions should be governed by several key priorities. These priorities do

not specify everything that must be considered in economic decision making. They do indicate the most fundamental and urgent objectives.

90. a. *The fulfillment of the basic needs of the poor is of the highest priority.* Personal decisions, policies of private and public bodies, and power relationships must be all evaluated by their effects on those who lack the minimum necessities of nutrition, housing, education, and health care. In particular, this principle recognizes that meeting fundamental human needs must come before the fulfillment of desires for luxury consumer goods, for profits not conducive to the common good, and for unnecessary military hardware.

91. b. *Increasing active participation in economic life by those who are presently excluded or vulnerable is a high social priority.* The human dignity of all is realized when people gain the power to work together to improve their lives, strengthen their families, and contribute to society. Basic justice calls for more than providing help to the poor and other vulnerable members of society. It recognizes the priority of policies and programs that support family life and enhance economic participation through employment and widespread ownership of property. It challenges privileged economic power in favor of the well-being of all. It points to the need to improve the present situation of those unjustly discriminated against in the past. And it has very important implications for both the domestic and the international distribution of power.

92. c. *The investment of wealth, talent, and human energy should be specially directed to benefit those who are poor or economically insecure.* Achieving a more just economy in the United States and the world depends in part on increasing economic resources and productivity. In addition, the ways these resources are invested and managed must be scrutinized in light of their effects on non-monetary values. Investment and management decisions have crucial moral dimensions: they create jobs or eliminate them; they can push vulnerable families over the edge into poverty or give them new hope for the future; they help or hinder the building of a more equitable society. They can have either positive or negative influence on the fairness of the global economy. Therefore,

this priority presents a strong moral challenge to policies that put large amounts of talent and capital into the production of luxury consumer goods and military technology while failing to invest sufficiently in education, health, the basic infrastructure of our society and economic sectors that produce urgently needed jobs, goods and services.

Chapter III
Selected Economic Policy Issues

172. As pastors we have seen firsthand the faces of poverty in our midst. Homeless people roam city streets in tattered clothing and sleep in doorways or on subway grates at night. Many of these are former mental patients released from state hospitals. Thousands stand in line at soup kitchens because they have no other way of feeding themselves. Millions of children are so poorly nourished that their physical and mental development are seriously harmed [26]. We have also seen the growing economic hardship and insecurity experienced by moderate-income Americans when they lose their jobs and their income due to forces beyond their control. These are alarming signs and trends. They pose for our nation an urgent moral and human challenge: to fashion a society where no one goes without the basic material necessities required for human dignity and growth.

173. Poverty can be described and defined in many different ways. It can include spiritual as well as material poverty. Likewise, its meaning changes depending on the historical, social, and economic setting. Poverty in our time is different from the more severe deprivation experienced in earlier centuries in the U.S. or in the Third World nations today. Our discussion in this chapter is set within the context of present-day American society. By poverty we are referring here to a lack of sufficient material resources required for a decent life. We use the government's official definition of poverty, although we recognize its limits [27].

1. The Characteristics of Poverty
174. Poverty is not an isolated problem existing solely among a small number of anonymous people in our central cities. Nor is it lim-

ited to a dependent underclass or to specific groups in the United States. It is a condition experienced at some time by many people in different walks of life and in different circumstances. Many poor people are working but at wages insufficient to life them out of poverty [28]. Others are unable to work and therefore dependent on outside sources of support. Still others are on the edge of poverty; although not officially defined as poor, they are economically insecure and at risk of falling into poverty.

175. While many of the poor manage to escape from beneath the official poverty line, others remain poor for extended periods of time. Long-term poverty is concentrated among racial minorities and families headed by women. It is also more likely to be found in rural areas and in the South [29]. Of the long-term poor, most are either working at wages too low to bring them above the poverty line or are retired, disabled, or parents of preschool children. Generally they are not in a position to work more hours than they do now [30].

a. *Children of Poverty*

176. Poverty strikes some groups more severely than others. Perhaps most distressing is the growing number of children who are poor. Today one in very four children under the age of six, and one in every two black children under six, are poor. The number of children in poverty rose by four million over the decade between 1973 and 1983, with the result that there are now more poor children in the United States than at any time since 1965 [31]. The problem is particularly severe among female-headed families, where more than half of all children are poor. Two- thirds of black children and nearly three-quarters of Hispanic children in such families are poor.

177. Very many poor families with children receive no government assistance, have no health insurance, and cannot pay medical bills. Less than half are immunized against preventable diseases such as diphtheria and polio [32]. Poor children are disadvantaged even before birth; their mothers' lack of access to high quality prenatal care leaves them at much greater risk of premature birth, low-birth weight, physical and

mental impairment, and death before their first birthday.

b. *Women and Poverty*

178. The Past twenty years have witnessed a dramatic increase in the number of women in poverty [33]. This includes women raising children alone as well as women with inadequate income following divorce, widowhood, or retirement. More than one-third of all female-headed families are poor. Among minority families headed by women the poverty rate is over 50 percent [34].

D. The U.S. Economy and the Developing Nations: Complexity, Challenge, and Choices
1. The Complexity of Economic Relations in an Interdependent World

254. The basic tenets of church teaching take on a new moral urgency as we deepen our understanding of how disadvantaged large numbers of people and nations are in this interdependent world. Half the world's people, nearly two and a half billion, live in countries where the annual per capita income is $400 or less [99]. At least 800 million people in those counties live in absolute poverty, "beneath any rational definition of human decency" [100]. Nearly half a billion are chronically hungry, despite abundant harvests worldwide [101]. Fifteen out of every 100 children in these countries die before the age of five, and millions of the survivors are physically or mentally stunted. No aggregate of individual examples could portray adequately the appalling inequities within those desperately poor countries and between them and our own. And their misery is not the inevitable result of the march of history or the intrinsic nature of particular cultures, but of human decisions and human institutions.

Chapter V
A Commitment to the Future

333. But as disciples of Christ we must constantly ask ourselves how deeply the biblical and *ethic*al vision of justice and love permeates

our thinking. How thoroughly does it influence our way of life? We may hide behind the complexity of the issues or dismiss the significance of our personal contribution; in fact, each one has a role to play, because every day each one makes economic decisions. Some, by reason of their work or their position in society, have a vocation to be involved in a more decisive way in those decisions that affect the economic well-being of others. They must be encouraged and sustained by all in their search for greater justice.

334. At times we will be called upon to say no to the cultural manifestations that emphasize values and aims that are selfish, wasteful, and opposed to the Scriptures. Together we must reflect on our personal and family decisions and curb unnecessary wants in order to meet the needs of others. There are many questions we must keep asking ourselves: Are we becoming ever more wasteful in a "throw-away" society? Are we able to distinguish between our true needs and those thrust on us by advertising and a society that values consumption more than saving? All of us could well ask ourselves whether as a Christian prophetic witness we are not called to adopt a simpler lifestyle, in the face of the excessive accumulation of material goods that characterizes an affluent society.

3. The Church As Economic Actor

347. Although all members of the Church are economic actors every day in their individual lives, they also play an economic role united together as Church. On the parish and diocesan level, through its agencies and institutions, the Church employs many people; it has investments; it has extensive properties for worship and mission. *All the moral principles that govern the just operation of any economic endeavor apply to the Church and its agencies and institutions; indeed the Church should be exemplary.* The Synod of Bishops in 1971 worded this challenge most aptly: "While the Church is bound to give witness to justice, she recognizes that anyone who ventures to speak to people about justice must first be just in their eyes. Hence, we must undertake an examination of the modes of acting and of the possessions and lifestyle found within the Church herself."[10]

D. Commitment to a Kingdom of Love and Justice

363. Confronted by this economic complexity and seeking clarity for the future, we can rightly ask our-selves one single question: How does our economic system affect the lives of people - all people? Part of the American dream has been to make this world a better place for people to live in; at this moment of history that dream must include everyone on this globe. Since we profess to be members of a "catholic" or universal Church, we all must raise our sights to a concern for the well-being of everyone in the world. Third World debt becomes our problem. Famine and starvation in sub-Saharan Africa become our concern. Rising military expenditures everywhere in the world become part of our fears for the future of this planet. We cannot be content if we see ecological neglect or the squandering of natural resources. In this letter we bishops have spoken often of economic interdependence; now is the moment when all of us must confront the reality of such economic bonding and its consequences and see it as a moment of grace -a *kairos* -that can unite all of us in a common community of the human family. We commit ourselves to this global vision.

364. We cannot be frightened by the magnitude and complexity of these problems. We must not be discouraged. In the midst of this struggle, It is inevitable that we become aware of greed, laziness, and envy. No utopia is possible on this earth; but as believers in the redemptive love of God and as those who have experienced God's forgiving mercy, we know that God's providence is not and will not be lacking to us today.

Notes for Appendix B
Economic Justice For All
A Pastoral Letter by the
U.S. Catholic Bishops

Because only selected paragraphs of the letter are included in Appendix B, the numbering of the notes below is not always sequential, however this does reflect the original numbering of the notes throughout the letter.

Chapter II Notes

[1] John XXIII, *Mater et Magistra*, 219-220, See "Pastoral Constitution, ", 63.

[2] Vatican Council II, *Decree on Ecumenism"*, 22-23.

[7] On justice, see J.R. Donahue, "Biblical Perspectives on Justice," in Haughey, ed, *The Faith That Does Justice* (New York: Paulist Press, 1977), 68-112; and S.C. Mott, Biblical Ethics and Social Change (New York: Oxford University Press, 1982).

[8] See Ex 22:20-26; Dt 15:1-11; Jb 29:12-17; Ps 69:34; 72:2, 4, 12-24; 82:3-4; Prv 14:21, 31: Is 3:14-15; 10:2; Jer 22:16; Zec 7:9-10.

[9] J. Pedersen, *Israel: Its Life and Culture*, vol. I-II (London: Oxford University Press, 1926), 337-340.

[10] J. Alfaro, *Theology of Justice in the World* (Rome: Pontifical Commission on Justice and Peace, 1973), 40-41; E. McDonagh, *The Making of Disciples* (Wilmington, Del: Michael Glazier, 1982), 119.

[11] Pope John Paul II has drawn on this parable to exhort us to have a "compassionate heart" to those in need in his Apostolic Letter "On the Christian Meaning of Human Suffering" (*Salvifici Doloris*) (Washington D.C.: USCC Office of Publishing and Promotion Services, 1984), 34-39.9).

[14] J. Dupont and A. George, eds., "*La pauvrete evangelique* (Paris: Cerf, 1971); M. Hengel, *Property and Riches in the Early Church* (Philadelphia: Fortress Press, 1974); L. Johnson, *Sharing Possessions:*

166

Mandate and Symbol of Faith (Philadelphia: Fortress Press, 1981); D.L. Mealand, *Poverty and Expectation in the Gospels* (London: SPCK 1980); W. Pilgrim, *Good News to the Poor: Wealth and Poverty in Luke-Acts* (Minneapolis: Augsburg, 1981); and W. Stegemann, *The Gospel and the Poor* (Philadelphia: Fortress Press, 1984).

[15] See Am 4:1-3; Jb 20:19; Sir 13:4-7; Jas 2:6; 5:1-6; Rv 18:11-19.

[16] See paragraphs 85-91.

[23] See paragraph 39.

[24] Josef Pieper, *The Four Cardinal Virtues* (Notre Dame, Ind.: University of Notre Dame Press, 1966), 43-116; David Hollenbach, *Modern Catholic Teachings concerning Justice* in John C. Haughey, ed., *The Faith That Does Justice* (New York: Paulist Press, 1977), 207-231.

[25] Jon P. Gunnemann, "Capitalism and Commutative Justice," presented at the 1985 meeting of the Society of Christian Ethics, forthcoming in the "Annual of the Society of Christian Ethics."

[26] *Pastoral Constitution*, 69.

[27] Pope Pius XI, *Divini Redemptoris,* 51. See John A. Ryan, *Distributive Justice,* third edition (New York: Macmillan, 1942), 188. The term "social justice" has been used in several different but related ways in the Catholic ethical tradition. See William Ferree, "The Act of Social Justice," *Philosophical Studies,* vol. 72 (Washington DC: The Catholic University of America Press, 1943).

[31] Pope Paul VI, "On the Development of Peoples" (1967), 19.

[44] On the recent use of this term see: Congregation for the Doctrine of the Faith, "Instruction on Christian Freedom and Liberation", 46-50, 66-68; *Evangelization in Latin America's Present and Future,* Final Document of the Third General Conference of the Latin American Episcopate (Puebla, Mexico, January 27-February 13, 1979), esp. part VI, ch. 1, "A Preferential Option for the Poor," in J. Eagleson and P. Scharper, eds, *Puebla and Beyond* (Maryknoll: Orbis Books, 1979), 264-267; Donald Dorr, *Option for the Poor: A Hundred Years of Vatican Social Teaching* (Maryknoll, N.Y.: Orbis Books, 1983).

[45] *Octogesima Adveniens,* 23.

[46] Address to Bishops of Brazil, 6, 9, "Origins" 10:9 (July 31, 1980): 135.

[47] Pope John Paul II, Address to Workers at Sao Paulo, 4, "Origins" 10:9 (July 31, 1980): 138; Congregation for the Doctrine of the Faith, "Instruction on Christian Freedom and Liberation", 66-68.

Chapter III Notes

[26] Massachusetts Department of Public Health, *Massachusetts Nutrition Survey* (Boston, Mass.: 1983).

[27] There is considerable debate about the most suitable definition of poverty. Some argue that the government's official definition understates the number of the poor, and that a more adequate definition would indicate that as many as 50 million Americans are poor. For example, they note that the poverty line has declined sharply as a percent of median family income – from 48% in 1959 to 35% in 1983. Others argue that the official indicators should be reduced by the amount of in-kind benefits received by the poor, such as food stamps. By some calculations that would reduce the number counted as poor to about 12 million. We conclude that for present purposes the official government definition provides a suitable middle ground. That definition is based on a calculation that multiplies the cost of USDA's lowest cost food plan times three. The definition is adjusted for inflation each year.

Among other reasons for using the official definition is that it allows one to compare poverty figures over time. For additional readings on this topic see: L. Rainwater, *What Money Buys: Inequality and the Social Meanings of Income* (New York: Basic Books, 1975); id.; *Persistent and Transitory Poverty: A New Look* (Cambridge, Mass.: Joint Center for Urban Studies, 1980); M. Orshansky, "How Poverty is Measured," *Monthly Labor Review* 92 (1969):37-41; M. Anderson, *Welfare* (Stanford, Calif.: Hoover Institution Press, 1978); and Michael Harrington, *The New American Poverty* (New York: Hold, Rinehart, and Winston, 1984), 81-82.

[28] Of those in poverty, 3 million work year-round and are still poor. Of the 22.2 million poor who are 15 years or over, more than 9 million work sometime during the year. Since 1979, the largest increases of poverty in absolute terms have been among those who work and are still poor. U.S. Bureau of the Census, *Money, Income and Poverty*.

[29] U.S. Bureau of the Census, Current population Reports, series P-60, no. 149, 19. Blacks make up about 12% of the entire population but 62% of the long-term poor. Only 19% of the overall population live in families headed by women, but they make up 61% of the long-term poor. Twenty-eight percent of the nation's total population reside in nonmetropolitan areas, but 34% of the nation's poor live in these areas.

[30] G.J. Duncan, et al, *Years of poverty, Years of Plenty: The Changing Economic Fortunes of American Workers and Their Families* (Ann Arbor, Mich.: Institute for Social Research, the University of Michigan, 1984). This book is based on the Panel Study of Income Dynamics, a survey of 5,000 American families conducted annually by the Survey Research Center of the University of Michigan. See G.J. Duncan and J.N. Morgan, *Five Thousand American Families – Patterns of Economic Progress vol. III* (Ann Arbor: University of Michigan, 1975).

[31] Congressional Research Service and Congressional Budget Office, *Children in Poverty* (Washington, DC, May 22, 1985), 57. This recent study also indicates that children are now the largest age group in poverty. We are the first industrialized nation in the world in which children are the poorest age group. See Daniel Patrick Moynihan, *Family and Nation* (New York: Harcourt, Brace, Jovanovich, 1986), 112.

[32] Children's Defense Fund, *American Children in Poverty* (Washington DC 1984).

[33] The trend has been commonly referred to as the "feminization of poverty." This term was coined by Dr. Diana Pierce in the 1980 Report to the President of the National Advisory Council on Economic Opportunity to describe the dramatic increase in the proportion of the poor living in female-headed households.

[34] U.S. Bureau of the Census, Technical Paper 55, *Estimates of Poverty Including the Value of Non-Cash Benefits: 1984* (Washington, DC, August 1985), 5, 23.

[99] Overseas Development Council, *US Policy And The Third World: Agenda 1985-1986*.

[100] Robert S. McNamara, *Address to the Board of Governors of the World Bank* (Washington, DC: World Bank, September 30, 1980).

[101] UN/Food and Agricultural Organization, *Dimensions of Need* (Rome, 1982). The U.N. World Food Council uses this figure consistently, most recently at its 11th annual meeting in Paris.

Chapter V Notes

[10] Synod of Bishops, "Justice in the World" (1971), 40.

Suggested Readings

Alfaro, J. *Theology of Justice in the World* (Rome: Pontifical Commission on Justice and Peace, 1973).

Beisner, E. Calvin. *Prosperity and Poverty: The Compassionate Use of Resources in a World of Scarcity* (Westchester, IL: Crossway, 1988).

Beversluis, Eric. "A Critique of Ronald Nash on economic justice and the state," *Christian Scholar's Review* vol. 9 no. 4 (1982) p. 330-346.

Burrell, David. B. "Justice? What Is It All About?" *Education for Justice: Occasional Papers on Catholic Higher Education 4* (Winter 1978): 12-17.

Burns, Camilla. "Biblical Righteousness and Justice." *Liturgical Ministry* 7 (1998): 153-61.

Clouse, Robert G, ed. *Wealth and Poverty: Four Christian Views of Economics* (Downers Grove: InterVarsity, 1984).

Collins, Joseph. "World Hunger: A Scarcity of Food or a Scarcity of Democracy," in Michael T. Klare and Daniel C. Thomas, eds., *World Security: Challenges for a New Century* (New York: St. Martin's Press, Second Edition, 1994).

Davis, John Jefferson. *Your Wealth in God's World: Does the Bible Support the Free Market?* (Phillipsburg, N.J.: Presbyterian and Reformed, 1984).

Donahue, John R. "Biblical Perspectives on Justice," in Haughey, ed, *The Faith That Does Justice* (New York: Paulist Press, 1977), 68-112.

Donahue, John R. "Two Decades of Research on the Rich and Poor in Luke-Acts," in *Justice and the Holy: Essays in Honor of Walter Harrelson*, ed. D.A. Knight and P. J. Paris (Atlanta: Scholars Press, 1989) p. 129-44.

Dorr, Donald. *Option for the Poor: A Hundred Years of Vatican Social Teaching* (Dublin: Gill and Macmillan/Maryknoll, N.Y.: Orbis Books, 1983).

Dorr, Donald. *Spirituality and Justice*. Maryknoll, NY: Orbis Books, 1984.

Duffey, Michael K. Sowing Justice, *Reaping Peace: Case Studies of Racial Religious, and Ethnic Healing Around the World* (Chicago: Sheed & Ward, 2001).

Finn, Daniel R., and Pemberton L. Prentiss. *Toward a Christian Economic*

Ethic: Stewardship and Social Power (Minneapolis: Winston, 1985).

Finnerty, Adam Daniel. *No More Plastic Jesus: Global Justice and Christian Lifestyle* (Maryknoll, N.Y.: Orbis Books, 1977).

Grant, James P. *The State of the World's Children* (Oxford: Oxford University Press, 1993).

Grant, James P. *The State of the World's Children* (Oxford: Oxford University Press, 1995).

Grassi, Joseph A. *Broken Bread and Broken Bodies: The Lord's Supper and World Hunger.* (Maryknoll, NY: Orbis Books, 1985).

Haight, Roger. "Spirituality and Social Justice: A Christological Perspective." *Spirituality Today* 34 (1982): 312-25.

Hamm, Dennis. "Preaching Biblical Justice." *Church* (Spring 1996): 17-21.

Haughey, John C. ed. *The Faith That Does Justice* (New York: Paulist, 1977).

Hengel, M. *Property and Riches in the Early Church* (Philadelphia: Fortress Press, 1974).

Hollenbach, David. Modern Catholic Teachings concerning Justice in John C. Haughey, ed., *The Faith That Does Justice* (New York: Paulist Press, 1977), 207-231.

Hopps, L. J. *Being Poor: A Biblical Study* (GNS 20; Wilmington: Michael Glazier, 1987).

John Paul II, *Centesimus Annus,* May 1, 1991 (Washington: United States Catholic Conference, 1991).

Johnson, L. *Sharing Possessions: Mandate and Symbol of Faith* (Philadelphia: Fortress Press, 1981).

Kammer, Fred. *Doing Faith Justice: An Introduction to Catholic Social Thought* (New York: Paulist Press, 1991).

Kavanaugh, John F. *Following Christ in a Consumer Society: The Spirituality of Cultural Resistance,* rev. ed. (Maryknoll, N.Y.: Orbis Books, 1991).

Klay, Robin Kendrick. *Counting the Cost: The Economics of Christian Stewardship* (Grand Rapids: Eerdmans, 1986).

Kreider, Carl. *The Rich and the Poor: A Christian Perspective on Global Economics* (Scottdale, PA: Herald Press, 1987).

Kvalbein, H. "Jesus and the Poor," *Themelios* 12 (1987) 80-87.

Malina, B.J. "Wealth and Poverty in the New Testament and Its World,"

Interpretation 41 (1987) 354-67.

Malina, B.J. *The New Testament World: Insights from Cultural Anthropology* (Atlanta: John Knox, 1981).

Massaro, Thomas. *Living Justice: Catholic Social Teaching in Action* (Chicago: Sheed and Ward, 2000).

McGinnis, James B. *Bread and Justice: Toward a New International Economic Order* (New York: Paulist Press, 1979).

Mealand, D.L. *Poverty and Expectation in the Gospels* (London: SPCK, 1980).

Morgan, Elizabeth. *Global Poverty and Personal Responsibility* (New York: Paulist Press, 1989).

Mott, S.C. *Biblical Ethics and Social Change* (New York: Oxford University Press, 1982).

Nash, Ronald. *Poverty and Wealth: The Christian Debate Over Capitalism* (Westchester: Crossway, 1986).

National Conference of Catholic Bishops (NCCB). *Economic Justice for All* (1986) in O'Brien and Shannon, eds. *Catholic Social Thought: The Documentary Heritage* (Maryknoll, NY: Orbis Books, 1992) #8.

O'Brien, David J. and Shannon, Thomas A. eds., *Catholic Social Thought: The Documentary Heritage* (Maryknoll, NY: Orbis Books, 1992).

Owensby, Walter L. *Economics for Prophets: A Primer on Concepts, Realities, and Values in Our Economic System* (Grand Rapids: Eerdmans, 1988).

Pilgrim, W. *Good News to the Poor: Wealth and Poverty in Luke-Acts* (Minneapolis: Augsburg, 1981).

Pobee, J.S. *Who Are the Poor? The Beatitudes As a Call to Community* (RBS 32; Geneva: WCC, 1987).

Porteous, Norman W. "The Care of the Poor in the Old Testament," in *Living the Mystery* (Oxford: Blackwell, 1967).

Schumacher, E.F. *Small is Beautiful: Economics As If People Mattered.* (New York: Harper and Row, 1973).

Sider, Ronald J. *Rich Christians in an Age of Hunger: A Biblical Study* 2nd rev. ed. (Downers Grove: InterVarsity, 1984).

Sider, Ronald J. "A Trickle Up Response to Poverty," *ESA Advocate*, March 1990.

Simon, Arthur. *Bread for the World* (New York: paulist Press, 1975).

Sine, Tom. *The Mustard Seed Conspiracy* (Waco: Word, 1981).

Stegemann, W. *The Gospel and the Poor* (Philadelphia: Fortress Press, 1984).

Thompson, J. Milburn. *Justice & Peace*. (Maryknoll, NY: Orbis Books, 2003).

Unger, Peter. *Living High & Letting Die* (New York: Oxford University Press, 1996).

Index of Scriptures